CW00349286

THE SECOND HUMDRUMMING BOOK OF HORROR STORIES

SELECTED & EDITED BY IAN ALEXANDER MARTIN

GUY ADAMS | JAMES COOPER

CHRISTOPHER FOWLER | GARY FRY

RHYS HUGHES | DAVIN IRELAND

ANDREW JURY | MICHAEL KELLY

TIM LEBBON | GARY McMAHON

MARK MORRIS | SARAH PINBOROUGH

SIMON STRANTZAS | JOHN TRAVIS

CAROL WEEKES | CONRAD WILLIAMS

THE SECOND HUMDRUMMING BOOK OF

HORROR STORIES

IAN ALEXANDER MARTIN has been frequently consulted for a wide variety of reasons, not the least of which involved the interpretation of *Menachmæ* as pottery-based performance art; examination of Shakespeare's First through Fourth Quartos seeking provenance for Æschylus's authorship of the works; and the construction of an anatomically correct 5:1 scale model of an cœlacanth made entirely from *œuf*-based *papier-mâché* using exclusively traditional æsthetics.

During the autumnal period of The Year of Our Lord Two-Thousand-and-Seven, he made his première appearance on non-North American soil by travelling *via* æroplane to Her Gracious Majesty's England and Spain. During this débâcle of a mêlée, he naïvely débuted a facility with the breaking of nations previously unknown to mankind.

He counts among his worthy associates, the Count Guy and Countess Debra of Moraira; Dame Jennifer of Moscrop-by-Hill; Baron Sean (who provided no legal advice for this volume) and Baroness Miranda of Brentwood-above-the-Bog; as well as large members of societies so secret that they themselves are not aware of belonging to them, yet who are aware of their largesse.

Upon his estate, he is currently engaged in the design and building of a temple-like feline hôtel — the façade and décor of which finds its inspiration in the Cæsarean period — which he intends to develop into a world-wide chain; all featuring restaurants with the widest selection of the freshest possible algæ. When he was asked why he was doing this, at the behest of the two cats who generously share the house with him and his wife, he answered simply: "because they wish me so to do."

www.humdrumming.co.uk

HUMDRUMMING TITLES BY IAN ALEXANDER MARTIN:

The First Humdrumming Book of Horror Stories [AS EDITOR]

The Second Humdrumming Book of Horror Stories [AS EDITOR]

Canada for Foreigners [EVENTUALLY]

Also available in this series:

THE HUMDRUMMING BOOKS OF HORROR STORIES (Vol I)

THE SECOND HUMDRUMMING BOOK OF

HORROR STORIES

Selected by

IAN ALEXANDER MARTIN

NONE OF THESE STORIES
HAS BEEN PREVIOUSLY PUBLISHED

GUY ADAMS
JAMES COOPER
CHRISTOPHER FOWLER
GARY FRY
RHYS HUGHES
DAVIN IRELAND
ANDREW JURY
TIM LEBBON
MICHAEL KELLY
GARY McMAHON
MARK MORRIS
SARAH PINBOROUGH
SIMON STRANTZAS
JOHN TRAVIS
CAROL WEEKES
CONRAD WILLIAMS

HUMDRUMMING LTD : LONDON

This collection first published in 2008 by
Humdrumming Ltd, Queens Road, London, 13B N11
WWW.HUMDRUMMING.CO.UK

HARD-COVER LIMITED FIRST EDITION
[100 copies, 'PPC' binding, signed by authors]
ISBN 978 1 905532 66 7

SOFT-COVER TRADE EDITION
ISBN 978 1 905532 62 9

Cover designed by Guy Adams
Edited and Typeset in "Bembo" by Ian Alexander Martin

Printed and bound in Great Britain by:
Biddles Ltd, Hardwick Estate, King's Lynn, Norfolk

TABLE OF CONTENTS

LATE RETURNS

CONRAD WILLIAMS

WITHOUT LOOKING AT her, Callaghan handed the book to the librarian and waited with the usual mild sense of guilt while she scanned his card. Even though he always returned borrowed items on time, he was unable to shake the feeling. The guilt extended to his opinions of these book-lenders. There was something about librarians that excited him, especially here in Didsbury. Something about their calm, their organisation, their restraint. He fantasised that once they had locked the doors on Wilmslow Road, they returned to the staff room, unpinned their tidily arranged hair, cracked open the *Rioja* and embarked on marathon Bacchanalian romps. It was as far as his imagination allowed him to go. He could never follow up any shiver of arousal with a concrete proposal. He had been given 'the look' during his life; women had favoured him. But he had never understood the signals. He had no in-built code-breaker. He played out the politics of sex within the pages of his beloved books. The moment it became something more physical than a conceit to propel a chapter, he was lost. A smile, a wink, a hand over his own — it might as well have been hieroglyphics made flesh, indecipherable. He had messed with the minds of so many women over the years, turned them upside down with his suspicions and reservations and reluctance, charmed and then disgusted them, that there seemed to have built up a protective layer around him, like horn. He was impervious. He was impenetrable.

Once outside he checked his watch, then set off for The Deli. He would not leave until he had read at least one chapter. Callaghan loved books, but he never bought them. He preferred to borrow from the library for any number of reasons. For a start, libraries offered an excellent public service and needed support. But there was also Callaghan's lack of disposable income and the shortage of space back at his rented terraced house off School Lane. Mainly, he loved to imagine other hands holding the same book, other eyes taking in the words. In this way, he felt less alone. He believed he was on the brink of understanding human behaviour. Maybe even women.

In the coffee shop, the same routine. He was glad to find a vacant window seat. He ordered a cappuccino and did not look at this randomly selected book until his coffee arrived. Now then... *The Matter of the Heart* by somebody called Nicholas Royle. A novel. According to the tagline, this was a 'nightmare road thriller'. He hoped that 'nightmare' was not meant pejoratively. The cover, beneath its protective Mylar wrapping, was of a headlight from a car. An unusual headlight, shaped like a number 8. The author photograph on the inside displayed a rather intense young man with kind eyes guarded by John Lennon-style spectacles, the ones worn by people who wanted to appear intellectual. Callaghan liked to imagine the kind of voice his chosen writer might own; it would flavour the narrative as he read it. This writer, he decided, would sound very much like Brian Sewell. He imagined that pompous, oleaginous voice now: *"On the highway between Geraldton and Perth I saw a man break his wife's neck in the door of his Mercedes," he said.*

Soon though, as the narrative gripped, he forgot his game and tucked into the story. At the end of the chapter, he plucked a bus receipt from his pocket and turned the page, intending to mark his place. But then he discovered that he did not need his ticket because there was already a piece of paper doing the job for him. Something was written on it in red pen. He unfolded it and stared. *Dashiell,* it read. Next to Callaghan's given name was a sketched love-heart.

He felt his own heart answer the message's call, filling his chest suddenly, as if someone had inflated it with a pump. His forehead prickled with sweat. The book had been an unwanted gift, he reasoned. This other Dashiell had donated it to the library without removing the personalised note first. He paid for his coffee and left for home, shocked by his reaction. A coincidence, he kept telling himself. *Yes, really.* His mother had named him after Dashiell Hammett, the American crime writer she had been so addicted to. He knew of no other Dashiells. Perhaps in America, but not in the UK. Not in *Didsbury.*

He tossed the fragment into the bin and by the time he was back home his thoughts had recovered themselves sufficiently to offer a more feasible alternative. A booklover had simply stated his or her admiration for a fine writer and left it in another volume, used it as a bookmark. This theory was made smoother by the fact that the Royle novel was also a thriller. It really was a coincidence. Nothing to worry about. Nothing to worry about.

Callaghan worked until seven – he earned a living as a freelance accountant – and prepared himself a meal. He listened to a radio programme about cloud goats in the Western Ghats of India. As with the books he read, he found himself lost in the details. Soon he could almost believe he had transported himself to the Nilgiri Hills, where the Kurungi flower blossoms once every twelve years, turning the countryside blue. The presenter described how the dominant male goats tended to drift away from the herd and become loners, occasionally releasing their energies through acts of violence and lust.

Callaghan switched off the radio and cleared away the plates. He took his new book to bed with him and read it until the words began to fail on the page. He dreamed of a cold, high place and something dark emerging through the mist.

* * *

Another week, another book. Another coffee. Another note. This time, the folded paper was less ambiguous. *Dashiell,* it read. *I watch you. I like you. My heart beats for you.*

It must be one of the librarians, slipping notes inside his borrowed items with the skill of a prestidigitator. His heart raced. He couldn't remember which of the librarians had served him last time. They were all charming. He thought about returning immediately and making some enquiries, but he realised that to do that would be to scare her off. He didn't want to ruin a late chance at romance, no matter how unconventional its beginnings might be. He skimmed this new novel, and returned to the library a few days earlier than usual. Once the book had been handed over, he sauntered towards the shelves, clandestine in his inspection of the staff behind the counter. He closed his eyes and selected a book from a different area of the fiction stacks. Now he took it back to the counter. He smiled at the librarian and watched carefully as she scanned his card, stamped the return date. She smiled back. He had not seen her insert anything between its pages. He scurried out, disappointed. She had noticed his scrutiny; perhaps she wasn't the librarian with an eye on him. He had spoilt it by returning too soon. There might be a librarian watching out for him on the days he usually attended, a scrap of paper turning warm in her hand.

Callaghan sat by the window in The Deli, ordered his cappuccino. The newspapers on the rack told of crimes of passion, shootings, knives in schools. Even the local papers screamed outrage over the stabbings which were occurring late at night with alarming regularity. A town out of control. A city in need. Callaghan's hands clenched and relaxed on the table top. Clenched and relaxed. Clenched and relaxed. He wasn't even aware that he was doing this.

When his drink arrived he took a sip, turning the borrowed book over in his hands. He had to laugh. *Walking on Glass* by Iain Banks. *Walking on eggshells, more like*, he thought. The cover puff from the *Observer* plucked at him: *Inexorably powerful... sinister manipulations and magnetic ambiguities.* "You and me both," Callaghan muttered. He opened the novel to the first page.

An hour later, restored by the magic of coffee and prose (the first three chapters of the novel devoured), Callaghan drew his faithful bus ticket from his top pocket and turned the page to mark his progress.

The scribbled loveheart. His name. *Come to me.* A date. A time.

He stared at the words, an ache building fast behind his eyes. He had watched the librarian without blinking, without breathing. She had not planted this note. The alternative would not sit in the centre of his thoughts. It kept sliding away from his grasp, like the final pickle in a jar.

Callaghan arrived home without realising it. He turned the key in the lock with a hand that felt too weak for the task. He climbed the stairs and lay in bed until darkness took away the shape of his room, the shape of his own body on the sheets. How did whoever it was know which book he was going to select? How did whoever it was know where he was going to stop reading? He groaned and pressed his fingers against his eyes as if that might force some believable answer. Fear fanned through him, like the pages of a book left on a table in the wind. And yet, there was excitement too. Someone wanted to see him. Someone was interested in him. He fell asleep to the radio. News. Dead tones. Bodies felled in leafy, well-to-do conurbations. He imagined the metallic music of a kitchen drawer yanked open. The oily play of high street colours at midnight played out on a wet blade. He imagined kissing someone; being kissed. Being loved. Was he yet asleep when it hit him (who else could have sucked in their breath at the shock?) that the last person to hold him close was his mother, twelve years dead?

* * *

His work suffered; he failed to respond to two urgent letters. These clients summarily dismissed him and went elsewhere to have their ledgers studied, their claims double-checked. He took to eating his prepared meals standing up in the kitchen, directly from their packaging. He could not focus on anything else. He woke up and stared at the pyjamas resting at the foot of the bed for a long time, realising that he wasn't wearing them because he had not changed out of his own clothes for two, maybe three days. He did not finish his latest loan from the library. He read the same line over and over as if it there were some physical object preventing him from moving on. All that existed behind his eyes was the cursive flourish of his own name and the worry over the kind of fingers that had penned it.

One day he rose early and went to his desk. He cleared it with one sweep of a stiff forearm. He placed a pad of paper and a pen on the blond wood and sat down, watched a dagger of dawn light threaten him from the wall. All around him were flat, bare surfaces that might have supported framed photographs of people in love.

He wrote, *Do I know you? Who are you? Don't be shy. Dashiell.* He tore that up and wrote, *Why me?* He tore that up and wrote, *Leave me alone.* He tore that up and wrote, *My God, my God.*

He dreamed of blue flowers opening on a mountain skirted with cloud. He looked down at his hands and saw blue buds pushing through the pores of his skin. The coin-slot eyes of thin, sinewy goats watched him. He gazed down at his feet, clustered with blossom. His head was filled with spicy perfume. He opened his mouth to speak and petals flew from his lips. He saw a figure rising through the basin of mist, bipedal, but climbing as fast and sure-footedly as one of the goats themselves. Its arms were outstretched, far too long for the body, although this must be some sort of illusion created by the shadows. The fingers were thin and elongated, ape-like. They raked against the skin of the mountain; he felt the tremor of the damage they did through the ground. He could not tear his eyes away from the thickening shape as it rose; soon it would be visible. He heard the moist splitting of buds as they opened. His eyes filled with blue as a head broke free of the cloud and swung its face towards him. The blue was so deep now that he could not extract any detail from the shadow. A sound of hooves; the goats breaking for cover. He was on his own, rooted. He felt the air move, compressing against his face as it came for him. He heard the tremulous whisper of a dozen voices cracked with sorrow: *I do.*

* * *

It was Friday, coffee morning at the library, and he gratefully accepted a cup and a biscuit from the librarian at the table. His hair was still wet from the shower; he had had to strip the bed and lean the mattress up against the wall it was so soaked through with his sweat. He strolled up to the shelves of DVDs and stopped just before the library opened up further to take in the children's section, the fiction and the computer terminals. It was a busy morning. He tried to remain calm as he assessed the people moving through these pacific zones. Could it be this woman in the short, green leather jacket and scuffed jeans? Or her, with her sandy blonde hair tied back in a *chignon*? Or this one, with her long skirt and voluminous cream blouse?

Callaghan decided to force the issue. At the very least it would prove he was not insane. He put down his cup and saucer and strode to the thrillers. He placed his finger on a spine and drew it towards him. *The Eros Hunter*, by Russell Celyn Jones. *Well, Russell, aren't we all?* On the cover, Jonathan Coe referred to it as "a terrific, contemporary thriller... fast, funny, merciless". First line: *My name is Alice Harper and I murdered my father, they say.*

He closed his eyes. The flavour of coffee was on his tongue. He could imagine sitting by the window, the endless stream of buses hissing past. The 4x4s and Bugaboo Frogs. The students. The sassy girls, all boho chic and clipboards offering discounts on beauty treatments. School uniforms from Beaver Road and Parrs Wood.

Callaghan opened the book at the end of the first chapter. Nothing. He flipped to the end of the second. And the third. He held the book by the spine and waggled it. No entreaty, no appeal fluttered clear of the pages. He thrust the book back into the row. He moved along, selected another. *Invisible Monsters* by Chuck Palahniuk. *Booklist* saw fit to describe it as "a wild ride of a novel". Chapter One. Nothing. Waggle, nothing.

"You've gone off me," Callaghan said.

"Sorry?" A woman in a soft orange cardigan arched her eyebrows. She was beautiful. Callaghan couldn't say that. He couldn't smile. Where was a way forward? He shook his head, grabbed another book and stalked back to the counter.

The Deli. The window. The cappuccino. The cover. *Tales of Love and Loss* by Knut Hamsun. Isaac Bashevis Singer reckoned that the "whole modern school of fiction in the twentieth century stems from Hamsun".

Callaghan read the first story, "A Lecture Tour". His enjoyment of it was banished by the scrap of paper that fell into his hand as he turned the page in order to mark his place. *Dashiell, find your way to my heart. Please.*

* * *

Wednesday came around too slowly, too rapidly. He didn't know what he wanted to do but realised, as he showered and lay clothes on the bed, that he was going to find her, despite the knots tightening in his stomach. Whoever she bloody was.

Romance was the farthest thing from his mind as he shut and deadlocked his front door. This early evening winter sky was battleship grey; he had war in his thoughts. How dare this person stalk him? Did she not realise the stress she was causing him? The simple pleasure of a borrowed book had become a stifling experience. Already he was thinking of getting a bus to Withington and using the library there instead. He guessed that would not protect him from her messages, though. It was getting to the point where he suspected books bought from the shop on Warburton Lane, or on-line at Amazon, would sit in his hands containing more paper than their authors intended. A future without reading beckoned. Maybe there would be invitations which flashed up on the television screen. Maybe the radio would whisper supplications at him. Perhaps, after all, he was simply mad. It suddenly seemed an inviting condition.

He reached the heart of the village before realising that the message had specified a time, but not a place. He glanced at his watch as if that might help him. Five to seven. Couples were sauntering along the pavements, holding hands. Women nestled against shoulders. He saw a man kiss a forehead. He heard the intimate exchange of laughter.

He headed towards the library, reasoning that she must be there, if she was going to be anywhere. It closed all day on Wednesday; she must be waiting for him outside. But there was nobody. He stood in the cold, his breath cocooning his face, waiting for sense to reveal itself. A shadow moved in the glass of the entrance but no traffic had whistled past behind him. He approached the door and, cupping his hands against the glass, peered inside. When he pressed his forehead harder against the frame to improve the tunnel of his vision, he was appalled and excited to feel the latch give way. Perfume breathed against him as the door swung open. From somewhere deep inside the library, he heard the brief trill of a woman's laughter.

Callaghan had no name to call. "Hello?" he said. "It's Dashiell."

He thought he could see, at the far end of the library, a jerk of movement, as if someone was trying to duck out of view. He cleared his throat, and said again: "It's Dashiell."

A moan or a sigh. He took this as encouragement and closed the door behind him. He looked around him for light switches but could see none. When he returned his gaze to the depths of the library, he saw a figure.

"Hello," Callaghan said. "It's me. I'm here."

The figure did not move. At this distance, it appeared to have its back to him, a grey wedge drawing shade towards it.

"We shouldn't really be in here," Callaghan said, trying to inject a little levity into his voice. "Why don't we nip across the road to the Dog? I'll buy you a drink. You can tell me how you became so interested in performing magic."

A whimper or a groan. Callaghan licked his lips. "Are you all right?" he asked. An incremental shake of the head, as if it was attached to something rusty, in need of oiling. Callaghan quelled the conviction that he had heard bone grinding against itself.

He was growing impatient. "You told me to find my way to your heart," he snapped. "Well I'm here, aren't I? Do you want my help or not?"

Now she was saying something, or trying to. She half-turned; he caught a glimpse of her face in profile, a black eye swivelling to fasten on him. The blackness swelled, enveloping him. It became the territory of his dreams, where the blue flowers shivered in the wind. They were all dead now, the petals black and shrivelled like burnt shreds of paper. He opened his mouth to cry out and pounds of black ash poured from between his lips. The goats, so chary but dominant here — a sinewy extension of the land — were dead, devoured; a dozen scarlet ribcages all that was left, arthritic hands beseeching the heavens. Her voice was something filtered through wet earth. He saw chopped shadow, creating itself out of the slender shape of her arm. She seemed to be riffling in and out of true, like a deck of cards shuffled in the hands of a seasoned croupier. He heard a mish-mash of words slithering against each other, eels in her throat.

He felt an itch in his hand and misread it as the need for physical contact. He reached out for her, and saw that the itch was down to a different kind of catalyst. He was bleeding. How had that happened? He inspected his palm, lifted his other hand to touch the skin and saw a knife gripped in his fingers. He stared at it for a while, as if it must be somebody else's limb, somebody else's weapon.

Dear Michelle, the woman finally intoned. Her voice was a tombola of varying tones and timbres. *Dear Kathy. Dear Olivia. Dear Belinda. Dear Claire.*

"What?" The names pricked him. From long ago. Long ago.

Dear Debra. Dear Sarah. Dear Amy. Dear Lorraine. Dear Joy.

She turned; light from the road fell across her face, slashing it to leaves. They swarmed with words, as if she were a book brought to life. But these were not the ordered lines of Helvetica or Sabon. This was handwriting; his handwriting. Glimpsed phrases: *I need... I want... You must...* Her eyes came alive, but would not remain constant: they changed colour, blue to green to hazel to brown, as if an optician were slotting lenses into a refractor head. She moved her hand to her face, but not before he saw a flicker-book of lips chase each other across her mouth, from plump to flat, rouged to chapped. Her long fingers rested against her cheek, the nails of restless colour. Her ring finger was abnormally long, encircled with a dozen engagement bands, all of which were tarnished, their stones chipped or cracked or lost. She slid them off and threw them at him; he raised an arm to protect his face, but a couple stung him. When he opened his eyes again, she was close, her other hand encircling his waist. He smelled so much perfume lifting from her — a cloying mix of ill-matched notes — that his eyes watered. She splintered in his gaze, as if into many different people, but it could only be his tears causing such an effect.

What a waste, she said, although her voice seemed to come at him from a multitude of directions. He didn't know if the words were a reference to him, or herself. He tried to step away but she had him fast in her fingers, surely too many for just one hand to possess. The voice, the voices, were weighed down with age, with regret. He recognised something of his own within them. It was a tiredness, a capitulation.

So it was that when he felt the mouths on his skin — and the teeth, as countless lips peeled back — he was unable to fight. The knife was forgotten, or forsaken. He might even have flung his arms up and allowed it to happen, perhaps the first time in his life he had thrown caution to the wind. He was not scared. They struggled into him like a pack of lionesses at a goat. He was dead before they reached the sawdust of his heart, but he hadn't even noticed the difference.

ABOUT THE AUTHOR

CONRAD WILLIAMS WAS born in 1969 and has been in print since 1988. He is the author of the novels *Head Injuries*, *London Revenant*, and *The Unblemished*; the novellas *Nearly People*, *Game*, *The Scalding Rooms*, and *Rain*, and the collection *Use Once Then Destroy*.

He is a past recipient of the Littlewood Arc Prize, the British Fantasy Award and the International Horror Guild Award. His new novels, due to be published in 2009, are *One* and (as "Conrad A. Williams") *Decay Inevitable*.

He lives in Manchester, UK, with his wife, three sons and a large, plastic bag-chewing Maine Coon.

www.conradwilliams.net
www.humdrumming.co.uk

HUMDRUMMING TITLES BY CONRAD WILLIAMS:
Rain Dogs [FOREWORD]

SEEN BUT NOT HEARD

GARY McMAHON

Cat got your tongue?

— Old English mariners' folk saying; broadly meaning, 'Have you nothing to say?'

THE BOY WAS waiting in the house when I returned from a meeting with a hack journalist who had first interviewed me several years ago, just after the accident. The man said he wanted to write a book about me, to study my 'gift' and try to understand exactly what it meant in the 'Great Scheme of Things'. I knew exactly what it meant: nothing. Nothing at all.

The boy was sitting by the unlit gas fire, his feet propped up in the low, tiled area below the appliance as if he was warming them. He looked to be about seven years old, and had longish blonde hair, rich green eyes, and hands that seemed somehow too big for his small frame.

Walking quietly across the room, I sat down in a chair facing the television. I stared at the boy's reflection in the blank screen, waiting.

When I could wait no more, I said: "What do you want from me?"

The boy remained silent. He did not even move. Then, after what seemed like an age, he turned his head towards me.

"What?" I said, wishing the boy would leave me alone.

The boy opened his mouth as if to speak at last, but no words came out.

He had nothing to say. The boy had no tongue. It had been cut from his mouth, leaving a small wriggling nub of purple flesh that was unable to form an audible sound.

Even now, after all this time, some of them are so weakly projected that they struggle to make themselves heard: this apparition was unable to speak by no choice of his own.

Slumping back into the armchair, I closed my eyes to block out the sight.

No matter how many times they come to me, I can never get used to the children. It hurts to see their old wounds and mutilated bodies; and a deep sadness always hangs about them like storm clouds gathering around mountain peaks.

It is the children that bother me most, because they remind me of my own dead child.

The boy stood up and went to the window. Darkness pressed against the glass, a roaming entity looking for company. His face was troubled, his entire stance speaking of unfinished business. When he raised a hand and pointed somewhere out into the night, I slowly nodded my head.

"Take me there," I said. "I'll do what I can."

But he did not take me yet. All that night the boy stood guard over my bed, waiting for a breakthrough. Often images came to mind without him having to try too hard, but this one was different. The boy's death was shrouded in so much violence and secrecy that I could establish no firm connection. All I was able to catch were brief images of pain and confinement. A terrified boy — this boy — locked in a basement room; the cries of other, long dead children; the confusion of the killer, and the dull thud of his heavy boots as he paced the earthen floor.

A kidnapping, then; followed by a sharp and messy demise. The missing tongue was important: it was a signature, a trademark mutilation. But I could recall nothing in the news about such a vicious act — perhaps it had been kept back, as a way of rooting-out false confessions by crazy attention-seekers?

Unable to sleep with the boy watching me so intently, I rose from my bed and connected my battered old laptop to the Internet, running a search for child-abductions, specifically those resulting in murder. I'm not the sharpest tool in the box when it comes to technology, but I know enough to get by.

The results came back in a flood of mostly useless information. I narrowed the search, keeping it local, and eventually found an article regarding the kidnapped son of a millionaire. The boy was still missing; there had been no sign of him since his disappearance over six weeks ago.

I closed my eyes and pressed an open palm to the rubbery screen. A subtle vibration ran along my wrist, climbing my arm to settle in my chest, near the heart.

This was the one.

Opening my eyes, I spun around on my office chair, the castors squeaking like inquisitive mice. The boy was no longer in the room.

* * *

Morning: a short drive out of town to the local "Millionaires' Row", where Mr. and Mrs. Lefine owned a palatial residence surrounded by several acres of land. The countryside rolled jaggedly by as if on castors, the clear sky above looking bright as a film set backdrop. Everything looked so unreal, so perfect. I knew from experience that this was a bad sign.

I was expected, so when I buzzed at the entrance and announced myself at the intercom, the great gates opened at once to allow me access. Coasting up the gravelled drive, I felt a deep pang of envy. Not for the money, but for the peace that these people enjoyed. Then I remembered the boy and envy quickly passed, replaced by an empathy born of a similar loss.

A butler let me in to the main house, and I stifled a grin. Nobody hired butlers these days; it was so bourgeois. I followed the man through an elegant reception hall, fine portraits hanging on the clean white walls. Houseplants shifted in a slight breeze, lowering their heads like respectful mourners, and I was aware of the grim aspect that had so recently invaded this beautiful home.

"Ah, Mr. Usher. Please come through to the library." The well-dressed man who appeared in the doorway looked drawn and tired; the strain was beginning to tell. Yet he retained an upright posture, and an air of good breeding. I glanced down at my own baggy pants and scuffed shoes, then back again at the man's expensively fitted suit. The two of us were worlds apart, each from a different social class in a dying social system, yet we were bound by a common grief.

"My name is Charles Lefine," said the man, flashing a pained smile. "I know you, of course. It's the only reason I took your call. I'm afraid my wife wasn't up to your visit, so it's just you and me."

I said nothing, pressuring Lefine into saying more.

"Your name is legendary in these parts since the Millington scandal. Even those of us who don't believe in the spirit world couldn't fail to be impressed."

"Thank you," I said, nodding slightly, "but that whole thing was solved by good police work, and not by anything I had to offer."

Candice Millington. Daughter of a local bathroom tycoon and part-time prostitute. Candy had taken her rebellion one step too far the night she accepted a lift from a serial killer, and the mental flashes of previous victims that I received had eventually led to the out-of-season holiday chalet where she was imprisoned. Luckily, the girl was still alive. A prosthetic arm had already been successfully fitted, and they said that she would eventually walk again. The mental scars, however, would never heal: the killer was still at large.

Lefine poured us both a brandy, despite the early hour. Then we sat facing each other in matching leather armchairs. Lefine leaned forward, betraying tension, whereas I was much more relaxed. A skinny black cat entered the room, looked around, and then scampered back out the door.

"I've come here with a message, Mr. Lefine."

"What kind… of message?"

I put down my glass, swallowed burning spit. "You say you know of my reputation, so you must know this: I am not here as a fraud, a trickster, or a con man. I require no payment for the information I bring. All I want is peace."

"Yes, I know that you are considered the genuine article, and that you've helped a lot of people."

"Some people," I said, wincing. "Others I have not helped at all. It doesn't always work that way — you see? I have no control over what I see, feel, hear. All I can do is watch, listen, and try to aid these poor souls in what they need to do."

"Go on," said Lefine, visibly restless: his left leg jittered arrhythmically and he made a fist with his free hand.

"A boy came to me last night. A boy I believe to be James, your son. He told me nothing because he was unable to communicate, but he gave me enough of a clue to his identity that I managed to track you down."

Tears moistened Lefine's eyes, and he finished the brandy in a single swallow. His chest hitched as a breath stuck there. Then he stood and moved to a desk in the far corner of the room. When he spoke, his voice was muffled, as if he were hiding his mouth with a hand.

"And why couldn't he communicate, Mr. Usher?"

I did not want to say it out loud, but felt compelled to do so. I was forced into a tight corner by a father's need to know. "Because he had no tongue. It had been… removed."

There came a soft thudding sound from the floorboards at my feet, as if it were punctuating my sentences.

When Lefine turned 'round, he was holding an antique pistol. The barrel was trained unsteadily upon me, aimed at my chest.

"I'd hoped that you were a fake, Mr. Usher. But sadly, your talents seem genuine."

When the boy appeared in the bay window, I finally understood. I had been used again, manipulated into a situation where I must bear witness. It happened again and again; time after time… the spirits toyed with me, pulling me this way and that. All I could do was follow and watch as the scene played out before my jaded eyes.

The commotion under the floor was repeated. It sounded like the banging of fists against the inside of a coffin lid — sadly, that was a sound I had actually heard before.

"I'm sorry," I whispered, both to the boy and the man with the gun. "So very sorry."

Lefine looked puzzled, and took a step back, bumping into the desk and pushing closed the drawer that had held the weapon. "I had to do it. I'm virtually bankrupt, and the insurance payoff will save my business… save my life.

It was such a simple plan... and a cruel one. Kidnap his own son and wait until his insurance brokers agreed to pay the ransom. Then, when the money was safely in his grasp, place the body somewhere far away, where some anonymous by-stander could discover it. An abandoned culvert running beneath a quiet stretch of motorway. A muddy ditch in some forgotten field. Somewhere it would not be associated with him until the police identified the remains.

"It's such a small price to pay: the life of a stupid little boy. He was mentally handicapped; brain damage sustained during birth complications. He would never have amounted to anything, and I would have been forced to keep him fed and clothed forever, like a sick dog."

The boy stepped slowly forward, smiling as he closed in on his father from behind, oversized hands reaching out to seize the man by the throat. The youngster's moss-green eyes were cold and hard, like tiny stones on a riverbed, his mouth a slit of darkness. In death, this boy knew everything, despite the mental inadequacies which had limited him in life.

The banging noises stopped, the silence proving even more deafening.

"It wasn't so hard," said Lefine, rambling now. "Not really. I practised on a few first; homeless kids that no-one would ever miss. I cut out their tongues so they couldn't scream. After the first couple, I actually began to enjoy it."

The others appeared on cue, rising and twisting like bands of mist through the floorboards from the basement where their corpses lay in shallow graves. Their hands were curled into ugly claws and their faces hung long and empty, bereft of any visible means of articulation.

Sometimes, I know, the ghosts return to make peace with the living; but sometimes — more often than anyone could ever imagine — they simply come back for revenge.

After watching as much as I could stomach, I quietly left the room. It would take hours, I thought, for the butler to scrub those stains off the heavily varnished wooden floor. There were no screams, no frenzied cries for help as I let myself out of the house. Lefine was rendered speechless, but it was no cat that got his tongue.

ABOUT THE AUTHOR

GARY M^C^MAHON HAS placed over 60 stories in magazines and anthologies in both the UK and USA. He is the author of the novellas *Rough Cut* (nominated for a British Fantasy Award, 2007) and *All Your Gods Are Dead*, as well as a short story collection titled *Dirty Prayers*, and the novel *Rain Dogs*.

His contribution to *The First Humdrumming Book of Horror Stories*, "Hum Drum", was honoured with inclusion in Ellen Datlow's *The Year's Best Fantasy & Horror #21*. Previously, he was lucky enough to receive two Honourable Mentions in *YBF&H #18*, and four more in *YBF&H #19*.

Gary lives with his wife and son in West Yorkshire, where he quietly rages against the society that spawned him. He wishes to inform us that the rumours about him are quite untrue; he was visiting friends in Amsterdam on the night of the murders.

www.garymcmahon.com
www.humdrumming.co.uk

HUMDRUMMING TITLES BY GARY McMAHON:

The First Humdrumming Book of Horror Stories [CONTRIBUTION]
All Your Gods Are Dead [NOVELLA]
Rain Dogs

PINHOLES IN BLACK MUSLIN

SIMON STRANTZAS

RUSSELL LOOKED UP at the night sky, at the single northern star around which everything rotated. Whenever he felt uncomfortable, Polaris was the one place to which he knew he could always turn: the one constant in his life. But he had not travelled four hours northward from Toronto to stargaze.

Philip had dragged him along on a weekend getaway. Russell had initially resisted, not because he did not know Philip well but because he had long ago realized that, though he had lost many friends over the course of his life, he had done little to gain any. Perhaps it would do him some good to be in the company of people rather than stars. He might then learn to forge new bonds to replace those that were broken long ago.

But he found doing so difficult as he sat around the campfire while the others talked and laughed. It was as though there were a thick wall protecting them from him, but in that wall there was a tiny hole between the bricks, just large enough to see through and observe the warm life existing beyond. The sound of the loons on Lake Tyson, even the crickets in the grass around him, seemed distant, as though they too were beyond that great barrier.

"Aren't you going to eat something?" Philip asked, and Russell looked at the fire and at the others surrounding it. No one else was turned his way, yet he could feel them watching, deciding what to make of him.

"I guess so," he said, and picked up the long skewer he'd been issued and went to the cooler. Inside, a package of meat floated on a sea of ice and water, beer cans bobbing around it.

"Hey! Pass me one of those," Daniel said, and his windbreaker rustled as he held out his hand. Russell reached into the frigid water and retrieved the can for Philip's friend. "Thanks... Russell, right?"

"Yes, that's right."

"So, Russell, how do you know Phil again?"

"We work together. At the bookstore."

"He works in the Science Department," Philip added. "It's the section right next to mine."

"Oh yeah? Wow. I failed science class, myself."

Russell put on a smile and nodded. He had no idea how to respond. Should he ask what Daniel did for a living? Was that the right thing to say?

Before he could answer, Daniel was speaking to his sister, Claire, again. About what, Russell had no idea, so he returned to his seat and fed the sausage he did not want into the flames.

It was hard for him, having an interest in something no one knew much about and being so disinterested in anything else. It made small talk difficult. He didn't understand the mechanics of it, nor why it came so easily to Philip. But that might have been the reason why he and Russell had been able to form any sort of connection in the first place — Philip had done all the work. It was a marvel sometimes to behold him, speaking to the customers as though they each were important to him, listening to their stories with what appeared to be genuine interest. Russell's own rare attempts felt stilted and awkward, and he worried his face betrayed his disingenuousness. How much easier the stars were, with their predictability and their silence. That far up north, he had seen lights he had never seen before — not past the blinding glow of the city — and he wished he could have spent time there alone with only his telescope and astral charts.

Yet it was interesting to be there with other people while the rest of civilization was so far away. If he thought about it, he could almost imagine they were all that remained of life on Earth — just these six people on the empty planet. He wondered what would happen if he were to actually pretend that were the case — would he then find it easier to interact with them? To befriend them? He had to do something, because as it stood he had nothing left in his life but the sky.

"You're pretty quiet," said Claire, who resembled Daniel so much the two had to be twins. "What are you looking at?"

Russell stammered as he spoke to her.

"The constellations. I'm trying to find Cygnus. I can't usually see it when I'm in Toronto."

The whole group looked up.

"Which one is it?"

"It's that cluster of stars, obviously," Trevor said, and Russell tried to modulate his voice to keep it sounding friendly.

"Actually, that's not it. It's the one that looks like a giant cross." He looked at Trevor for a reaction. The man said nothing, but looked bored by the answer. His girlfriend though, did not. Annie looked fascinated, an effect intensified by her blonde curls being lit so brightly by the fire.

"I'm amazed we can see it," she said. "There's so much pollution in the air it's a wonder the sky isn't permanently covered with smog."

"That's why we have a hole in the ozone layer." Trevor smirked at his own joke.

"Actually, there isn't really a hole," Russell said, but even as he spoke he wished he hadn't. No one could possibly care about what he had to say. "The layer is thinning, but not completely gone yet."

" '...Yet'?" asked Philip.

"Give it time," Claire said. "Pretty soon, there's going to be nothing left alive on this planet."

"Ah, who needs ozone anyway?" Trevor laughed while Annie punched him.

"It protects us from the universe, you jerk!"

For the first time that night, Russell's smile was genuine.

Still, as the evening wore on, he didn't find making friends of the people any easier. They were so unlike him — so gregarious and full of life — and as they progressively became drunker, he felt increasingly alone.

Russell heard the fire hiss as it burned out, and the chill of the breeze intensified. Annie wrapped Trevor's arm around her and squealed. Russell caught Claire's eyes roll.

"We should get inside," Trevor said. Somewhere over the lake there was the distant sound of thunder. A loon cried once in the darkness beyond them, and then went silent.

* * *

Trevor's cottage appeared smaller once the lights were turned on, its two bedrooms squeezed together along the western wall.

"Are you sure you and Russell don't mind sleeping out here on the couches?" Annie asked. Philip waved his hand.

"I've slept in plenty of worse places, with plenty of worse people."

Russell could think of nothing to add.

"We'll switch tomorrow," Claire said. "Dan and I can sleep out here and you two can get the beds. Russell shouldn't be forced to stay on the couch both nights." She looked at him as she spoke, and he was keenly aware of how warm his face had become.

After everyone had turned in, Russell lay awake in the darkness. The windows were open, their curtains pushed aside, and he could see the tiny points of light that made up the Milky Way. There was no noise but the hiss of leaves gently shaking while water lapped the shore. He wondered idly when the crickets had stopped chirping.

He was unsure if or when he had fallen asleep under the blanket of darkness, but he awoke at some point in the night with the strange sensation of being watched. He tried to convince himself it was not true, but could not dismiss it. Then the floorboards creaked and he sat up.

His throat was so dry he could barely whisper.

"Who's there?"

The footsteps multiplied and became less cautious. Russell shrank before he could be seen.

"It's Trevor," a voice whispered back, but in the darkness Russell could not be sure it was true. "Who's that? Philip?"

"No. It's Russell." He wondered if the name would mean anything.

"Sorry, buddy. Did I wake you?"

"No," he lied, and then struggled for what to say next. "I don't sleep very well outside my own bed."

"Yeah, that whistling is keeping me up, too." What whistling? Russell thought. "I'm going down to the lake, in case anyone else wakes up."

"Okay, I guess."

There was a heavy sigh, though Russell could not be sure if it came from Trevor or the sleeping Philip, and a moment later there was the sound of the door opening. A faint rectangle of stars appeared in the nothingness. Then Trevor's body filled the hole and the room fell dark once again.

When Russell next awoke there was light, but it came from a clouded sky, and he could not tell for a moment just how early or late it was. His face felt swollen, his eyes sticky, and for the briefest moment the anxiety of being so far from home was intense.

Philip was still asleep on the other side of the room, and the doors to both bedrooms were closed. Russell recalled his encounter with Trevor in the darkness, and wondered if it had been a dream of his sleep-deprived mind; there was no way to be sure. He checked his watch. It was just past ten.

He always hated the morning, hated knowing the stars were out there, up in the sky, but too hidden to see. In his apartment in Toronto he would have spent the night looking at those heavenly bodies, tracking their course on his map, then sleeping-in the next day. At the cottage, he could not keep that schedule — he had to follow that of the others, and as a consequence he found himself with nothing to do but listen to the others as they slept.

It all felt eerily still. The sounds that should have been so clear during the day were muted, as though everything but he were submerged beneath the murky water of Lake Tyson, and all he could hear were its waves lapping the shore. He shuddered in the stillness, and felt its oppressing weight. Perhaps everyone's dreams were seeping into the air, accumulating to form clouds overhead that erased the stars from the sky.

Daniel was the first of the others to wake, but the sound of the opening bedroom door roused Philip as well. The former appeared no different than he had the night before. Philip, however, looked as though he'd been beaten by his dreams, and his face looked as Russell felt.

"What time is it?" Philip asked, the last word becoming a yawn.

"It's half past ten."

"Christ! I wanted to get out on the lake before it got too warm. Do you think we should wake the others?"

"No, let them sleep," Daniel said. "Trevor will get angry if we disturb him."

"Um — I think he's already gone."

"Gone where?"

Russell shrugged.

"Probably for a swim," Daniel said. "That's all he could talk about on the way here. Should we go down, boys? We can leave a note for the girls to join us when they wake up."

"Sounds good."

The three men walked down the tree-covered hill toward the lake. It looked much different in the daytime, and Russell could scarcely believe it was the same lake they had spent hours sitting beside the night before. The remnants of the campfire were still right where he remembered but everything else seemed wrong. The lake was rougher, and there was an electrical smell in the air like that after a thunderstorm. Wind was shaking the trees, and he thought for a moment he could hear the whistling Trevor had mentioned in the night.

"It's quiet this morning," Philip said, "and cloudy. I can't even see where the sun is."

Russell looked up and Philip was right. The empty slate grey sky deepened the sensation of being trapped in a timeless limbo. Daniel, however, seemed to be adapting.

"You can still feel the heat," he said. "Do you guys see Trevor anywhere?"

Russell looked, but saw nothing on the empty beach save for the canoe which was tied-down between two trees, just beyond the fire-pit. From somewhere above there came a strange hum, like an engine running far away, though its intensity wavered. At times the hum was so faint he wasn't sure he was still hearing the sound and not just the memory of it.

"I don't even see any footprints," Daniel said. "Russell, was it still raining when Trevor left?"

"Um..." he stalled, trying to remember the night before, but every second it took to recall the details only increased his nervousness, until he couldn't speak any words at all. Philip intervened.

"Look at the ripples in the sand." He pointed. "What does that?"

"I don't know," Russell said, and it was true. There was only so much he understood about the earth sciences, and even then only how they related to astronomy. What he did know was the wavy patterns in the sand had left him uneasy for a reason he could not fathom. He watched the grains creep across the beach under strong gusts of wind, and though that wind made the water roar, behind it the same hiss — that same whistling — continued, though finally loud enough that he was sure it was there.

"Can you guys hear that?"

Philip looked back quizzically, but Daniel seemed too distracted.

"I'm sure Trevor's just taking a walk. Last time we were up here he spent half a day walking around in the woods. Right now, I'm more worried about getting that boat in the water. I don't know how much longer the weather is going to hold out, boys. Russell, you want to go on the water, right?"

"Okay. Sure." Should he have said more?

"That's the spirit, I suppose." Daniel chuckled. "Philip, help me flip the canoe over. It looks like some sand got into it during the storm." Philip grabbed the other end while Russell watched, and the two shook the small boat until the sand fell out and was blown out across the beach.

The canoe did not appear large enough to hold three people at one time, but Russell said nothing. He could only assume Daniel and Philip knew what they were doing, as he understood virtually nothing of the world of camping and cottage living. So many others he encountered spoke that outdoors language though, and it was not the first time he felt excluded by his ignorance.

Perhaps he could learn it, if he tried harder to understand.

"Do we... um... don't we need oars... or something?"

"Actually, we need paddles. Oars get locked into the side of a boat." Philip made circular motions with his hands, mimicking rowing. "But you're right. Where are the paddles?"

"They can't be far." He started kicking the sand around where he stood. "Maybe they're buried? Split up, boys, and help me look."

The three walked away from each other, Daniel into the trees behind, Philip and Russell on the sand. It didn't take long for them to find something.

"Russell, come here and look at this," Philip said.

He was standing over a dark shape, about twenty feet or so from the water. Russell approached.

"What is it?"

"I think it's a towel."

It looked like it had been in the water for ages. It was covered in dark dead algæ, and its balled shape suggested it was wrapped around something small, about the size of a cantaloupe. He could not bear the thought of touching it to see what was inside.

"It must have washed up on shore."

"But it's so far from the water."

"Hey, I found them!" Daniel's voice carried from the trees. Philip looked at Russell with a moment of concern, then forced a smile and clapped him in the shoulder. "Let's go!"

He ran to Daniel while Russell rubbed his bruised shoulder. Somewhere above there was a wide field of stars hidden behind the blanket of clouds.

Philip and Daniel came across the sand, canoe held above their heads. They looked excited, and Russell couldn't help but feel infected by it.

"You'll love this, Russell. Last time we were up here, I wanted to spend the whole day on this thing. Okay, ready Phil? We'll flip it on three." He counted off the numbers, and then they flipped the canoe over and placed it on the edge of the water. "Okay, we'll push it out and then —"

Someone behind them was shouting. Russell could barely hear it over the waves in the lake. The three of them waited and listened. The shout came again. He saw a shadow move among the trees at the top of the hill. Russell squinted, but could not tell who it was.

"Hang on, boys. I'll be back in a second."

"If you're not back in five, I'm taking him out without you."

Daniel smiled broadly, then turned and trotted off, stumbling up the hill and into the trees. Philip watched him go, and then turned back to Russell with a worried look on his face.

"What's wrong?"

"Hm? Oh, nothing. Help me carry this boat out. We aren't really going to wait for him."

They each took a side and waded into the lake. It was colder than Russell had expected, and murkier. He supposed he was used to the water from the municipal taps.

"Okay, put it down. Now, get in while I hold it." Russell climbed in awkwardly. When he did, water shot up in a small jet from the bottom of the craft.

"Damn it!" Philip said, and Russell looked down at the water streaming in through the tiny hole, filling the otherwise empty boat. "Come on, we aren't going anywhere. Let's carry this thing back and then go see where the hell everyone is."

Russell got out cautiously and the two of them carried the boat back to where they'd found it. Philip tied it down again, and then they began to walk back up the hill towards the cottage.

"I wonder if Trevor's back yet," Philip said as they climbed.

Russell said nothing.

At the top of the hill, Daniel and Claire stood talking. They both turned and then looked disappointed when Russell and Philip emerged from the trees. The reaction hurt Russell when he saw it, especially coming from Claire. Then she spoke, and Russell did not know what to feel.

"Annie's gone."

"She and Trevor probably went off somewhere," Daniel said, rolling his eyes. "You know what they're like."

"I wonder how we missed Trevor," Philip said. "How did he get past us?"

"I didn't see him, either," she said. "Annie was still in bed when I left the room to take a shower. When I got back, she was gone."

Daniel did not seem concerned. "I've been telling her; I'm sure they're going to show up later, all full of smiles."

Something about it did not seem right, but Russell couldn't put his finger on what was wrong. Perhaps it was the lingering smell of ozone in the air, or maybe the sensation of sand underfoot though they were so far from the beach. Or, was it that damned noise? The sound of wind rushing past? Surely it was the cause of all the strange things he'd heard.

"Let's go inside. It looks like it's going to rain any minute. Trevor and Annie can take care of themselves."

But Russell didn't join them. Instead he sat on the deck of the cottage for the next few hours, beneath a sky that grew murkier with each moment, and watched the trees for sign of Trevor and Annie. He could hear the other three inside as they spoke, though the words seemed distant. Even the sound of the wildlife had diminished, and he wondered why he could not hear any birds with so many trees around him. Any indication of a world beyond the cottage had gone, and it left behind an oppressive cloud-filled void. But he could see a break in that cover, a small hole in the sky through which light shone. That had to represent some kind of hope, didn't it? Something to indicate things were going to be okay? Even the rushing sound of the wind picking up could not take that from him.

Claire's sudden appearance at his side startled him. He felt clumsy, and fought his body's urge to flee.

"What are you looking at?"

"Oh, um, the sky, I suppose. Just at the clouds."

She looked up and he saw for a moment the spot where her long neck touched her chest.

"Phil tells me you're into astrology."

"Astronomy," he said, and she laughed.

"That bugger. I knew he was lying to me."

Russell smiled with her, and struggled for words, but she did the work for him.

"Do think there are other people up there? Like us?"

"You mean like aliens?"

"I suppose so," she shrugged.

"No. Not really."

"Why?"

He took a breath and held it while he considered lying to her.

"In order for life to have formed on earth, there first had to be hundreds of millions of protein molecules shaped the right way. Do you follow me so far?"

She nodded.

"Given the size of Earth, though, do you know how long it would take for a single one of these to appear? Roughly ten to the two hundred and forty-third power billions of years. Not only is that older than the Earth, it's older than the whole universe. The odds of it happening twice are too astronomical for me to imagine."

"So, you think we're alone?"

Russell hesitated.

"Go on. You can tell me."

"I think there's nothing out there but cold darkness. Nothing but an endless vacuum, and it's only by a freak chance we're alive to know it."

"Do you think it's jealous of us?"

Words caught in Russell's mouth. Claire laughed again and touched his arm. "It's okay. I'm messing with you!"

Philip and Daniel emerged then, wondering what the laughter was about. Claire just looked at Russell and smiled. "He just told me a joke."

Russell felt strange inside, as though a wall were crumbling.

"Well, maybe he can tell us later. Right now, I'm getting worried about Trevor and Annie."

"I still think they're okay," Daniel said. Philip shot him a look. "Well, I do," he murmured.

"They've been gone too long, and that sky isn't getting any better."

"There's a hole," Russell said, but when he looked up it was gone.

"Do you really think something's happened?" Claire asked.

"I think we should go look for them."

"But we don't know where they went."

"We'll find them. I don't want to wait until it's too dark to see."

Russell felt a chill and rubbed his arms. Then he was outside himself, watching as he stood there on the deck of a summer cottage, surrounded by people who were joking with him, preparing to step off on a walk through trees and across beaches. How far he was from the bookstore, from his field-guides and telescope. He felt a million miles away from his regular life, and he could almost hear it spiralling away. He wanted to reach out, but did not know if he wanted to catch it or push it away.

"I think maybe we should go now," Russell said, ignoring his doubts. Then stronger: "We should go now."

"You boys are wasting your time."

Claire put her had on her brother's shoulder. "Don't be long," she said, and Russell tried to smile.

The two men made their way down to the beach, and then up again through the trees surrounding the cottage, yet they found no sign of Trevor or Annie. It was as though the couple had lifted both feet from the ground and vanished. Neither Russell nor Philip spoke much as they walked among the strangely quiet trees. The animals must have known something was coming, for at no point did Russell see a single hint of wildlife. It was as though the animals had all gone, and what was left was less a forest and more the representation of a forest — as though he and Philip were walking through one of the displays he saw in the department store windows along Queen Street on his way to work.

The wind returned with a strength which was beyond anything Russell had ever experienced, moving through the trees and throwing branches up into the air. The two of them stopped as grains of sand flew like tiny missiles into their faces, and Russell closed his eyes for protection. The sound the wind made was terrible — like a scream that would never end. Russell's heart raced with the noise, and then he reached out for Philip to assure himself that he too would not disappear.

When the wind died down, Russell slowly opened his eyes. Philip was rubbing his own, and looking ahead in the near dark.

"We should turn back," he said, though it was clear he did not want to do so. "It's six o'clock, but it looks more like eleven."

"Maybe Trevor and Annie are there now."

"Maybe," Philip said.

The two men made their way back through the woods, moving quickly to avoid the rain they were sure was coming. Through the canopy, Russell could see the hole in the clouds had reformed, and beyond it a star shone brightly. For a moment, he thought it was Polaris, but its position in the sky was wrong. He looked down when he realized Philip had stopped. He was pointing, and at first Russell saw nothing.

Then, something up ahead moved.

He wondered if it were Trevor or Annie, but just before Philip called out, Russell knew it was neither.

"Claire? What are you doing out here?"

"I don't know," she stammered, visibly upset. She looked as though she was about to fall, and Philip ran to hold her up. Russell was ashamed of his own inability to act. "I was inside, and then I thought I heard you two coming back. I went outside to check on you, and then there was this sandstorm or something. I think it cut my face," she said, and Russell could see the tiny drops of blood that had formed there, like a lattice of wounds. "I couldn't move — I could barely breathe. Then, I went back inside —"

Claire burst into tears, and the sound filled Russell with dread. He did not want to hear the rest.

"I went inside and he was gone. Daniel was gone!"

Philip held her, and tried to reassure her with calm words, but as she continued to sob he turned and looked at Russell with confused terror. Russell did not doubt he looked the same.

The cottage door was open when they returned. Stepping inside, the first thing Russell noticed was the sand — the floor was covered with it, as were the counters and the furniture. The windows were wide open, the sheer drapes hanging before them waving wildly. Philip closed each in turn, excluding all but the loudest howls of the heavy winds. Claire's sobbing had lessened, and Russell led her to the couch while Philip checked both bedrooms. When he returned, he looked at Russell and silently shook his head. "Don't worry, Claire. I'm sure he's just gone looking for the others."

She sniffled. "What's going on? Where is everybody?"

"I don't know."

No one spoke. The only sound was of the outside world spinning around them. The air felt heavy, weighing down as though they were under water. Russell went to the window and looked at the dark world. The sky was filled with clouds, and they all seemed to swirl around that tiny patch of empty sky in which hung that tiny light. Was it Sirius, perhaps? Could he somehow be mistaken about where that star should be? The trees below it swayed wildly, their dark shadows like dancers against the night sky, supplicants calling down some ancient god.

Then, the unearthly howl returned and grew louder, as though a dam had broken, and something large and vast was rushing towards them. The walls of the cottage shook, the windows rattling as though they were about to break. Then something rained upon the roof, striking so hard Russell thought sure it would break apart. He put his arms around Claire, as did Philip, trying to protect each other from whatever was trying to get in. The storm continued to push at the windows and at the door, but somehow the small cottage stayed standing, and eventually the wind and sand that had raged like a river eased. Claire slowly lifted her tear-swollen face and looked at Russell.

"I want to go home," she said. He would have kissed her were he not so afraid.

"But the others —"

"The others aren't coming back," Philip stood and brushed the sand off his clothes, "and we can't stay here any longer."

There were no arguments. They packed their belongings quickly, doing their best to ignore the whistling howl as it built again in the background.

Philip led them out of the house and toward his car parked a few metres away, while Russell watched the horizon closely, hoping for some warning. The wind coursed around him and he could feel its pull, but he held tight to Claire, sheltering her under his arm. When they reached the car, Russell froze in disbelief; while they had been inside the cottage, the car had been buried to its doors in a drift of sand, as though it were some relic from the past. Russell wondered, briefly, if the storm was intentionally trying to stop them.

"Come on!" Philip said, and was kneeling, digging the drift away with his hands in a crazed frenzy. When she saw this, Claire joined in the effort, while Russell continued to watch the dark clouds swirling overhead around that one empty space which framed the universe beyond. He had to squint to keep the sand and the wind from blinding him, but the stars he saw there bore no resemblance to anything he knew.

"Okay! Let's go!" Russell barely heard Philip's words over the deafening wind, but the car door was open, its interior light insignificant in the dark of the storm. Philip and Claire were already inside, and Russell got in. Once the door closed, the pressure in his head eased somewhat.

"We'll come back in the morning. Maybe the others will be back at the cottage by then." Philip did not sound confident, but Russell and Claire nodded, and Russell tried to convince himself he agreed.

Philip turned the ignition key and the engine revved to life, but only for a brief instant before it sputtered out. He turned the key again and there was the awful screech of metal against metal. "What's wrong?" Claire said, an hysterical edge to her voice. Russell and Philip looked at each other, and then Philip silently pulled a release beneath his dashboard and stepped out of the car. The wind blew his hair wildly as he lifted the hood, and Russell watched Philip's ten fingers appear over the top of the metal slab. They flexed as Philip disappeared behind the hood and Russell looked at the strange cloud coming towards them. Then Philip slammed the hood back into place and climbed back inside the car. For a moment, all he did was stare at that same cloud.

Then he turned.

"The engine has seized. It's full of sand."

The three of them sat quietly; wind pushing against the car. Outside, there was a sound so deep Russell was not sure at first it was there, but he felt the vibrations in his chest. Then the entire car rattled.

"What are we going to do?" Claire asked.

Before he could answer, the air became denser — as though under a great pressure — and through the window Russell saw the tree branches pulled upward while sand swept through the air and pounded into the car's windows. In the darkness, the debris looked like a hand with too many fingers, long tendrils waving. They closed around Philip's car, and then the vehicle started to rock back-and-forth in its grip.

"We're going to roll over," Philip said. "We have to get back inside the cottage!"

"It's too far!" Claire screamed, her hands pressed against the sides of the car to keep from falling.

"We can't stay here," he kept repeating. "We can't stay here!"

Russell tried to open his door but the wind pressed it shut. He kicked it repeatedly until it opened and the wailing sound filled his head again. Claire reached her hands out and Russell and Philip yanked her free just as the door slammed shut with a crunch. Then the car buckled as though squeezed. Philip screamed something Russell could not hear and the three of them ran towards the cottage without looking back at what chased at their heels.

They were on the porch in seconds, and Philip struggled with the door while Russell covered his ears to block the noise of whatever was racing towards them.

"Help me," Philip yelled and the two men put their full weight against the door while it splintered around them, its tiny window cracking.

Then door broke without warning, and Russell was thrown forward by the strength of the wind at his back as it rushed to fill the void. He landed awkwardly on the wooden floor, Philip on top of him, and he felt his knee grow cold on impact and then the pain took hold a moment later. The gust that swept over him and filled the cottage stole the scream from his lungs.

Philip did not notice what had happened. Instead, he was spinning his head, trying to stand as he frantically asked, "Where's Claire?" over and over. Russell winced and tried to follow before the pain made him collapse. He squeezed his knee tight to keep it together and from the floor looked through the broken door and glass into the mælstrom of debris that rose into the sky. He saw what Philip was staring at. Claire was there in the distance, struggling as though being dragged by unseen forces. Then she fell backwards and in an instant she was gone, yanked into the dense shadows of the towering trees.

"She's going towards the lake!" Philip said. A thought crossed Russell's mind: Why does everyone keep leaving?

Philip looked down at the crumpled Russell clutching his knee tightly, and said, "Wait here," before he was gone, hurrying towards the trees and the beach beyond.

"Wait!" Russell called out, and then started to give limped chase after the last of his friends.

The blasts of wind and the airborne debris made it difficult to see, but Russell continued toward the spot from which he had seen Claire disappear, following as close behind Philip as he could manage. The dark clouds overhead spun faster and faster, all being drawn into the small hole in the sky. He could feel the pull even from the ground, a sense of lightness to his step as though he weighed less the farther he went. The pull was almost unbearable, and as long streams of sand crossed in front of him like clenching fingers, he recoiled, allowing Philip to travel farther into the darkness. Then, as Russell watched horrified, Philip was lifted off the ground as though he were nothing.

At first, Philip did not seem to realize what had happened; his legs continued working, trying to push him faster and farther. Then, he began to tumble, and realized something was wrong. Russell tried to run to him, but the swirling winds prevented him making anything more than a few steps. By then Philip was far out of reach, spinning in the air as though caught in a funnel, circling faster and faster as he moved towards the one bright spot in the sky. Over the roar of the storm, Russell heard something, but did not know if it was Philip screaming, or something far worse.

There followed a cracking noise, deep and thunderous, and one by one he saw the trees along the ground ripped free of their roots, pulled upward by an impossible force. Beyond them, a giant funnel of water rose from the lake into the sky and it too circled the small opening in the clouds.

Unable to watch any longer, Russell turned and ran. He ran as fast as he could, but even as he did so, he could feel the cold hunger of the universe behind him, peering through the hole it had made in the barriers protecting the world. It was insatiable, wanting its fill of life, though Russell understood it would not be enough. It would never be enough to fill the vast emptiness.

He ran as hard as he could, driven by the knowledge that if he stopped it would be the last thing he ever did. He ran despite the pain that shot through his knee with each step. He ran until his breath tasted of blood, and his body was screaming for relief. He ran until his knee cried out for him to stop, and then until it decided to stop on its own, throwing him forward.

But he never hit the ground. Instead, Russell ascended slowly towards the stars to meet his new friends once again.

ABOUT THE AUTHOR

SIMON STRANTZAS WAS born in the dead of the Canadian winter and has lived in Toronto for more than thirty years, making a name for himself writing tales of the strange and the bizarre, tales that examine the illusions that mask our malignant and corrupting universe. Over twenty of these have been sold to places as *Cemetery Dance*, *Postscripts*, and *The Mammoth Book of Best New Horror*, from where they spread their sickness into unsuspecting minds.

There. Did you feel that? You too have just been infected, and there is no cure but death.

www.strantzas.com
www.humdrumming.co.uk

HUMDRUMMING TITLES BY SIMON STRANTZAS:
The First Humdrumming Book of Horror Stories [CONTRIBUTION]
Beneath the Surface [COLLECTION]

FALLING OFF THE WORLD

TIM LEBBON

AT FIRST THEY all came running after her, panic sewn onto their faces and a stitch in their sides. She could have been a stone plucked from a pond in defiance of gravity, and they were the ripples in reverse, flowing in from all directions to the point of her egress. All colours, all shades, sunburnt or pale, bald or long-haired, they ran with their hands held out to catch the trailing rope. She had not been lifted that high yet, and the end of the rope still kissed the ground below her, drawing a snaking trail in the dusty ground surrounding the lush field. One man leapt and missed the rope by a finger; he stumbled and fell, and Holly smiled. Dust rose around him in a cartoon halo. A woman managed to grab the rope but then let go, screeching as it ripped through her hand and burned the skin. She blew on her palm, and Holly laughed out loud, waiting for the smoke and fire. Other people jumped for the rope and missed, and somewhere a woman screamed. But by then the breeze had Holly held in its breath, and one great gust clasped the balloon and made her truly airborne. Holly looked up at the balloon but this made her dizzy, so she looked down at the ground again, at the people slowing from a run to a walk behind her, then from a walk to a standstill, hands on hips, faces pointed skyward but darkening quickly as their owners looked down to their own level again. Some of them turned and walked away, shaking their heads as if forgetting what they had been doing. Others started chatting now that circumstance had brought them unexpectedly together. One face remained aimed upwards at Holly. The shape waved its arms over its head, and she heard a distant voice. She did not understand the words. They were of the ground and she was of the air, and their language was wholly alien.

She drifted westward towards where the sun would set in a couple of hours, and thought that maybe she would beat it there. It hung high in the sky before her, a yellow smudge behind the hazy cloud cover. It was so slow. She concentrated on the sky next to it, trying to detect the sun's movement out of the corner of her eye, but it must have known she was looking because it did not move. There was no way it would beat her. She was travelling so fast. The wind had her firmly in its grasp now, tugging hard at the flabby pink balloon above her, dragging the two of them across the sky and leaving only a trail of her sighs behind. The rope was long and old, frayed here and there where it had been tied an unknown number of times, worn by constant striving for ærial freedom. It was stained too, darkened by the sweat of a thousand people who had tried to hold the balloon down. But, old and frayed, rough and dark though it was, still the rope sat snugly and comfortably beneath Holly's armpits, encircling her twice around the chest and shoulder blades, tied in some random fashion in front which seemed to mimic the very best knot she had ever been taught in Brownies. Those knots had been designed to restrain and hold back; ironic that now, here, they gave her such freedom.

Holly twisted and looked back over her shoulder. She could just make out the field in the distance: a splash of deep green in a patchwork of otherwise pale, wan fields and meadows. A firework rose above the field and splashed a red smear across the sky, much lower than she, but obviously so high up to those observing from the ground. Another followed the first one up, and then another, silent explosions flowering in the air like reflections from oily water.

The rope tugged at her once, hard, and she turned her attention forward again.

The show was going on without her, it seemed. She could hardly blame them. It was not as if they had meant this to happen, and guilt, as her mother often muttered between remorseful silences, was such a waste of time.

Holly was growing cold. She had come to the show dressed in summer finery: a flowery dress, sandals, a sun hat which had been flipped from her head the second the balloon's rope had broken from its mooring, wrapped itself around her chest and tugged her hard at the sky, even though there was no discernable breeze that day. No wind, no gale, no breath in the air, except when the balloon needed it. She looked up, but the pink balloon did not stare back down. She shivered, then smiled as they entered a stream of warmer air. It rushed by her face faster than before, lifting her hair from her forehead, and it was warm and comforting. She even began to feel tired.

Holly looked down, and between her dangling feet she saw a splash of water. It could have been a paddling pool in someone's back garden, filled to the brim at the break of day and slowly draining as the sun made its traverse of the sky, the black flecks drowned insects, the pool ignored already for some more urgent plaything. Or perhaps it was a lake, a mile across at its widest, speckled with insect-like boats tearing at its surface tension in their eagerness to sport or fish. She kicked off one of her sandals to see how long it took to fall, but the balloon moved her faster across the sky and she lost sight of it before the splash came.

She imagined some lonely fisherman mourning a dearth of catches that day, amazed at the footwear in his net. She giggled. Then she wondered what the little boy in his pond would think at the floating footwear, and she laughed so hard she wanted to pee.

She could, she supposed. There was no one here to see. But she held back, because modesty was really all about herself.

Holly's arms were aching slightly, and the rope had begun to chafe her armpits through the thin summer dress. But the sensations were not unpleasant. Sometimes after a day riding her bicycle or running through the woods with her friends, she would ache, muscles burning, face scorched by the sun, but it was always a good feeling. It was the evidence of a day well spent. Here and now, that feeling was more profound than ever.

The ground grew dark before the sky. The fields and roads faded into uniformity, and here and there the speckled lights of civilisation marked unconscious territory against the wild, the dark, the unknown that lived everywhere. It was as though the ground was fading away into nothing, and only these isolated pockets of humanity held out for a few hours more, their artificial light cementing them to reality. Holly had always been aware of the unknown, so near that it touched her every day, so familiar and so much a part of life that it was almost impossible to make out from everything else. She talked about it to her mother, but her mother sighed and shook her head and lit another cigarette, not knowing that the smoke made languages in the air. Holly would run through the garden, brushing by plants and flowers and letting them coat her in pollen. Her mother's shout from the kitchen doorway would dislodge the pollen from the fine hairs on Holly's arms, perhaps drifting to find other plants, aiding the spread of flowers. The land had language, and Holly was keen to translate.

As the sun dipped down into the west, winning the race, she looked up and saw several bright specks hanging in the air around her. They could have been stars but they seemed much closer, close enough to reach out and touch. She started to stretch her hand but the rope bit in. By the time the pain faded away, the sky had grown dark and whatever the setting sun had been hitting high up in the atmosphere had cloaked itself in night.

* * *

For Holly, night was a time of revelation. Lying in bed at home, clouds covering the sky, streetlights turning off at midnight, she had always imagined darkness to be a blanked canvas of history upon which the new day could be drawn. There were always noises linking the day passed by to the new one to come, but whatever made them were more secretive and self-conscious, more aware than when the life-giving light illuminated them. The sun had shunned them after all, spinning its way beyond their land to bless faraway places. They should be shamed at its leaving them. They should be humbled at its return.

And then the new day would dawn, and all night fears would burn away in the sun.

Here, now, above the clouds, Holly knew that true darkness must exist only in death. Because above the sleeping land, starlight made her shine. The light of the sun was minutes old, her mother had once told her, reading in stilted sentences from a book. That had made Holly feel grimy and grubby with age, but then her mother read that the light from stars was years old, centuries, millennia, five billion years, and that most of what you saw in the night sky was no longer there. The feeling of grime had been swept away by time, turning Holly into little more than a fossil. She was an artefact waiting to be found, a blip in time, and that idea of immateriality pleased her immensely. As her mother closed the book and left the room, Holly had stared from her window, straight out and up at one particular star. She wondered whether she could be staring directly into the eyes of a little alien girl a trillion miles away... and she knew that if this was the case, that alien girl was a long time dead and gone. All Holly could see of the universe were echoes. Nothing was quite as it seemed.

Stars floated here. They were the specks of light from which the sun had glanced as it dipped down to bed, reflective shapes in the sky, and now they caught moon- and star-light, shedding the primeval radiance without a care. Holly tried to steer their way. The breeze had her up here, and she was submitted to its will, but she still thought that if she leaned to one side, left, left, she could edge herself that way. She looked up but the balloon was merely a shadow blocking out a circle of the night sky.

Holly was cold and hungry, and she closed her eyes as her bladder let go. Her pee warmed her legs for a time, but then she thought it had turned to ice.

One of the shapes seemed to manifest from the silvery night, drifting closer to her as if steered by someone else, and it was as dawn exploded leisurely in the east that she saw it was another balloon.

There was a boy hanging beneath this one. He seemed excessively tall, as if stretched by however long he had been hanging up here, and though at first Holly thought he was waving, perhaps it was simply his limp, dead arm swinging in the wind. His balloon was a bright silver, as if it had swallowed and retained the starlight. It veered, taking away the boy so that Holly could not make him out in any great detail, for which she was glad. He had looked very thin.

As the sun rose once again, warming her back, she looked around at the reflections or dark specks which marked other shapes. She was amazed at how many people seemed to have been taken by balloons and blown up here. Perhaps somewhere, there was someone she knew.

When she was eight one of her school friends, Samuel, had gone missing. His parents had come to the school with red-rimmed eyes and thin, sunken faces, their hands so tightly twisted into each other's that they looked like an old knotted tree. They had sat on the stage with the headmaster during morning assembly and then, when called upon, Samuel's mother had made a tearful plea to the children to tell them where Samuel may be. Holly had been shocked. She had no idea why Samuel's parents would assume that someone like she would know where their son was. She had looked around at her friends, and they all appeared to be thinking the same.

Samuel had never been found, and Holly had soon cast him from her mind. But now maybe she would see him again. Perhaps he was up here, with all the other people caught beneath balloons, and perhaps even now her own mother was standing red-eyed on a stage, pleading with a hall full of children for Holly's safe return.

She looked down at the new ground created by this sunrise, and far, far below she could see a road. It had no dimension from this altitude; it was merely a grey line stretching across the land. It twisted here and there, avoiding hills which she could not see. Branches sprung from it and snaked away to places where few people went, withering eventually to nothing. Holly thought that was strange. All the roads she remembered went somewhere, not nowhere. Maybe there were many more roads left untravelled, there simply to exist. There were no signs of cars travelling these routes, but then maybe she was too high up to see. They would certainly not see her, she was sure of that. She kicked off her other sandal, giggled as it span away below her, and she watched until distance had swallowed it up. Its eventual fate would remain a mystery.

She warmed up nicely in the morning sun, though her arms and legs had grown stiff during the night. The rope was still making her armpits sore, but the worst pain now came from her shoulders and chest, stretched and strained as they were by the unaccustomed weight they were supporting. The rope was holding her in position, true, but it was her shoulders taking most of the strain. She tried to shrug herself into a more comfortable position. The rope shifted. She smiled, satisfied, and then screamed out loud when she realised that the rope was still shifting. It was slowly pulling her arms up, as if forcing her to flap the slow wings of a wounded butterfly, and if that happened the loop would slip over her arms and past her head, and the balloon would no longer have her.

Holly forced her arms down, crying, screaming out at the unknown people in the unseen cars far below to help her. The sandal must have landed by now, surely? They couldn't just ignore it, could they? Swerve around the footwear that had bounced across the concrete road, clip it with their wheels, send it skimming into the ditch to rot there and become home to ants and woodlice and other things?

It took all her strength to stop screaming and squeeze the rope to herself. It tightened. The wind caught the balloon and snapped it this way and that, and the rope tugged, and it tightened some more. Whatever unseen knot held her here must have been twisted and knotted again, because suddenly she felt safe once again.

She looked down at the strange ground far below, glad she had not gone. Things were much nicer up here.

Minutes later, and the brief scare seemed a lifetime ago. The speckled sky of night felt like two lifetimes, and the memory of those people chasing the rope as the balloon whisked her away was someone else's entirely. She may have been up here forever. She wondered what she ate and drank, but she felt neither thirst nor hunger.

The sun was chasing her. The breeze carried her westward, ever westward, but after yesterday she had serious doubts over whether she could ever beat the sun. It was gaining on her even now, furtively following its path of old and aiming to bypass her to the south, arc over her head and win the race again. She could see it if she glanced over her shoulder, feel its heat on her left cheek, arm, leg. She willed her balloon on, but will was not enough. There was wind, and the balloon's own improbable desire, and that was the only power her flight was allowed.

As the sun reached its zenith Holly saw another balloon drifting in from the north. Its path seemed to match hers for a while, several miles away but clearly defined by the reflected glare from its filled expanse. Holly crossed her arms and watched its progress. There was a shape hanging below this one too, a long thin shape dangling apparently lifeless, though it was still too far away for Holly to make any rash judgements as to its true status. She would have to wait, see if it came any closer, and make up her mind then.

It did come closer. Slowly, almost indefinably, its approach only apparent in the fresh detail Holly could make out. Like the hour hand of a clock she could not perceive its movement, yet still that movement was obvious. Her own internal clock was not attuned to such subtle changes. She wondered at all the intricacies of the world she missed because of this; the growth of plants, the blossoming of flowers, the lengthening of her own hair, the aging of her skin, the erosion of a rock, the melting of glass. If she could speed up time she would see all these things, like a time-lapse film showing the birth, life and death of a mayfly. But time would not be changed by the likes of her. She would have to change herself.

Holly closed her eyes and tried to blank her mind, think of nothing, focussing on one single point of light in her mind's eye. When she opened her eyes again, the balloon was noticeably closer, and the shape below had resolved into a hanging body. She closed her eyes again, that spot of light — nothing else — the light, the light.

Eyes open, reality crashed back in a welter of sensations, and the other balloon was closer to hers. The body had turned its head. It had a skeletal face, skin dried and pressed to the bones by the breeze. Long hair flared around its skull. Some of its clothes had been ripped off, and those that were left were bleached by the sun. Holly could not tell whether it was a boy or girl. Not even when it spoke.

"Hello," it said.

"Hello," Holly replied. She had observed the other balloon's journey and perceived its dangling cargo's progress across the skies. So much else must have changed that she had not noticed, and she looked around to see what. Down below, the road had vanished and the ground was smothered in a silvery sheen of distance. She wondered how high up she was, and how much higher she could go.

"Don't you think it's amazing," the hanging body said, "how many people are taken by balloons and carried up here?"

Holly nodded, went to speak and realised that there was no need. The person looked away, seeming to agree with her. There was not that much to say.

They drifted together for some time, until the sun had overtaken them once again and was on its homeward descent. Holly used her new-found talent to close off time, concentrate on the light, the light... and when she opened her eyes again, she had seen that the sun had moved. She wondered if the Earth was aware of those things upon its surface or floating way above, or whether it was so old and slow that these fleeting things were all but invisible to its grand perception. She and the body glanced at each other often, and she even smiled. The other person's balloon looked larger than Holly's, but perhaps that was a trick of the light, or distance deceiving her again.

She thought of the many things she could ask: How do we get down? What is down? Has there ever been a down, or did we dream it? But she did not wish to spoil the moment with awkward questions. So she closed her eyes for a time and watched the Earth moving beneath them.

* * *

At some point the other balloon must have been tugged away by an errant breeze, because when Holly looked again, it was gone.

She thought about falling. It was not the falling that killed, she remembered her mother once telling her, it was the impact. Looking down between her feet now, the ground hidden by a layer of cloud, she thought that maybe she could fall forever.

That did not frighten her. What frightened her was immobility, apathy and an absence of wonder. She knew that she had a choice. The rope slipped again as if to remind her of this; if she raised her elbows and pointed up at the balloon, the loop would slip over her shoulders and head and she would begin her new journey.

She raised one hand, felt the rope slide up her arm and lock at her elbow. It would be as simple as that.

She hung and watched the sun set, specks of light emerging across the heavens as star- and moon-light picked out other balloons. And she closed her eyes and concentrated on the light, to see whether she would feel herself making that choice.

ABOUT THE AUTHOR

TIM LEBBON IS a talented, highly-respected author, and the winner of the British Fantasy Society's "August Derleth Fantasy Award for Best Novel (2006)" for *Dusk*, the first of his "Noreela" fantasy saga. It was followed with the 2007 releases of *Dawn* and *After the War*, then *Fallen* in 2008.

Mr. Lebbon is the co-author with Christopher Golden of the novel *Mind the Gap: A Novel of the Hidden Cities.* He also wrote *Hellboy: Unnatural Selection*, and *The Everlasting.*

Mr. Lebbon is also the author of *The New York Times*-best-selling novelization of the terrifying horror movie *30 Days of Night*, which recently won a Scribe Award for "Best Novel (Adapted)" in the category of "Speculative Fiction".

Several of his novels and novellas are currently in development as movies.

www.timlebbon.net
www.noreela.com
www.humdrumming.co.uk

HUMDRUMMING TITLES BY TIM LEBBON:

The Reach of Children [NOVELLA]

QUADROPHOBIA

GUY ADAMS

OF COURSE, HIS mother had told him that he would never amount to anything. Sat in her armchair, like a tobacco-stained marshmallow stinking of Mackeson's Stout, she would offer forth these nuggets of affection. Dark and bitter things they were, the kind of comments you'd draw on if you caught the dog shitting on your carpet.

She was dead now and if Rupert Silkin had been the sort of man prone to dancing he would have proved it at the memorial service with a short routine, maybe a light shoe shuffle or something Latin American, on the lid of the coffin. Nobody would have complained; no one in the church that day had liked her. The entire service had a pleasant upbeat feel to it; many of the congregation having thanked him afterwards, saying how much they'd enjoyed it.

No, Doris Silkin hadn't been loved, nor was she particularly right in her predictions. As a Chartered Accountant within the respected firm of Buxton and Booth, Rupert was earning £42,000 a year (before tax), which was, as he was happy to tell anyone who asked (say at one of the social functions his wife would insist on holding), "Not exactly peanuts, even when one does take into account deductions and the standard depreciation of the pound in unruly fiscal climates."

Inevitably he would go on to talk about portfolios and the benefits of financial diversification. This would be followed with polite nodding, awkward silence and a sudden and desperate need on the part of the listener to hunt out small pieces of cheese and pineapple speared on cocktail sticks. In one particularly profound state of panic, an elderly relative of their next-door neighbour had resorted to an Angina attack, although it's possible this was a genuine medical emergency and not related to the fatal boredom being inflicted upon them.

* * *

Rupert wasn't stupid and knew the low regard with which most people held him. He was boring. He was also completely straight and no use when you wanted to fiddle your tax returns. Conversationally he just had nothing to offer which is why he loathed his wife's parties with such a passion, never knowing what to say or, indeed, *how* to say it. Over the years he had slowly given up trying and now he could most commonly be found hiding in the kitchen.

Which is where he first met Philip Jasper.

Jasper was a new face amongst his wife's extended social circle, the boyfriend of a woman Rupert couldn't have told you the name of, however hard you pressed. The names and faces at these evenings changed with such regularity that he had long ago resolved to simply smile, shake hands and pretend he knew them all well. So few people talked to him that he was never caught out.

Jasper was the sort of man Rupert congenitally distrusted, the sort who never wore ties but often hair product, who would listen to popular music and drive cars that didn't come in hatchback. He appeared to be in his early thirties; therefore, at most, ten years Rupert's junior. There may as well have been centuries between them.

Rupert was caught grazing on the finger food before taking it through to the guests. "Hello there," he mumbled around a mouthful of corn snacks the packaging assured him were both 'tangy' and 'cheesy'. He brushed his hand on a tea towel to try and rid it of the glutinous powder flavouring and offered it for shaking.

"Hi." Jasper replied, taking the offered hand in both of his and patting it in a way that confused Rupert, a fan of the simple up / down tug. "You must be Rupert, Valerie's husband."

"That's right."

"Philip Jasper, Debbie's boyfriend."

"Oh *right!*" said Rupert, as much in the dark as before but practiced enough not to show it.

"Good of you to invite us."

"Not at all, glad you could come."

Then came the reassuring pause, the chasm of awkwardness that sent most people scurrying for cover in another room. Jasper stayed, leaning back on the work-top with his arms folded and a gentle smile on his face. Rupert began to panic, it had been so long since someone had deliberately loitered in his company that he was uncertain what to do.

"I believe you're in accountancy?" Jasper asked.

"Yes, Chartered Accountant for Buxton and Booth,"

"Fascinating"

Rupert struggled to hear the irony in Jasper's voice; baffled, he conceded there wasn't any.

"Well," he struggled to reply, "it's not the word most people would use."

Jasper chuckled, "I'm not most people. You must be a very brave man working with numbers."

"Hardly..."

"Numbers have a power," Jasper leaned in close as if imparting a secret, "they are the building blocks of everything. They keep us safe in the air or on the road, stop our houses falling down around our heads. They allow us to measure time, distance, mass and speed. Nothing would function without numbers."

"True," admitted Rupert, rather surprised at his guest's enthusiasm for the subject, "but that hardly makes them dangerous does it?"

"Oh you think? Imagine for a moment what would happen if we were to lose a single number, just one solitary digit, tell me Rupert, where do you think that would get us?"

"Yes, well, it couldn't happen though could it?"

Imagination was not one of Rupert's skills.

"Don't be so sure." Jasper looked him straight in the eyes, "One, two, three... don't forget... five." Rupert suddenly felt rather hot and uncomfortable, a rime of sweat working its way around the collar of his sensibly plain cotton shirt. Then Jasper laughed. "Sorry mate, just messing about."

Rupert tried to laugh back but he found it difficult. "I'd better get these dips through to the other room," he said, hoping to escape.

"Want a hand?" Jasper asked patting him on the shoulder.

Rupert shuddered at the physical contact and shook his head, "I can manage, honestly." He looked at the little ramekin dishes for a moment. Of course he didn't need a hand there were only... three or... you know. Taramasalata, Tomato Salsa, Cheese and Chive, Sour Cream... not three. More than that; *one* more than that...

* * *

Valerie's guests dwindled away by half past eleven and Rupert was in bed by twelve. There was a throbbing behind his eyes and the couple of aspirin he had swallowed seemed unwilling to do anything about it.

It took him a while to drop off and when he did sleep it was troubled. In his dream, the tick of a clock combined with the bellowing of his bloated mother. The nagging of his wife mixed with Jasper's smug laughter and a repetitive flow of number cycles. Great armies of π marched through his head, tussling with other digits in perpetual motion. Odd, even, factored and prime square-bashing their way through until dawn.

* * *

He awoke a little after six feeling neither refreshed nor cured of his headache. After an unusually haphazard round of washing and dressing he sat and stared at a bowl of Cornflakes for a bit.

* * *

Leaving for his bus he brightened a little in the cool suburban air. By the time he reached his stop he was beginning to feel better.

The bus pulled around the corner and he rifled in his jacket pocket for his travel card. Glancing at the sign on the front the pain behind his eyes returned with sufficient force to make him drop his briefcase. Where there should have been a number there was just an unintelligible smear of grey. Everything around it was perfectly clear; the destination, a poster advertising a musical his wife was badgering him to take her to, even a couple of streaks of pigeon muck. Everything but the actual number. Which was ridiculous, Rupert knew the number of the bus he took to work every day, it was the one just above three before you got to five, y'know, *that* one.

He couldn't even think it, not precisely, knew where it was in the general scheme of things but could neither visualise its shape nor the sound it would make if you said it out loud.

Trying not to panic he stumbled onto the bus, showed his travel card to the driver and took a seat somewhere near the back.

Eventually his heart rate slowed. He began to convince himself that it had been a momentary lapse brought about by his rough night; maybe even something he had eaten. There had been some spiced pickled onions he'd sampled, dark and exotic things stewed with brightly coloured herbs and peppers, he should have known they'd be trouble.

Calm now, he rested his briefcase securely on his lap and glanced out of the window. They were everywhere: great swathes of unintelligible space as if the street was an oil painting violently smeared by fingernails while the paint was still wet.

He turned away from the window screwing his eyes shut. He dug his nails into the plastic leatherette of his briefcase, desperate for anything tangible. What was happening? *Why* was it happening?

Tell you one thing, he'd think twice before eating pickles again.

Not daring to look out of the window normally, he snatched a series of glimpses at the road ahead, just enough to keep track on where he was. By the time he reached his stop he was feeling more than a little travel sick.

* * *

He negotiated his way to the office by keeping his eyes mostly on the pavement. Once inside he felt safer, shivering a little as his humid body met the air conditioning of the foyer. He nodded at the reception desk, managing a brief smile as always, and headed straight for the lift.

Which was going to be a problem.

He held back for a minute, pretending to straighten his tie in the mirrored wall opposite the steel doors, hoping for a familiar face to glide by and save him from the ludicrous terror of the lift buttons.

"Morning Rupert." Thank God! Alan Davis, from a couple of offices down the hall.

"Morning." He hung back, letting Davis press the button for their floor then dashed into the lift keeping his back to the control panel.

"I say, you feeling alright Rupert?' Davis asked, 'You're looking a little green around the gills if you don't mind me saying."

"Fine Alan, just a little peaky. Dodgy pickles."

Alan looked at him strangely before chuckling and inching his hands rather nervously into his trouser pockets.

"Tricky buggers," he said, as if it were a common problem, a day-to-day inconvenience.

"Hmm." Rupert fidgeted with his tie, trying to think of something normal to say. "You never know where you are with the onion."

There was a pause so large it transcended the laws of Physics just by fitting inside the lift.

"True. Bastard things, really," Alan said eventually, just as the welcome sound of a bell announced that they'd reached their floor.

Rupert hurried out and continued straight down the corridor, hoping to get into his office and safe behind his desk before he embarrassed himself further.

Danielle, his assistant, a girl as unsuited to accountancy as a whale to stilts, caught him just before he'd got through the door.

"I've got those spreadsheets for Dobbins and Clark you wanted." She said around the wedge of chewing gum she eternally stored in her mouth.

"Thank you," he mumbled trying to take the file she was offering without being seen to look at her prodigious cleavage. She had got into the habit of wearing bras so thrusting Brunel might have engineered them. He had a feeling it had something to do with the new junior they had taken on a few weeks ago. Whatever the cause he wished she would stop it, it was most disconcerting.

Managing to get the file under his arm with only the briefest of glimpses he darted into his office and closed the door aggressively enough to halt Danielle's gum chewing.

"It's a bloody pleasure," she muttered before heading back down the corridor, her buttocks shaking with a vigour normally reserved for Mexican percussion.

Rupert sat down behind his desk. Drumming his fingers on the closed file for a few moments he got to his feet again and filled a cup of water from the cooler in the corner. A sign of importance that cooler, only staff above a certain salary could expect one of their very own; as sure a sign of rank as a Captain's stripes. Now was the first time he'd used it since the water heavy few days after they'd first put it there, his initial excited guzzling having faded once the smugness had worn off and the repetitive need to urinate had become something of an irritation.

The water calmed him, the very act of filling the plastic cup and then draining it a soothing process. He filled the cup one last time and sat back down.

It was neurosis triggered by his conversation of the night before. Work related pressure bringing it on perhaps.

He just had to work through it, force himself back on track.

He opened the folder Danielle had given him, steeling himself for the pain in his head.

The numbers flowed, some recognisable, some not. He focused on those he could see. Calculating, multiplying and dividing.

It was like a mental maze, every few steps in a certain mathematical direction would lead him running into a brain-crunching barrier. The pain in his head built and built until it became white noise; an incessant whine that forced tears from the corners of his eyes. Still he tried to focus, tried to push through it. Then other numbers started to tumble away and, as one brick had been loosened, the whole wall threatened to collapse, the blind spots increasing until the entire page was a scar across his eyes. Just as he thought his head would split, he felt a pain in his left hand. Investigating, he found he had punctured the web between forefinger and thumb with the large stapler he kept on his desk. He watched as two small rivulets of blood appeared, a red circle turning purple in the centre where a buckled staple bit into the flesh.

There was a knock on the door. He pulled at the staple, wincing as his nails scraped at the wound.

"Come in," he said, trying to keep the panic from his voice.

Danielle put her head around the door.

"You all right?"

"Fine, just a little accident that's all." He dropped the bent staple into his wastepaper bin and pulled a clean handkerchief from his trouser pocket with the right hand.

Danielle's eyes lit up as she saw the blood and, damn her, she stepped into his office pulling the door closed behind her.

"How did you do that?" She came over to the desk, took the handkerchief from him and wrapped it around his hand.

"Honestly," he pleaded, "It's nothing, I can manage."

"Don't be silly," She dabbed at the punctured bruise, glancing down at the spreadsheet on his desk. "Don't tell me my math's drove you to it." She joked, "I went over it a couple of times and you were right about the inconsistencies."

She moved to the water cooler to rinse the hankie,

"If you look at the returns for March they're all wrong, they've filed..." Her voice suddenly dropped out to be replaced by a high-pitched whine, electric feedback, the figures she was quoting an unrecognizable scream to his ears.

He clamped his hands to his head. His vision blurred. There was the distant feeling of vomiting and a sense of movement, although he wasn't aware of trying to stand up.

The noise stopped and his eyes focused on Danielle's face. He was stood directly facing her, the front of his shirt covered in vomit. His right hand was drenched in blood from a hole in her throat. The hole the letter opener he was holding must have caused.

The letter opener had been a gift from his wife on their fifth wedding anniversary, gold plate with the engraving 'Who's the Boss?' on the handle. He hadn't been blind to the double meaning of the question, or foolish enough to mistake himself for its answer. He had smiled and thanked her with a dutifully subservient peck on her cheek and slit his letters open with relish ever since, only occasionally imagining its blade parting juicer matter than gummed paper.

He tried to read the engraving now but the rhythmic pump of blood from Danielle's Carotid artery obscured it.

The wet handkerchief fell to the floor at their feet.

He stood there for a moment, unable to move. The only sound was the laboured whistle of air escaping from Danielle's windpipe as she tried to breathe.

Then the moment broke and he threw himself back, the letter opener staying firmly fixed in the puncture wound of Danielle's throat.

He began to cry, all rational thought vanishing as he watched her bleed. She opened her mouth as if to speak, then toppled forward onto the carpet.

He cowered in the corner of his office, hiding behind the fronds of the potted palm that had been placed there. Office research showed that a potted plant made the worker feel more comfortable, more relaxed; the act of watering and tending it creating an emotional bond to the working environment, instilling a proactive sense of calm.

It had let him down today but he hugged it nonetheless.

* * *

Of course his mother had always told him that he would never amount to anything, but — as he was happy to tell the number of specialists that visited him over the years — she'd been a silly cunt and he'd never liked her much anyway.

He had to admit, though, that his life had undoubtedly taken a turn for the worse in recent years, but was reassured that things were getting better: they allowed him a small plant these days and, while still a little hazy, he was pretty sure that the number on his cell had a three in it.

ABOUT THE AUTHOR

GUY ADAMS HAS written so many books about TV show *Life On Mars* he risks entering a coma himself. Still, they paid the mortgage which means a lot to him as writing is his livelihood. Silly man.

He is also the author of the two novellas he refers to — somewhat exaggeratedly — as "the Deadbeat Series". These books are well thought of by some which means even more to him than having the mortgage paid (although not so much by his family who like food more than praise).

With two teenage boys and a wife in mind then, he is currently working on: two novels based on TV shows other than *Life on Mars*, a replica of Doctor John Watson's scrapbook (covering a handful of the cases he shared with his good friend Sherlock Holmes), a humorous novel about a Polish immigrant, a children's novel featuring giant squid and sea zombies, and an adventure series aimed at twelve-year-old boys.

He is bloody tired most of the time.

www.guy-adams.com
www.humdrumming.co.uk

HUMDRUMMING TITLES BY GUY ADAMS:

More Than This
The Imagineer [as 'Gregory Ashe']
Deadbeat I: Makes You Stronger [NOVELLA]
Deadbeat II: Dogs of Waugh [NOVELLA]
Deadbeat III: Old Bones [NOVELLA; FORTHCOMING]
The First Humdrumming Book of Horror Stories [CONTRIBUTION]

NIGHTMARE ALLEY

RHYS HUGHES

A PERFECTLY NORMAL man was Mr. Ogerepus and he travelled to the perfectly normal town of Porthcawl by imperfectly normal means. The omnibus discharged him with his suitcase and cramps into a day of medium greyness. Then he sought to work out his bearings, first by listening for the sea, then by asking an old man who hobbled past. A finger was pointed and Mr. Ogerepus strode in that direction.

As he walked, he struggled to remember why he was here. The weight of the suitcase eventually refreshed his memory. It was heavy because it was full of books, many copies of one book. He was a salesman. In this case, why was he heading for the sea? The answer took a few minutes to bubble into his awareness: because there was no castle in Porthcawl. And no great wall. Not even one penal colony.

Yes, that was why. His boss had ordered him to target coastal towns without showing mercy or restraint to potential customers. Aggression was certainly not Mr. Ogerepus' style, but he was prepared to be very persistent with his work. He was already forty years old and new jobs were hard to find. Somehow he must sell every single book in his suitcase, following the rules of engagement without significant deviation. He would smile, frown and cough in all the right places.

The very best salesmen went much further than that, of course. Mr. Ogerepus knew colleagues who could wiggle their ears, touch their noses with confident tongues, even dislocate shoulders and knees for the sake of an impressive display. But his envy of these achievements remained mild and never triggered heartburn. He worked with a minimum of the obligatory theatrics. Perhaps he was more old-fashioned, as well as physically less supple? Who knew with any degree of certainty?

He continued to walk, but the sea refused to make its appearance. Somebody must have been telling lies about Porthcawl, for even the salty tang of brine on the air was absent. Further ahead, stumbling closer with each step, was the same old man who had earlier given him directions. It was too late to cross the street and no other course of avoidance could be convincing. Mr. Ogerepus might stoop to un-tie and re-tie a shoelace, or count the loose change in one of his pockets, but the timing involved in these operations demanded a precision beyond his competence.

He had no choice but to confront the old man. And why should he be given a choice in these circumstances? The very luxury of the idea suddenly irritated him as a noxious waste. Fortified by this boost of anger, he stopped in his tracks and glared at the approaching figure, who raised his hand slowly to point in a different direction, almost certainly random. Mr. Ogerepus forestalled these antics by shaking his head in a masterful way and addressing the old man as follows:

"You strike me as a hale and hearty fellow, a typical worthy citizen of this fine town. Perhaps all you lack is a small dose of culture. I have in my suitcase an omnibus volume of the most important works of the writer Kafka. Or do I not? The sum I want in exchange for such a handsome and edifying volume is trifling. You have been waiting all your life to own this book, to wallow in its wisdoms, but you were never aware of the fact. Now your chance has arrived at last!"

The old man spat on the ground and reached into his pocket for an antique hearing trumpet, which he thrust into his ear with all the force of an automated execution apparatus. His entire body shook, the long slender trumpet oscillating like the leg of a distressed insect on its back. Mr. Ogerepus could not bring himself to repeat his speech word for word and so gasped a condensed version:

"And why should you refuse to own a copy? You misdirected me. All his best works, not just the acclaimed novels. Consider yourself a sly one, do you? Beautiful binding. A purple ribbon to keep your place, if you have one. Large print, generous margins."

Drooling and weeping, the old man lowered the hearing trumpet and turned his face derisively away from the suitcase. By this gesture, Mr. Ogerepus understood that the man had already read most of Kafka's works, perhaps even written an essay on him for some church hall newsletter. His luck clearly was not going to be good today. Shrugging, he abandoned his customer. But before he had taken more than six steps, the old man called a piece of un-wanted advice at his back; even the bare words seeming slobbery and thick with undigested food:

"Whichever way you go to the sea, avoid the shortcuts. Even the longest ones. They are not worth the trouble!"

Mr. Ogerepus turned on the spot and jutted his lower lip. "You dare to speak to me about 'worth'? Acid free paper, a new font designed especially for this edition, a previously unreleased photograph of the author on the back flap... I call you ignoramus, lunatic, buffoon, recidivist, duffer, charlatan, deceiver! But thanks for the warning..."

Then he turned back and hurried away, keen to move out of sight. It was just feasible that the old man would demand payment for his advice, an intolerable impudence! Mr. Ogerepus reached an area of the town where many lanes and alleys existed, most of which served the rear gardens of terraced houses. He ventured down one, an extremely long alley that dwindled to a point with the aid and guidance of sheer perspective. At least here would be no corners, nothing maze-like. Impossible to get lost down a straight line! This alley was on a gentle incline, a good sign that it led to the sea. Or, if not a good sign, then a sign of some sort, and Mr. Ogerepus loved signs. In fact, he collected them.

This fact, or quirk, reminded him of his latest acquisition. He slid a hand under his un-buttoned jacket and removed what was secured behind his elastic braces: a bronze representation of the number eight. It had once adorned the front door of a house. Storms or rot had caused it to fall to the pavement, where Mr. Ogerepus had scuffed it with the toe of his shoe before deciding to pick it up and cherish it forever. Opportunistic theft? By no means! First he had sought to return the object to its rightful owner. It was clearly the property of the eighth house in the street. Mr. Ogerepus was unable to locate the home in question. There was a number seven and a number nine, but only a blank door between. Conscience satisfied, he moved away with his trophy.

Unlike most other men — including technical school graduates — he did not regard it merely as a symbol of a finite integer. Not at all. When turned on its side it became something much bigger, far odder, excitingly advanced, almost mystical in essence. Infinity, the symbol of. Mr. Ogerepus knew two facts that his rival salesmen did not: firstly that the capital of Turkey is not Istanbul, secondly that infinity is equal to zero divided by any whole number. The implications of the latter secret were truly awesome. At a dinner party with no food, for example, the emptiness on all the plates would have to be divided by the number of guests. The result: plenty for all! A choking surplus, in fact. The end of all hunger, but massive suffocation and vile nutritional landslides. The bronze gleamed and Mr. Ogerepus curled away a melancholy smirk. All in good time.

He looked around. He had already walked a hundred paces down the alley, too late to turn back without shame. He felt that he was in a gutter which drained the lower-middle-class cosmos, traversing a conduit which served a specific urban landscape that belonged to only one generation: the clerks and accountants whose fathers had been dockers and miners. The brick and stone walls on either side were too high to peer over, but he knew that the gardens were full of sheds and sprouting cabbages and rotary washing lines. He sensed this subconsciously, but his bleakness was minimal. The old metal bins, most without lids, clanged as he kicked accidental stones at them. A lid for a shield, a stick for a sword; how he had enjoyed playing archaic games of war in his childhood! But what was the past to him now? Indeed, what had it been at the time? Just an opportunity to create nostalgia for future use, a sump of unhatched sickly sentiment.

No, he was free of such nonsense, Mr. Ogerepus, the perfectly normal — but thick skinned and hard-headed — salesman. Copies of Kafka to sell; all else was superfluous. Reaching the sea would be a start. What kind of start he was not yet sure; but are you sure? Not even his boss was. Not even a starfish. Porthcawl was a town close to the sea. The sea, unseen, must be near. Mr. Ogerepus believed he would wade out as far as his knees in the scummy waters, it seemed the right thing to do, both for himself and his customers. It is not entirely necessary to be an educated man or woman, a technical school graduate, in order to read books. Omnibus volume. All the best work in one thick tome, astonishing!

Mr. Ogerepus decided to risk taking a short rest, perhaps even to read for ten minutes. It was surely wise to be familiar with the product he hoped to sell. He opened his suitcase, extracted one copy, closed the case and used it as a low chair. Then he flicked through the book at random, stopping at a curious page. The omnibus discharged its words with their allusions and hints into a mind of medium greyness. Imperfect symmetry. The book was too heavy and cumbersome to read with any degree of comfort. Mr. Ogerepus angrily replaced it, resumed his trudge, looked over his shoulder. Not content with owning one end of the alley, perspective had taken over the other end too, focussing it to a bright point. "This is all very well," snapped Mr. Ogerepus to nobody in particular, "but personally I consider all optical illusions bland and pathetic. Geometry is no friend of mine, not even a pet. I live with angles simply because I have to, not through active choice. I am too busy to pay attention."

And with this resolve firmly in place, he refused to glance again over his shoulder. But something he had read in the book continued to bother him. Unable to ignore it he was forced to pause once more, open his case, take out the volume and search it carefully for the relevant enigmatic page. Here it was! Mr. Ogerepus frowned. His lips moved as he read the oddly brazen passage: YOU DOLT! HAVEN'T YOU SOLD THIS COPY YET? GET A MOVE ON! Mr. Ogerepus felt betrayed by a long dead hero of literature. How could Kafka do this to him? Then he realised that the page in question was actually a note that had been inserted at a later date and had nothing to do with the original binding of the volume. His trickster boss was always playing jokes of this nature. L-D was the official pseudonym of his boss and his refusal to give himself a proper name was just one more example of his capricious and riddling character. Mr. Ogerepus slammed the book shut, stood with grim determination.

Yes, it was true: he was already behind schedule, having sold a grand total of none so far. It was time to accelerate his pace. The soles of his feet hurt, but what of that? He cast an envious eye at one of the metal dustbins. A younger fellow might consider turning the rusty cylinder on its side, climbing inside and rolling down the remainder of the steady gradient. But Mr. Ogerepus could not countenance the inevitable dizziness. An engineer might insert a smaller bin mounted on a gyroscope as a contra-rotating cabin, but such intricate measures were outside his sphere of operations. Mass, velocity, torque: what did such scientific variables have to do with slinky patter? Walking was his sole recourse and one he would take without rancour, riding no bins.

And yet, with this pledge to tramp firmly embedded in his brain, he had the good fortune to be offered a sophisticated alternative, to be urged into a different mode of forward movement. A bicycle stood in the middle of the alley, propped up by a small pile of loose bricks. Gripped by a series of powerful reflexes, Mr. Ogerepus crouched forward, furtively looked left and right for the owner, mouthed the word "Locked!" to himself in disgust. But in fact the bicycle was unsecured. More indeed, for a slip of paper gleamed in the late afternoon haze, a message slipped between the spokes of the rear wheel, and it offered the machine for free to whoever wanted to claim it. A further mordant joke of L-D, his malignant boss? FOR THE USE OF ANY TRAVELLER. No, the script was different.

He plucked the bicycle from its lean, wondered how to balance his suitcase on the skeletal frame, finally decided to lash the object to his back with the aid of his belt: his trousers would have no use for it while he was perched on the saddle. Then he gently sniffed the leather, a habit acquired in the school sheds many years ago, nodded without comment and pushed off. A slight wobble due to unfamiliarity with the model and the uneven surface and fading light, but then he was accelerating away, changing up through the gears, wincing as a breeze that smelled of boiled cabbage and creosote combed his unsatisfactory hair.

His exultation lasted almost twenty minutes before souring abruptly into a subdued panic. At this speed he should have reached the exit of the alley by now. Somebody or something was a liar: not he. But there was no real urgency, he reassured himself. The haste imposed on him by his boss was artificial and conceited. On no account should he be intimidated by L-D more than his original work contract specified. After all, where was his boss now? Probably at home on the sofa, eating potato crisps. Or forcing his reflection into a selection of teapots. The usual. Not in this alley, that much was certain. Mr. Ogerepus was safe for the time being. His pneumatic tyres and confidence bulged.

Mr. Ogerepus continued to pedal at high-speed, until sore ankles and poor visibility compelled him to proceed more cautiously. It was astounding how rapidly darkness fell in these parts, with what gross efficiency, filling the alley with intangible ink. The greyness of the sky now blackened perceptibly minute-by-minute like an unpeeled, gangrenous toe. He groped for an electric lamp attached to the front of the bicycle, but the battery was dead. Clearly, to continue would pose a risk: there were too many deep holes in the surface, too much debris overflowing from some of the older bins. It was time to dismount.

Reluctantly, he braked and climbed off the saddle, resisted the urge to sniff it again, stretched his freelance limbs, rolled his smooth tongue in his commercial mouth. He cared not to walk all night, pushing the bicycle. But where to sleep? There was nowhere even remotely comfortable. Had he brought a hammock and tools, he might have suspended a temporary bed right across the alley, driving the supporting nails into the wooden doors. Perhaps he should try to stealthily enter a garden, find refuge in a shed or on a mound of grass cuttings. The idea was worth pursuing. But every door was locked and the walls were high, lacking suitable footholds. A younger man, more agile, more springy, might be able to accomplish the feat. Having said that, why would a younger man be travelling down this alley at this time with a suitcase full of Kafka? It made little sense, perhaps none. Not one in a hundred thousand youngsters had even heard of that writer, at least not in Mr. Ogerepus' experience. Not lacking courage and rashness, he next attempted to force the lock of one of the more feeble looking doors. He bruised his shoulder: his only success.

He sat on his suitcase and muttered words of annoyance to himself, but these words were disconnected and strange. An editor would query or delete them. Probably.

No blankets, no food, no means of making fire: not that he cared to draw attention to his presence. He was being sold coldness and irritation and had no choice but to pay through the snivelling nose. His suitcase was a reasonable stool, but would scarcely suffice as a bed. No matter. He would prioritize his head and shoulders: the rest of his body would have to 'grin and bear it'. Pulling rank on body parts like this showed ruthlessness and sharp business acumen. Mr. Ogerepus was not a victim; by no means. On the contrary, he was a chip off the L-D block, a mineral fragment. Greasy schist.

Sleep did not come. Not even for one minute. He lay on his back, his shirt having somehow ridden high, exposing his lower back to chill grit and woodlice interference, but he dared not move to adjust it for fear of creating a disturbance elsewhere. To pass the long, hostile night, he indulged random memories; most of them his own.

His interview for the position of salesman. How long ago it seemed, and yet was only a matter of weeks. The waiting room with its solitary chair, the slow electric ceiling fan, the guard at the door who repeatedly denied him access to the office of L-D. The time booked for the interview came and passed, the guard remained stubborn. Mr. Ogerepus continued to wait until the lights were switched off. Then the guard stepped forward and leaned over Mr. Ogerepus to whisper in his ear, "The door to the office existed just for you. Why did you miss your interview? You should have ignored me and walked past." But Mr. Ogerepus was asleep on his chair. In that case, how did he remember what the guard had said to him? It was another mystery. When he awoke, the building was deserted and he stumbled home through empty streets, reaching his sagging bed just as the first light of foul dawn licked the filthy window. He felt like a magnified mole.

Nonetheless, the following day he began work for L-D, and no longer remembered the details of how contact was established. Maybe there had been a telephone conversation. He took possession of his first batch of books, one hundred in total, and was obliged to buy them from L-D and sell them at a higher price to the public. Or was it a lower price? The advantages of working as a salesman over being chronically unemployed were grotesquely small. But at least there was dignity: stuffy, soiled and drenched with mucus. Awful esteem.

Intense cramps assailed Mr. Ogerepus. He shifted position at last, was racked by chills, compelled to stand and hop on the spot, rubbing his hands together vigorously. His mouth throbbed and his stained teeth were like the keys of a piano for little pains, played by an unshaven criminal. Sleep was out of the question. He had to resume his journey. How many hours had he managed to kill by his stratagem of reclining on his back? Difficult to be certain: it might be one or eight. Riding the bicycle was not feasible and in a fit of pique he vowed never to push it. No, he would walk, in the manner of walking things: dung beetles, puppet shadows, hands that pretend to be spiders for black comedy purposes.

Almost at once he began to feel better, his stiff joints becoming more loose and warmer. Then his trousers fell down. He had forgotten to replace his belt. A sudden horrible thought assailed him. He wore braces, that was his style. Could it be possible that he had caught the omnibus to Porthcawl while wearing two different systems of trouser suspension? How *gauche*, how disreputable! No wonder he was trapped part of the way down an alley that stretched to infinity! The punishment was understandable. He pulled up his trousers and forgave himself.

To distract his mind from boredom and revulsion, he honed his patter, experimented with variations on the traditional formulæ, modified his tone of voice in new and unusual ways. "Look here, my friend. No favour you are doing me. Omnibus volume, it is. Man turns into a giant insect. Read all about it. Not for nothing has the word Kafkaesque entered the language. Sprightly does it. Where did you get that hat?"

A dog howled in a distant garden, a lonely sound which brought a small measure of comfort to Mr. Ogerepus, but so small it was unnoticeable. At the same time, he yawned and shivered. For long hours he proceeded in this manner, then the sky began to grow light again. Ahead was another bicycle, somehow different. No, not a bicycle, but a motorised scooter. A note glued to the front mudguard declared: YES, THIS ONE TOO. DO I NOT LOOK LIKE A CHARITY? The key was in the ignition. Mr. Ogerepus felt vaguely like an Italian girl as he mounted and started the engine. His experience was modest but sufficient. The scooter was old, but in good condition and not too noisy. Increasing amounts of rubble made it necessary to swerve often. Far more comfortable than the bicycle: his prospects were improving. Apart from his hunger, thirst, cramps, chills, stench, despair, horror, fatigue and abysmal misery, he was doing well.

Mr. Ogerepus, as already stated, was a perfectly normal man, but the contents of the compartment under the saddle probably were far from perfect. How to be sure of this assertion? He cut the engine, dismounted and checked for himself. A pair of binoculars, a figurine that proved to be a bizarre version of the Statue of Liberty with a sword instead of a torch, one blade of a broken pair of scissors. Yes, useless. Onwards he went, drowsy and almost in a trance. Then he spied movement far ahead, only a blurred dot at first. He risked a glance through the binoculars without stopping. The old man! The old man who had given him directions. So the end of the alley must be close after all. How delightful!

"Stand still where you are. I do not intend to destroy you much. You should buy a book immediately. Is the sea still this way? I come in peace from civilisation. A sucker is born every minute: the regularity of octopus breeding habits remains a source of wonder. Show me the colour of your money: I will display my Kafka in return. You may touch it, dirty degenerate that you are. Hello!"

The old man heard none of this, did not even notice the oncoming scooter. He dipped in a pocket for a key, inserted it in the lock of one of the wooden doors, and then passed through into a littered garden. Mr. Ogerepus arrived just in time to hear the shooting of bolts. He dismounted and pounded on the door with a fist which was soon just as bruised as his shoulder. Then he paused and pressed his ear to the grimy wood. The old man was talking to himself as he lurched up a path, punctuating his discourse by crunching snails under his mouldy shoes:

"Fried me a sausage as long as a whip, she did. Good old woman. Snapped her dog's head off, I did, with it. Always a trowel in the cupboard under the stairs. Dug the head a grave with that. In other circumstances, if time was less linear, the twist would be that I was an older version of the salesman: after he emerges from the alley, a lifetime later. But there are currently no circumstances at large."

Mr. Ogerepus fell back with savage glee. He had not met his future self after all, there would be no implausibly ironic loop! He swung the binoculars around his head on their strap, let them go when they had attained maximum velocity, watched them spin over the wall. With luck they would brain the old man. But the margin of error was too wide. Mr. Ogerepus heard the smash and knew they had fallen short or long. The old man and his thumbs would remain alive to misdirect and burble for many more days, even weeks.

The scooter welcomed him back with all the imaginary affection that a singing mouse feels for a gramophone stylus. No sleep generally means mild delusions. He puttered off and gradually increased his speed to 'quite extreme'. Without making precise calculations based on the old man's average walking speed, length of stride, tendency to deviate and dribble, Mr. Ogerepus felt certain that the end of the alley had to be less than one hour's further ride. And then the sea, his knees. But what was this ahead? Another obstacle! A car almost as wide as the alley, blocking his path. He dismounted to inspect this new vehicle. A rag of cloth tied to the rear bumper did not snap like a flag in the non-wind.

Fumbling with the knot, Mr. Ogerepus read the message on the stained linen. He smiled viciously. YOU AGAIN, HUH? WHAT A SURPRISE! GO ON, TAKE IT AND BE OFF! Mr. Ogerepus was given to wondering if using the car was worth the effort. The exit of the alleyway must be close. The old man could not have walked far in his present state. But what if he had originated from another garden, rather than from the far end of the alley? That cast matters in a different light, cast them so that they tumbled like heavy dice and the light was broken. Life was never easy: nightmares only marginally less complex and chaotic.

Preferring to keep the scooter, but lacking any method of getting it past the car — being too physically feeble to lift it over the roof — Mr. Ogerepus opened the driver's door as far as it would go and squeezed into the seat. The interior was putrid. All the dashboard instruments — including odometer, fuel gauge and radio — were broken. Electric wires sprouted. There were no blankets on the back seats, no food in the glove compartment; not even a bag of travel sweets. But the engine started without too much stuttering and the gears crunched less than those garden snails.

It was dangerous to drive too quickly, because the tyres implausibly flicked small stones at the windshield. Too much force, and the glass would shatter under the attack. Gritty realism. Mr. Ogerepus watched the sky. Already the light was fading again. At least he now had a more elegant place to sleep, not much warmer than outside but psychologically more stable and comforting. The headlamps did not work; Mr. Ogerepus drove for twenty minutes in the dark before stopping. He scrambled to the back seats, the gear stick ramming between his legs as he wriggled and thrashed. He was exhausted and more hungry than he had ever been. He was also thirsty, yet he dreamed more about food than drink. This was clearly a technical oversight.

What did this frustratingly long alley represent? What metaphor was causing him so much anguish? Was it a symbol of life itself; of curiosity; ambition; abandonment; despair? Was it entirely fair that unexplained dark events should automatically happen to a Kafka salesman? And did the old man have no real place in the narrative, even less than his boss did: were they both unnecessary additions? Why was he, Mr. Ogerepus, so concerned about understanding the nature of his situation? It was of no great consequence, so why did objectivity matter at all? Somebody must have been telling lies about the value of truth. This was clearly a clerical error.

In the morning, he suddenly decided that breakfast was now his first priority: a question of life and death and toast. But he resolved to settle for a raw cabbage. He drove steadily for one hour. How much petrol was in the tank? He had no way of telling. A sudden impulse — perhaps one of mine or yours, rather than his — caused him to press hard on the accelerator. Then he deliberately steered at a sharp angle into a brick wall.

The impact was less fatal than it should have been. Bricks crumbled into dust, the car crumpled slowly. Mr. Ogerepus rose up and down in a graceful wavelike motion, striking his chin on the steering wheel and biting his tongue, his first taste of meat for days. He attempted to reverse the vehicle but the wheels had buckled. He flung open the door, and staggered into clouds of red particles that settled rapidly. Behind the smashed wall was a bare space perhaps ten feet deep, contained by another brick wall and another locked door. The accident had failed.

Reaching inside the wrecked car for his suitcase, Mr. Ogerepus stumbled away, his knees aching but the rest of his body surprisingly relaxed. Action, excitement, the very negation of stasis! That brick wall had been no castle, no trial, no door to the law: it would not take the investigations of a dog to deduce those conclusions. No, indeed. He was cheered, still an utter captive of this absurdly cruel joke, but more free then he had felt himself to be. A collision was no variant of delay. He knew he was, or was not, bleeding, even without looking.

Curiosity pulsed in his head. What would his next mode of transport be? The progression must continue to be logical. When would it come to an end, with what contraption in particular? Hovercraft, jumpjet, teleportation device? Or was regression the order of the day? He was amused by a vision of himself mounted on a pogo stick, rusty springs squeaking, rubber contact pad bleeding black pus. He walked for hours. Did days and nights pass like squares on a chessboard? Hardly. Never would he regard himself as a pawn and no other piece seemed even remotely suitable. Cancel the comparison! I bought the hat in a market. Stolen.

The answer to his question was solid and honest: a train. In fact it seemed more like a hybrid between a steam locomotive and a tram than anything a genuine railway company would dare to whistle to the next station. L-D washes his socks in a tub of spit. Mr. Ogerepus walked around the big machine, inspecting tracks as warped as the humour of a comedian locked in a tea chest for a month. On the cowcatcher, inserted between the thick bars of the iron grille, was an envelope. He tore it open. A LITTLE TEDIOUS NOW. BE OFF WITH YOU, I'M NO LONGER INTERESTED. Mr. Ogerepus climbed into the cabin.

The train was extremely easy to operate. He pulled a long lever and an automatic process took over. Water boiled somewhere, chunks of coal suspiciously shaped like books flared, cogs turned with unwise wisdom teeth. Down the tracks the machine accelerated. Mr. Ogerepus went into the carriage behind, hoping it might be a buffet car of some kind. And so it was. Did this mean his luck was in?

Not quite, not truly, not at all. L-D thumbs his nose only when he is unable to toe his chin. There were bottles of flat lemonade and trays of sandwiches. The only problem was that every sandwich had a bite mark in it. Mayonnaise oozed like senile pus into the indentations made by incisors in the pale, stale bread. For the first day of travel in this manner, Mr. Ogerepus could not face eating such food. He drank but chewed nothing. Then the discomforts of weakness compelled him to munch. The crusts tasted like the guts of ugly puppets.

Maximum velocity was attained, and the train swayed and groaned. Lacking relevant ability, Mr. Ogerepus avoided the cabin. He sang train songs to himself, classics originally rendered by Ringo Starr and George Gershwin. He felt at peace with vapours and camshafts. No ticket inspector came, no Emperor of China. The absence of an obviously logarithmic purpose to the narrative grew more irritating to him. He stomped up and down the buffet car, indulging in remembered, anticipatory, or imaginary conversations with his boss, sometimes interrupting himself with extreme rudeness:

"After all, I could live and work in a large glass jar if I really had to. Or in a disused canoe. What is the meaning of your nose? I appreciate the index and scholarly notes and agree that they constitute a strong selling point. Porthcawl should be arrested without having done anything wrong. Not the citizens but the material town, yes."

When he was unsure who was speaking, he tried the opposite tactic, refusing to utter a single word, and even attempted to repress coughs and belches. He eventually worked through all the sandwiches and lemonade. He became aware that the train was slowing down. Over a period of an entire afternoon it trundled to a stop. He jumped out, stretched his legs, and learned that the uneven tracks ended here, at a large buffer. Was this his ultimate destination: the sea? No. The alley continued as before, dwindling to a point of zero dimensions, ungratefully.

He set off, shifting his suitcase between hands. He had not thought to put the train into reverse. It did not matter. He somehow felt certain it would never move again. What would be the next vehicle? A curious depression filled him. He stopped and rested, walked some more, slept, rose, walked. At last he encountered the next note, a bedsheet strung across the alley. The words on it were written in lipstick. there's further to go than you've already come. Mr. Ogerepus sighed, crouched under the sheet, spluttered as its lower edge clammed his face. He realised now how wrong he had been. Every metal bin resembled a dislocated turret. One castle infinitely spread. Like fortified butter.

He walked away the weeks. He walked into weakness. Blisters wanted to halt his progress, and they were very insistent. Thrusting his hand into a pocket he counted his loose change. Did he have enough money for a copy of his own? Yes, just about. He bought one, thankful for the lack of patter, the ease of the transaction. Not that he was a gullible customer, far from it. He sat on the closed suitcase and balanced the open book on his knees. With one hand he traced the words and mouthed them silently with his lips. His other hand was extended far out, thumb upraised, to beg a lift or grant life, he remained unsure which.

NOTES

- The braces didn't hold up Mr. Ogerepus's trousers after he removed his belt because he had forgotten that he was wearing braces. Had he remembered they would have held up his trousers. The scene with the belt and braces serves the function of reinforcing the general solipsistic effect — that everything is a solid mirage created by Mr. Ogerepus. Or so he claims.
- Greasy schist is a slimy form of medium-grade metamorphic rock.
- Things that don't seem to belong to the paragraphs they are in should actually be there because it was part of Kafka's style (or rather the style of his first translators into English) and Mr. Ogerepus is trying to recapture some of that off-key ambience. The non-sequitirs and sudden breaks in the flow are all part of the 'Kafkaesque' thing. Even without asking, I know that you either trust me or don't trust me on this point (that's another example: it's logical but pointless: which is one of the main disturbing qualities of Kafka's work: that even when the pointlessness is logical it's still pointless! Quite often, however, it's not logical).
- When Mr. Ogerepus says things like, "Stand still I do not intend to destroy you much..." the slight incorrectness of the sentence (the 'much' is contradictory) is also there to create a sense of Kafkaesque dislocation. You do believe me, don't you? Even without subjecting you to interrogation I know that you do or do not. The use of 'less fatal' is another example of this...
- Random references to Kafka's many stories include: the magnified mole, the model of the Statue of Liberty, the automated execution apparatus, the Great Wall of China, the investigations of a dog, the singing mouse, etc.

- Yes, rotary washing lines are lines. They are lines hung on a rotary mechanism. All these separate lines are customarily referred to as a 'line' (singular). At least in my house they are. Not that I have a house. But various people I've lived with do. Sometimes I've slept on a sofa or an inflatable mattress in such houses. Small comfort for many people, but last summer I lived in a tree. Everything is relative: even Einstein, especially when he was an uncle, cousin, brother, etc.
- The question remains: for readers who don't know Kafka, will these allusions be interesting? I hope they will be but I can't say for sure. You are the reader and so now must ask yourself how much you enjoyed the story. You did enjoy it, didn't you? I know without asking that maybe you did or perhaps you didn't.
- I started writing short stories seriously when I was 14 years old. The very first was called "The Journey of Mountain Hawk". Everything I wrote between then and the age of 22 was lost. I won't go into details of why, but I still feel a little angry at the circumstances. My juvenile writing wasn't especially polished or sophisticated but I flatter myself that it contained some powerful and unique ideas, or rather a series of archetypal images and situations among the most resonant I've created. I have a good memory, so now I make occasional efforts to rewrite those lost stories, preserving the images but rendering them in more advanced prose. "Nightmare Alley" was one of the most difficult of these rewrites, partly because this fable about a man travelling down an infinitely long alleyway was one of my earliest concepts. I feel relief and satisfaction at the completion (or rescue) of this lost story, which was an adolescent reaction to my discovery of Kafka. Somehow I have settled an unresolved issue from the past, taken a small revenge on the bad luck that affected me at one youthful stage of my life. It feels worthwhile.

ABOUT THE AUTHOR

RHYS HUGHES IS one of the most prolific and successful authors in Wales, although his work has rarely been available in his own country. His earliest publications were chess problems and mathematical puzzles for newspapers.

His first short story was published in 1992 and since then he has embarked on a project that involves writing exactly one thousand linked 'items' of fiction, including novels, to form a gigantic story cycle. Many of these individual items have appeared in magazines, journals and anthologies around the world and his books are currently being translated into French, Spanish, Portuguese, Russian, Serbian and Greek.

His latest novel, *The Postmodern Mariner*, is available from Screaming Dreams; who also have released *Dead Ends: Anthology* containing his story "Degrees of Separation".

rhysaurus.blogspot.com
www.humdrumming.co.uk

HUMDRUMMING TITLES BY RHYS HUGHES:
The First Humdrumming Book of Horror Stories [CONTRIBUTION]
The Less Lonely Planet [COLLECTION]

THE VELOCITY OF BLAME

CHRISTOPHER FOWLER

"THE BEST WAY to get rid of a really big Cambodian cockroach is to wrap it in tissue paper, drop it in the toilet and pour *Coco de Mer Body Butter* over it so it can't climb the walls of the bowl, because the buggers have clawed feet and can really shift. Even then, they sometimes manage to shuck off the paper and use it to climb back up out of the toilet into your bathroom."

That's what Dorothy's guide book said. She was always reading me passages from the damned thing. It had a bunch of tips for dealing with the kind of problems you encounter over there. When they didn't work, she added her own twists. It was one of those guide books obsessed with hygiene and the strength of the dollar, and so paranoid about being ripped-off that you lost faith in human nature the longer you kept reading it. I made her throw it away when we decided to stay on.

I'll admit, it took us a while to get used to the bugs in South East Asia, but I thought they'd turn out to be the least of our problems. There would be other issues to deal with. The food, the people, the heat, the past, the politics. I should have added another problem to that list: lack of communication.

We came to Siem Reap to do the tourist thing, hire bikes and see the temples of Angor Wat at sunset, climbing over the temples of Ta Keo and Ta Prohm, where great tree roots entwine the carvings until it's impossible to tell what is hand carved and what is natural. We wanted to ride elephants, hang out in bars where you could still smoke beneath slow-turning fans, drive along the endless arrow-straight roads to the floodplains of the Tonle Sap Lake, eat fat shrimps in villages which had survived through the horrors of the Kmer Rouge; but no-one had told us about the people, how kind, placid and forgiving they were. No other country in the world could have survived so many horrors and still have found such power to forgive. It didn't make sense to me, but then I come from a land that specialises in Christian vengeance.

It was our first visit to South East Asia, and we immediately fell in love with the place.

Siem Reap was little more than a dusty crossroads crowded with ringing bicycles, lined with cafés and little places where you could get a foot and shoulder massage. There were covered markets at each end of the town selling intricate wooden carvings, pirated books and gaudy silks, and barns where farmers sat on the floor noisily trading their produce, with their kids running everywhere, laughing and fooling around, the closest definition I'd ever seen of real community. That's a word we're fond of using at home, but there it means something entirely less friendly.

After watching Chinese dealers testing gemstones that had been dug out of the mountains, running little blowtorches over rubies to prove their integrity, I bought Dorothy a ruby for thirty dollars.

'I'm not going to have this made into anything,' she said happily, 'I just want to keep it somewhere in a box so I can look at it and remember.'

Instead of frying ourselves by the hotel pool we wandered around the streets, where every merchant was calling out, trying to lure us into their store with special offers. Not so pushy that they were annoying, just doing business and quickly leaving us alone as soon as they realised we didn't want to buy. Now that Cambodia was finally stable, the Russians and the French were competing to build along the town's main road, and ugly concrete blocks were going up behind the 1930s colonnades. No plumbing, no drainage, but plenty of internet access; welcome to the new frontier, where you could use an ATM machine but still had to step over duelling scorpions to do so. A national museum had opened, absurdly high-tech, half the interactive exhibits not functioning, as though some rich outsider had insisted that this was what the town needed to draw tourists. Less than a decade of peace and the nation was embracing its future with a kind of friendly ferocity, but you feared for the transition process, knowing that everything could still be lost overnight.

And I was finally vacationing with my wife. Gail and Redmond had married and left home and were now living in Oakley, Virginia, which left me and Dorothy rattling around the house in Washington with too many bedrooms and memories. I'd been promising Dorothy that we'd eventually travel, but it proved harder to get away from work than I'd expected. After thirty seven years of marriage — during which time we'd hardly ever left the country — I decided 'enough was enough' and applied for two months' leave, although I eventually had to take it unpaid. Of course, whatever time you pick to go away is never the right time, and this proved to be the case; there was an election pending and everyone was expected to help, but Dorothy put her foot down and told me she'd go by herself if I didn't step away this time and make good on my promise to her. She said; 'Politicians are like policemen, the work never stops and they never make much of a difference, so take a vacation.'

So I booked the tickets and off we went.

When I first saw the officials at Siem Reap airport emptying their collected visa-cash into leather suitcases right in front of the tourists who paid them, I'll admit I thought the worst, that the corrupting influence of past dictators lived on — and maybe it does in other ways — but after that day I saw nothing else like it and we had a wonderful time.

On one of our last trips out beyond the river we found ourselves in a town almost completely surrounded by dense jungle. The Tonle Sap lake is tidal. For most of the year it's barely three feet deep, but during the monsoon season it connects with the Mekon River and reverses its flow, flooding the surrounding plains and forests, filling a vast area with breeding fish. The Vietnamese families living in the floating villages at the lake's edge aren't much liked by the Cambodians, but on the whole everyone rubs along. The effluvial soil is rich and the landscape is lush with vegetation. On that day we stopped in a village so small that no-one living in it could decide what it was called, and that was when we saw the house.

It was just a white brick box in a small square of cleared grass, but the surrounding forest canopy glowed emerald even at noon, and it looked like the happiest place on earth. What's more, the little house was available to rent. I mentioned it to Dorothy, who dismissed the idea at once, but I could see she was excited. A light had come into her eyes that I had not seen in years. Dorothy never went out without makeup and jewellery. She cared about appearances, and what people thought of her. She was concerned about making a good impression. It's a Washington habit. But I could tell she relished the thought of not having to bother, even if it was just for a month.

'Well, I guess it wouldn't hurt to take a look,' she said finally, so we visited the owner, a tiny little old lady called Madame Nghor, and she showed us around. It was just about as basic as you can get. There was really just one room with a single small window, because the kitchen and toilet were kind of outside. They stood on a half-covered deck with a wood rail that overlooked the fields and the forest. There was also a plank terrace at the front facing the road. Life was lived mainly out of doors.

The monsoon had recently ended, leaving the jungle green, but fœtid. On its far side, palms had been cleared to build a factory, but the breeze-block building had never been finished. The village was so perfect that it could even keep progress at bay. Madame Nghor agreed to rent us the property for one month. The price seemed absurdly low, but maybe it was extortionate to her. We didn't really care.

We checked out of the Borei Angkor, the fancy hotel where we had only met other Americans, and moved right in to the tiny house. When we got in the taxi to leave, the driver automatically assumed we were heading to the airport and very nearly dropped us there. He was real surprised when we redirected him into the countryside.

Our tickets home were open so there was nothing else to do but tell our family that we had decided to stay on awhile. Gail thought we were behaving kind of weirdly, but Redmond congratulated us when we told him.

"I won't be making many more calls," I warned him. "The charger we brought with us doesn't work out here. But we have our health and our money, and the change is doing Dorothy a world of good."

'Just don't go native on us, Dad,' Redmond laughed.

Obviously, staying in the house was very different to being in the hotel. There were no fresh towels or little gifts on the pillow, and there was no room service or air-conditioning, but we loved it all the same. Madame Nghor offered to prepare food for us, and we took up her kind offer. On our second day, she called around with the other villagers to formally welcome us. The women peeped shyly around the door and wouldn't come in. The men sat in a circle outside and offered us a strong, sour, yellow drink they'd made themselves. I didn't like it much, but it wouldn't have been right to refuse it.

We were sad to see so many of the children missing an arm or a leg. They danced about dextrously with just a stick or two to lean on, and Dorothy and I felt compelled to give them a few coins even though we knew we shouldn't. There was this kid called Pran, a skinny little runt about seven years old, who had lost both his legs and one arm. There were still thousands of landmines buried in the countryside around the village, and we were warned about straying from the marked paths when cycling to the next village for provisions. The damage of war always outlives the fighting, sometimes in ways we can never imagine.

The younger villagers spoke some English, and all were anxious to ensure that we would have a happy stay. Madame Nghor was especially thoughtful, and would bring us small gifts — a mosquito coil, candles, a hand fan — anything she could think of that might make our stay more comfortable. Her husband had died in tragic circumstances — I heard from one of the villagers that he had been murdered by a Kmer resistance unit about fifteen years earlier — and pain was etched deeply in her face, but now her life was simple and safe and she made the best of it; her story, we felt, was to have a happy ending. She and the villagers lived by the principles enshrined by their religion, peace and acceptance and harmony, and we found it a humbling contrast to the way we lived at home. You try to do the right thing, but life in the West is complicated and hypocritical.

There were times when we felt like disoriented Westerners, not understanding what we were seeing. On a trip into Siem Reap we saw a fight explode out of nowhere between two men who were whisked away so quickly by police that I feared for their survival in the cells. Then, an hour later, we saw them in a café together laughing and drinking. Some of the food gave us fiery stomach cramps — we weren't used to eating such quantities of spiced vegetables without any dairy products — and the insects particularly plagued Dorothy, who would find herself bitten even though she tightly wrapped herself at sunset from head-to-foot. One night as I watched this ritual of protection, I found myself fearing for her. She seemed so much more fragile here. Dorothy caught me looking, and told me not to fuss. She always had confidence in me.

The bugs were at their worst after a humid rainstorm broke across our new home one night. They flew into the shutters at such a lick I thought they might crack the wood. The next morning the warm, still pools under our decking were filled with giant centipedes and every type of crawling creature, some with pincers, some with horns and stingers, many as big as an adult fist. I shifted one multi-legged horror from the bedroom with a stick, and it caught me by surprise when its shiny black carapace split open and two vibrating iridescent green wings folded out. It lifted lazily into the air like a cargo plane, and I guided it toward an open window.

The following evening we opened a bottle of warm red wine and sat beside each other on the rickety wooden terrace, watching the sunset, Dorothy and I. Silence fell easily between us, but it was also a time for asking things we had avoided discussing all of our married life.

'Tell me," she said after a long pause for thought. "Do you ever regret working for the doctor?"

It was a question I had asked myself many times. "I was young," I replied. "I was ambitious. We were denied information. We didn't know many of the things we know now."

"But if you had known, would you still have worked for him?"

"Why do you need to know?"

"Because there were others who stood their ground." There was no reproach in her voice.

"They knew more than I ever did. He kept us in the dark."

"You knew about the carpet bombing. Everyone in Washington knew."

"We didn't know what it would lead to. How could we? But to answer your question: No, I wouldn't have worked for Kissinger."

As we were dressing, Madame Nghor brought us a ceramic pot and shyly set it on the low dining table. She looked uncomfortable about bringing it. "This for protection – for –" and here she rolled one forefinger over the other in an explanation I could not understand. I looked into the pot and found it contained an oily red butter that smelled like copper and petrol.

"How do I use this?" I asked.

"Not for you," she told me gently, "for your wife."

I figured that explained her awkwardness. For the last day or so Dorothy had been suffering from cramps. Madame Nghor held her hand out over the edge of the floor and made a soothing flat-palmed gesture.

"Put it at night. You rub it like this to stop them from coming," and again she did the finger-rolling thing that I took to be an indication of cramps. 'You have no trouble from them after, they stop and die. You must keep lid on pot tight. You want me to show?" I thought she looked mighty uncomfortable with what she regarded to be a personal subject, and by this time her embarrassment had spread to me, so I hastily thanked her and showed her out.

We were planning our first trip into the jungle, but Dorothy had not slept well, and was still in some pain. "We'll postpone it to another time," I told her. "Besides, it's been raining and now it's hot again, so God knows what kind of insects will be out and about."

"No, we'll go. I feel a lot better now, really. I'm not going to be a killjoy on this trip." I explained to her about rubbing on Madame Nghor's home-made potion but it seemed too oily and liable to stain, so she decided it would be better to use when we got back. After tucking our shirts and socks tightly into our trousers and boots so that no insect could find a way in, we set off into the woodlands, clambering over great tree roots, stopping to listen to the calling of birds in the jungle canopy. The going was a lot tougher than we had expected, and after an hour we decided to turn back.

We had been hoping to stumble across one of the many overgrown temples that lay almost entirely buried by the returning jungle, and in one patch of cleared ground I rubbed away a layer of thick green moss to find the scarred stone face of an Apsara dancer staring up at me through the soft soil. With her raised eyes appearing above the leaves, it looked like she had been swimming through the grass and had just broken through the surface. As if she had been waiting for someone to come along and awaken her.

"You've let the sunlight fall on her face again," said Dorothy.

"We could uncover the rest of her," I suggested.

"You don't understand. The moss was protecting her from damage."

We walked on. Dorothy was particularly exhausted by the journey, so we stopped by a stream and listened to the sounds of the forest.

"We should have done this years ago," I said, taking her hand. Dorothy's hair had greyed a little and she had tied it back into a ponytail, but in the yellow light that fell through the branches she looked blonde again.

"The time was never right before, you know that," she replied. "At least we got to do it now.'

She looked down at her boots, lost in thought. There was a leathery scuffle of wings, and a bird screamed high above us, then it was silent once more. The stream was so clear that you could count the pebbles on the bottom. Dorothy looked down at her white tube sock and began to rub it. 'Damn.'

"What's the matter?"

"Nothing, maybe a scratch." I looked and saw a small crimson stain the size of a penny. "I don't think anything could have got in, these socks are really thick. I'd have felt it."

"Better let me have a look." I rolled down her sock. It was full of blood. "I think you got a leech in there," I told her. "It won't hurt, but we'd better get you back." I knew that leeches produced an anæsthetic in their bite so they could continue to suck their host's blood without being felt. They also have an anticoagulant in their saliva, so they can carry on feeding until they're fully gorged. Then they drop from the body to seek water, through which they can travel to find a new host.

"It could have carried on and on without me knowing it was there," said Dorothy.

"No," I told her. "In the natural world parasites don't kill their hosts, because they'd ultimately kill themselves."

"You mean it's only humans who do that."

Soon the cover thinned out and the jungle opened onto a road that led back to the village. As soon as we reached the house we took off our socks and shoes. I found one leech attached to my ankle, and Dorothy had two. They were small and black, as soft as slugs but far more elastic and lively. They left splattery trails of blood as they twisted about on the bathroom floor. I stamped on their bloated bodies, sacs of blood that burst messily over the cracked white tiles. I had a sudden suspicion that there might be more of them on us.

"Turn around," I told Dorothy. "Take off your shirt." As she peeled off the wet cotton, I saw two more on her back, between her pale shoulder-blades.

When she saw the thin streaks of un-clotted blood in the mirror, Dorothy yelped. I picked off one of the creatures and examined it. As I did, it stretched and swung around, trying to bite me. I was surprised at the speed with which it moved. I could see two sets of tiny hooks like pin-points, set on either end of its body. When I dropped it on to the sink it flipped over, end to end, like a slinky. It climbed the sheer sides of the bowl in seconds and disappeared into a wet corner.

"Let me light a cigarette," I told Dorothy, "I think you're supposed to burn them off."

"No," she said, trying to sound un-panicked, "they bite deeper if you do that and tear the skin when you pull them. I think you're meant to flick them off with a fingernail." She had read about them in her travel guide, and was right. A nail under the leech's body was enough to make it come away. My back was clear — I think they found Dorothy's blood sweeter. The harder part was catching them once they fell. You expect anything that looks like a slug to move slowly. I placed my finger above one and watched as it stretched and waved about like an antenna, desperate to reach me. There was something grotesque about its obviousness, as if I was automatically expected to forgive its uncontrollable hunger.

The sun was setting and the sky had turned a spectacular shade of crimson. Out on the balcony, the warm moist air was thick with flying insects. I felt as if our environment had subtly turned against us, as if it was saying We've nearly had enough of you tourists now, time to go home. You've pretended to be like us, but you really don't belong here.

Dorothy was tired and in unusually low spirits. She hardly ate anything from the tray of pork and noodles Madame Nghor had left for us. She was still suffering from muscle cramps, and opened the pot of oily, rust-coloured ointment, patiently rubbing it into the tops of her legs and over her belly until the room stank.

My calves and thigh muscles were sore from the expedition. We were not so young now, I thought, and would have to make adjustments to the way we behaved. It had been foolish of us to just take off into the jungle like that without telling anyone where we were going — what if we had gotten lost, what would we have done? Just how quickly could things go wrong here?

I turned out the lights and we went to bed. The blackness was complete, but soon I saw lightning crackle above the tree-line. It looked like an electric trolley was running through the forest. The temperature started to climb, and within minutes it was unbearable. Dorothy was twisting and turning in her narrow bed. I was sweating heavily, and could not get comfortable. I went for a smoke on the terrace and stood at the rail, listening to the noises of the night.

Dorothy's questions about my life had bothered me. There were no easy answers. Had Kissinger's illegal bombing of this astonishing country opened the way for everything that followed? We went into other countries and created a vacuum that had to be filled by something. Every day took us further away from being the innocents we had so long pretended to be.

I reached the end of the Marlboro packet. I left the terrace door wide to let some air in and came back inside. It seemed more stifling than ever. I lay down on top of the bed once more.

An hour later, rain broke and fell hard, pounding on the roof of the little house. The temperature began to fall. It rained and rained until the sky wore itself out. Calm returned, and I must have dozed.

Dorothy cried out suddenly, making me start. I tried to find a light, but it seemed the electricity was out, and the candles were somewhere in the other room. I knew at once that something was amiss.

Dorothy was struggling to sit up. She called for me and I grabbed at her wrist, only to find her skin slick with sweat. "What's the matter?" I kept asking. I probably frightened her with my shouting. I found my lighter, flicked it and tore back the thin sheet. Her nightdress was stained scarlet, and the material was shifting as if alive. I could smell something bad, like an infected open wound. She and I scrabbled to tear off the wet material.

As it ripped, I saw what was wrong; the area from her navel to the tops of her thighs was a black squirming mass of tiny bodies, slick and shiny with her blood. Leeches, it seemed that there were hundreds of them, sucking her life away from her.

I thrust my hand into them and instantly they began to flip onto my wrist and arm, attaching themselves, finding veins and biting hard. Dorothy screamed as I grabbed at them, trying to squeeze whole handfuls at a time, but they slipped through my blood-slick fingers. As fast as I flicked them away they came back, driven by their hunger for blood.

I needed something else. Finding the lighter, I struck it and thrust the flame into the wriggling slimy nest. Too late, I remembered that the ointment contained petrol. There was a soft pop of ignition and she was enveloped in thin blue flames. I grabbed my shirt and threw it over her stomach.

In the moment before the flickering flames were extinguished, I saw the horrific mess on her body, blood and burned leeches writhing everywhere, Dorothy shaking in pain and terror, and I...

It shames me to think back to that moment. All I could think about when I saw her was the roaring anger of the blame, someone to blame. Madame Nghor had given us the oil, she had somehow discovered who I was, who I had worked for in Washington, and had made up this concoction to draw the leeches to us. She was taking revenge for the loss of her husband, for the destruction of her country, for me being an American. That was my first reaction, the seeking of blame.

The screams brought Madame Nghor — and half the village — to our door. She put on the light, and I realised that in my panic I had simply failed to find the switch. I thought she had come to gloat and take pleasure in this bizarre revenge, and I must have rushed at her. I remember grabbing her thin shoulders and shaking her very hard. Two men who turned out to be her sons ran forward and pulled me away from her.

"What did you do to my wife?" I yelled in her face, "What did you do?" I said some other things that it pains me now to remember. When she saw the pulsing mass of leeches that still quivered and crawled on Dorothy, Madame Nghor ran back down the steps and returned with something that looked like a can of lighter fluid, squeezing it wildly all around until every last one of the leeches had fallen away and shrivelled up.

Chaos. In the exposing glare of the overhead bulb, my wife lay sobbing, bloody and naked on the bed before the shocked villagers. I stayed frozen in one place until Madame Nghor had pulled a sheet over her.

"You stupid man," she scolded, wagging a cartoonish finger at me. "This all your fault, not mine! This! This!" She picked up the pot she had given us. "You put it on —"and when she made the smoothing gesture again I realised she meant I should put the oil on the floor, along the edges of the room, to keep the leeches out after the storm. It was not meant to be put on the skin. And the rolling fingers, she was simply showing us how the leeches moved and why it must be applied. I had misinterpreted so blindly, so badly. One of her sons dipped his finger in the mixture to show me. The thick red oil had cattle blood in it. The coppery smell attracted them, and they got stuck.

In shame and shock I started to laugh. I couldn't stop myself. Was this really how things went wrong in the world? Were mistakes always this fundamentally stupid? How could I have thought this tiny village woman might know I once worked for a political oppressor? It was absurd. Guilt, like some barely-visible fish resting in deep water, could surface without warning.

We took Dorothy to the hospital, but the burns themselves were superficial and there was no real damage. However, a ragged black patch of discoloured skin was left behind from the burned edges of the unhealed wounds, and her blood could not coagulate over the scratches my fingernails had left as I tried to dig the leeches from her. The doctor told her she would be left with scars.

Dorothy hardly spoke to me that day. We returned to Washington as soon as we could get a flight, slinking out of the village like criminals. The villagers watched us go in silence and embarrassment.

Seven months later my wife became ill and died. To this day I do not believe what the doctor said, and have convinced myself that her death was the result of some kind of blood poisoning, a delayed reaction to what happened that night.

Just before the year ended, I took early retirement. A new phalanx of eager young recruits was entering politics for the first time, and the thought just made me tired.

I know at heart that I am a good man. I have made mistakes in my life, but the worst that night was the speed with which I sought to blame.

ABOUT THE AUTHOR

CHRISTOPHER FOWLER WOULD make a good serial killer. He's charming and English and lives in a white penthouse with a view of St Paul's Cathedral, and you'd think butter wouldn't melt in his mouth until you read his dark urban fiction — 17 novels and over 120 short stories so far.

His œuvre divides into black comedy, horror, mystery, the odd revolting death and a set of novels unclassifiable enough to have publishers tearing their hair out. Emerging from a film industry background, he has come painfully close to having movies made of his novels *Roofworld*, *Spanky*, *Psychoville* and *Calabash*, but oddly it was his short story "The Master Builder" that became a film called *Through the Eyes of a Killer*, starring Tippi Hedren and Marg Helgenberger.

He is currently writing the 'Bryant & May' mysteries, featuring two elderly, argumentative detectives, but his latest book, *Paperboy* is autobiographical. His graphic novel for DC COMICS was the critically acclaimed *Menz Insana*.

He also achieved three pathetic schoolboy fantasies, releasing a pop single, being used as the model for a Batman villain, and acting as a stand-in for James Bond.

www.christopherfowler.co.uk
www.humdrumming.co.uk

HUMDRUMMING TITLES BY CHRISTOPHER FOWLER:
Wife or Death [FORTHCOMING]

IT SOUNDS A BIT LIKE...

GARY FRY

I THINK THERE'S something wrong with my Dad, but in fact it's worse than that; I think it's spreading to *all* of us...

Sorry, I'm a bit nervous. Let me provide a bit of background information.

My Mum died about two years ago: cancer got in her spine. The hospital didn't spot it early enough, even though she'd had some routine tests after complaining about back pain. She'd always been a smoker, so we were naturally concerned. Still, when the results came back clear, we were happy, despite all the problems we'd always suffered between us. Bloody NHS! Then again, it wasn't the authorities' fault that we were a... yes, I guess you'd call us a *dysfunctional* family.

I was an only child. I secretly think my Mum had wanted a boy, or maybe a girl who matched her ideas of what a girl should be. But I was always more of a tom-boy. It wasn't that I'd associated more with my Dad or anything, because he worked a lot and I rarely saw him, but as far back as I can remember, I'd always preferred climbing trees and playing with noisy toys and other stuff. I liked sport, too, and at school I was always the best, particularly in athletics — running, mainly.

Anyway, my Mum didn't like this, was kind of embarrassed by it. But my Dad, he was proud: despite his long hours, he used to come to all the track events and cheer me on. However, I was never really allowed to get *close* to him. Whenever I tried, my Mum would intervene. If I asked him to come into my bedroom to kiss me goodnight, she'd always be standing there; the same whenever I phoned home: she'd always answer, and only reluctantly pass me on to him.

If it was jealousy, I couldn't understand why — she was probably neurotic or something. She was an edgy sort, whereas Dad and I were calmer. Neither of us smoked, and we hated the habit; she was a forty-a-day woman. And her influence was like an invisible force over me. Even when I did well in school tournaments, I could hear her voice at the back of my head saying, "That's not what women *do*, Jenny." I hated her calling me 'Jenny'. *Hated* it.

It got worse. When I was sixteen, whenever I looked in the mirror I saw *her*. We were alike in appearance, even if poles apart in outlook. I'd just discovered boys — or rather they'd discovered me — and for many months I was juggling my sporting aspirations with my social life. Yeah, feminism and all that stuff has allowed women a chance at doing whatever they wish in the modern age, but it's still not easy. My first boyfriend always moaned whenever I had to train first thing on a morning and then last thing at night. So I chucked him. But guess what? My Mum had *liked* him. At least on our various dates, she'd had my Dad to herself, though what did they ever do together? *Nothing*. Still, that was obviously enough for both of them.

He loved her; he's a simple man, not very good at dealing with people. He'd always worked alone, on building jobs. He was forty-seven when they had me; Mum was thirty-eight. There were certainly some strange family dynamics going on, but I never understood them. Maybe they'd struggled to have a child when they were younger — I don't know. I might have been a late decision or a mistake… I don't know that either.

Anyway, I got rather sick of coming between them all the time. I had a chance at getting in a UK running team for a tour of the Far East, but by then I'd taken the softer option. My second boyfriend — Alan, my husband now — had his own flat, and I'd spend as much time there as I would out training. He's a decent, attractive man whose own family is comparatively stable and straightforward. Of course I was drawn to this. Even though family was important to him, and he couldn't understand the issue I had with mine (having kept most of it to myself), he finally persuaded me to marry him, planning for children and a mortgage — the *usual* stuff.

Well, when I put the athletics career on hold, Mum was delighted. However at this point she'd been begun to complain of those back-aches. Dad was frantic. I think he feared, now that I was gone (Alan and I moved into a nice, small terrace about four years ago), that he'd be left alone in the world: remember, he was then in his sixties by then; just a few years off retirement. So he insisted on Mum going to the Doc's. It was quite a fight: one of the few occasions I've seen him so wound up. He even had a go at me, because he thought I wasn't expressing enough concern. But it wasn't that I wasn't worried, rather that I'd had enough of Mum's malingering — she'd always used it to get the better of me, to attract Dad's sympathy. I thought I knew her better than I actually did in the end.

But the next time I saw them, she was hunched over terribly. Dad was walking with her in the park, while I was out jogging (I'd decided to give the running another shot, despite the fact that Alan and his family kept harping on about kids). And I was shocked. This time, I joined in with my Dad's demand for a medical assessment. Mum was still smoking heavily, and her face when I examined it in broad daylight was all wrinkly. It scared me. I imagined my face like that in thirty years or so, perhaps as a consequence of the pressures of bringing-up children, and it didn't appeal at all. So I took her to the hospital. "No, no, I've just slipped a disc or something," she protested, her voice hacking on smoke. "It'll pop back in. This happened before, when I was younger; I did it when I... I..."

We never did find out how she hurt herself, because that was when she collapsed. I called Alan on my mobile and he came straightway — he liked my folks. And here's the ironic thing: when we drove my mum in to the hospital, I also had a funny spell; fainted or some such. All I know was that when I came to, my husband was there, beaming down at me, and he'd also brought his own parents. And they were all smiling.

Yep, you got it: I was *pregnant*. I was stunned. However, all I could think about was whether my Mum was okay, or rather how my Dad was coping with this episode. I kept my news to myself, and made Alan's parents promise to do so, too, as I went to find my own. And they were simply waiting to leave. A few tests had been done; results pending; nothing to worry about, the young male doctor told me. He looked about twelve. Still, perhaps that's the state of the country, isn't it? You'll see that it *certainly* is after I tell you the rest.

Excuse me, this is the hardest bit for me to explain. Give me a second, will you…?

* * *

Right, thanks. Let me go on.

Time seemed to pass too quickly. Before I knew it, I was already *showing*: two months of morning sickness and bad moods had led to Alan working even longer hours at the supermarket where he's a Branch Manager. Anyway, one day I went round to my parents, because I fancied a walk as much as anything else. I couldn't have run if you'd paid me! My own back was hurting, but I still couldn't imagine what Mum must have been through.

I already knew that the tests had come back all-clear (just a little swelling around the vertebræ or something, easily treatable by tablets) so I was reasonably unconcerned when I entered their bungalow which is situated in one of the nicer areas of Leeds. By now, they knew about the baby, of course, and Mum had been delighted, despite her obvious pain. Dad's response had been more — what's the word? — more *ambiguous*. He'd certainly smiled when Alan and I had related our news while driving them home from the hospital, though I'd also sensed a kind of… oh, I don't know… a kind of *regret*. Maybe he was still concerned about Mum.

And soon I realised that he had good reason to be.

She looked *horrible*. She could barely stand up straight. Her voice was like it was full of dirt, and she'd clearly neglected the housework. Since Dad had retired, perhaps he should have helped out with chores, but he didn't have a clue. She'd always done everything for him. Bloody men!

Anyway, I called Alan, who — bless him — skipped a meeting and drove us to the hospital at once. My Mum couldn't even walk from the car park; her back seemed to have locked; she was in agony. When we got inside, I demanded to see a specialist, since Dad had never been any good at asking for anything. Mum was taken to a room and they did stuff to her — God knows what. And *then* the devastating news.

It was cancer.

The doctor who told us could only assume some test results had got mixed-up. In response to this, Dad had another of his rare tantrums: he called the NHS every dreadful name he could think; he got so bad that even I started to think I should leave in case my unborn child absorbed any of it... the things you think when you're under stress! Dad had said that he'd paid his taxes all his life, and was *this* his reward? I think he went a little *mad* that afternoon. You'll see in a moment what I mean...

Mum never came out of hospital. The tumour had spread to her blood, and then to her brain. She died at about midnight the same day. Dad just sat in silence, while Alan rubbed my back.

Well, things were rather subdued for a while. It took me a long time to come to terms with our loss — I mean, my Mum and I had never really got on, but she was still my *Mum*, wasn't she? Alan was supportive, but it was my Dad I was worried about. Whenever I'd go round there, as my belly grew bigger and bigger, he'd take only a cursory interest in his future grandchild, while paging through old photo albums and handing me pictures of Mum, as if to say, 'Don't forget her, Jennifer. And make sure your girl or boy knows where she or he comes from, too.' Of course I nodded at the right moments. In the past, we'd become adroit at communicating *via* gestures, and even now without interfering Mum around, we still did this. It was like a habit. Weird, eh?

But not as *weird* as the few years that followed... oh, good God, not at all! And this is the main bit of my story. So let me start by outlining what happened after my son — Harry, we called him: a beautiful, healthy boy — was born.

Things were okay for a while. I got back into shape by running on an evening after Alan had stumbled in from work. Whenever I returned, I'd see him stooping over our child, showing him photos and repeating the names of the people in them again and again. I think he was determined for Harry's first word to be 'family'.

I used to call in to see my Dad, now in his late sixties, about twice a week, and he'd generally be sullen and quiet, though always ready to greet his grandson with a childish prank or a daft comment or some silly language of his own devising. This cheered me, but I didn't realise that *these* might have been the early signs...

After a year had flashed by (*don't* they just?), I became a bit worried by Harry's eating habits: the only thing he'd entertain with any enthusiasm was bananas. He'd turn his nose up at proper food, while dribbling cereal or toast or whatever down his chin. But with bananas he'd just sit there, munching for hours. I wasn't sure this was healthy. I read books on the subject. I consulted Alan's folks. I even asked my Dad, whom I'd somewhat neglected since becoming such a fretful mother... and *then* I realised what I was up to.

I was being as fussy and neurotic as my own Mum had been! *That* couldn't be good, could it? I didn't wish to repeat *those* patterns; I wanted Alan, Harry and me to be happy together, and not to bear any of those strange complications my family had suffered. Is that natural? Do all parents go through this? Trying to make sure their own efforts at bringing up kids are better than their predecessors until surely one day the perfect family is produced? I mean, are we always trying to strip away the bad influences of previous generation? Well, perhaps that's partly true. But I also know that it's never as simple as that.

My first realisation that matters were very wrong was when I received a phone call one morning, about a month ago now. Alan had the day off and was talking to Harry, who'd yet to say his first word and who wouldn't eat the mashed meal I'd prepared. Exasperated by this, I told my husband to give him a banana while I escaped for a moment to shut up the ringing, which was pricking my nerves.

"Hello?" I said, possibly a bit sharply. But the reply didn't seem concerned about that at all.

"It's your Mum," the person at the other end of the line said.

Imagine what I thought then. There I was, up to my neck in the inevitable problems of motherhood, and now I was hearing a voice from beyond the grave! Except that it was no such thing; in fact, if anything, the truth was far *worse*.

Once I'd calmed down a little, closing the door to silence Alan (who was again going through a photo album and naming every person we knew), I recognised the harsh tone, which had indeed sounded like a woman's after a lifetime of cigarettes.

It was only my Dad.

"What do you mean?" I asked, suddenly very uncomfortable. I hadn't been jogging in weeks, and I felt tired and rundown.

"She's come back!" Dad told me, his tone so bright it might indeed be a woman's... or a child's.

Of course I went round there immediately. I asked Alan to look after Harry, and I ran the short distance across the village in which we all lived.

Dad had just got up: what little grey hair he had left was all spiky, and his eyes had a sad, rheumy look. He'd obviously been dreaming.

I was able to settle him, even though he still insisted that my Mum *had* visited him. By this stage, I'd begun to suspect that this behaviour might not just be senility... that he might be getting seriously ill. Dementia? Alzheimer's? Something like that.

It's easy to understand why I was reluctant to phone a doctor! In the event, however, I got in touch with Social Services, whose male representative suggested that my Dad might be best off selling his home and moving in with us... Yeah, *sure*: in a two-bedroom terrace and with a baby! I mean, my husband was doing okay at the supermarket, but with house prices the way they are lately, we were stuck there for the foreseeable future. So thanks for nothing, authorities!

Instead, I decided to keep an eye on my Dad... not always face-to-face, since I had Harry to look after (who, at twenty months, still hadn't spoken and still had that annoying eating habit), but I'd call Dad at least once a day, making sure he had everything he needed.

The next creepy episode occurred about a fortnight later. To be honest, racing over to my Dad's that day had given me back the running bug. I was keen to return to my former aspirations. Oh, I don't mean in any professional capacity — I was way past that — but there are various amateur organisations for less ambitious people, and after spending all my time at home with Harry, I was keen to get out there, have some kind of life of my own.

I'd said all this to Alan the night before *that* call. We'd argued, and I hoped our son hadn't overheard. I didn't want his first word to be 'selfish' or the phrase 'bad mother'. Still, these are what my husband had called me. So I was extremely wound up when I rang my Dad to make sure at least *he* was okay.

Someone answered, and when I said, "Hi, Dad. Dad? *Dad?*" the line went silent for a moment. Then I heard my Dad say, "All right, love, I'm coming," but his voice was faint, as if… as if he was speaking from the other side of the room. But how could that be when he would be holding the handset? I heard footsteps approaching, and then my Dad replied, "Hello, Jennifer? Sorry. Your Mum answered first — just as she used to. Still, it's so nice to have her back, isn't it?"

I felt as if she *had* returned. I was going crazy at the time. After exchanging a few carefully worded pleasantries, I got Harry out of bed and fed him his usual banana: "Say 'banana'," I instructed, almost by rote as this stage; "Say 'banana' — come on, say it! *Say it!*" I was hardly in my right mind. Once I'd settled him in front of the telly, I phoned Social Services about the possibilities of care.

I was so frantic that I initially dialled the wrong number and got put through to the employment office. Mind you, the woman there had used to work in housing, and she was able to explain a few details. Apparently, if older folk had savings (and my Dad did; he'd always been careful with his money), then they must live on these, since they weren't entitled to benefits or a relocation to sheltered accommodation. I was also told a load of other stuff too complicated for my tired brain to take in.

I just needed a *run*, to blow out the cobwebs. I'm afraid I lost my temper with this woman, whom I later realised was simply toeing the line of government policy. She'd told me that the law had just changed, that care of the elderly was no longer an entitlement for all, that each case was 'means tested', and blah blah blah. I hung up angrily.

When Alan came home from work, I left at once, having strapped on my trainers to take several laps of the nearby park. This overlooked my Dad's house, but I didn't have the confidence — or I was too scared — to visit. So as soon as I felt more collected, I trudged home, resolved to talk it all through with my husband.

He had Harry on his lap and another photo album open. I was dismayed to see that the picture both he and our son were staring at was one of my Mum, just before she'd become ill. Perhaps it was the resemblance between her and me that attracted Harry's attention so lengthily; he'd even flung aside his second banana of that day. Alan had been just about to repeat the names of the people on the pages — I'd have called her 'Grandma', but his family used another term of address — when he turned to me to say, "We've got to talk."

We did, for several hours. We decided that we couldn't afford to look after my Dad in our current circumstances, though if we re-mortgaged the house and combined the cash with my Dad's savings, then we might be able to get him a place in a nice rest home, where he'd be cared for "by professionals". These were Alan's words, and naturally I was sceptical, yet come the next day — a Saturday — we visited the nearest home for the elderly. I felt bad about doing this behind Dad's back, but he'd always been led by other people and had never protested — my Mum had seen to that... when she'd been living.

The place impressed me, even though I experienced several unsettling episodes with some of the residents. I rapidly felt as if I was surrounded by children — the old folk were all so simple, so innocent, so carelessly jolly... Did I really want to leave my Dad here? However, maybe he was headed the same way; perhaps that's what awaits *all* of us. Anyway, after I'd instructed my husband to take Harry into the garden to play, someone called me by name.

It was an aged woman whom I vaguely recognised. Once I'd crossed to her seat, she grinned up at me, bearing immaculate dentures, and introduced herself as Mavis Hall, an old friend of my Mum's. I smiled back, and then became engaged in various reminiscences which almost brought a tear to my eye until I remembered how much of the really strange behaviour in my family had been kept behind closed doors. It's the same with all families, I imagine.

But then Mavis made me *scream*.

She said, "Your Dad hasn't wasted much time, has he?"

I asked her what she meant.

Every fortnight, I was told, the old dears were taken to the local park, the one in which I jogged, to see the ducks and to get a bit of fresh air. It was during one of these trips a few weeks earlier that Mavis had seen my Dad... with another woman.

"Still," Mavis finished, "I dare say he's being charitable as much anything else. The poor lass! Stooped over like *that* — I didn't get a good look at her; the sun was in my eyes. Tell me, dear, does his new lady-friend have something wrong with her back?"

I didn't stop shaking until Alan drove me home, and then not for another few days. We argued again, my husband and me, and on this occasion Harry *did* overhear. Alan grew so infuriated (I said some terrible things, such as that my marriage had stopped me doing what I'd always wanted to do, and that I regretted having become tied down: I was very confused) that he drove off to work on the Monday as if our relationship was over. It wasn't, of course, but the voices in my head wouldn't let me get the whole situation into any perspective. When Harry cried, I just gathered him from the floor in front of the telly, spilling the photo album he'd been holding open, and then grabbed one of his precious bananas from our fruit bowl, before charging out of the house; I was determined to put an end to all this mess.

I didn't stop running until I reached my Dad's bungalow. It was still early. He'd forgotten to pull on the curtains in his bedroom and I could see only the headboard; weak April sun made the glass all waxy. Shamefully, I was terrified to enter the building.

"Dad!" I called, almost waking the street, whose residents were mostly elderly. "Dad! *Dad!*"

And then he appeared... or *someone* did: a figure bent upwards as if from a severe back injury. What with the light on the pane, this person was just a hazy shape. When I squinted, with my son's arms wrapped around my neck to prevent a good view, I saw... I saw *my Mum* sitting up in the bed.

Oh, but *no*, I was mistaken. What I was actually seeing was my own reflection projected onto my Dad's face, his wrinkles making mine look *older.*

Still, I jumped on the spot, so severely that my son looked at what had caused the fright.

"Nana," he said, as the image disintegrated or my vision refocused; and indeed there was just my Dad staring dreamily, forlornly, out of the window. "Nana, nana, nana," my son went on.

Just then, I was too delighted by Harry's first word for much thought. So I gave him his usual feed — you've guessed what: the thing I believed he'd asked for — and then went inside and spent several hours crying in my Dad's arms.

It was only later, after I'd got home and started to tidy the house before my husband returned from work, that I began to wonder what my son had *actually* meant. The family photograph album had been left open on the carpet, bearing a picture of my Mum. In Harry's company, Alan had never referred to his own Mum as 'Grandma', but the one alternative — the word I can't bring myself to write here.

It sounds a bit like...

Forgive me, my son's hungry; I must go and feed him. That's what mothers do, isn't it?

ABOUT THE AUTHOR

GARY FRY HAS a PhD in psychology, though his first love is literature. He's had around 60 short stories published all around the world, and his first collection *The Impelled and Other Head Trips* (Crowswing Books) was released in 2006, with an introduction by Ramsey Campbell in which Gary was described as "a master."

His second book was a collection of cosmic horror entitled *World Wide Web and Other Lovecraftian Upgrades* (Humdrumming, 2007; introduction by Mark Morris), and his third is the collection *Sanity and Other Delusions: Tales of Psychological Horror* (PS Publishing, 2007; introduction by Stephen Volk).

Gary also runs Gray Friar Press, and amid his publishing schedule is currently working on several novels and more stories.

www.grayfriarpress.com/gary-fry/
www.humdrumming.co.uk

HUMDRUMMING TITLES BY GARY FRY:

World Wide Web (& Other Lovecraftian Upgrades) [COLLECTION]
The First Humdrumming Book of Horror Stories [CONTRIBUTION]

BAD CALL

MARK MORRIS

MY BOSS, RIK, has got a Chinese dragon tattooed on the side of his bald head. It's one of the things I like about my job. Other things I like, in no particular order, are: the bakery next door, which makes the best egg custards in the world; the shrink-wrap machine, because it's so satisfying to turn the hot-air blower on to the cellophane and watch it seal itself tightly around whatever it's covering like a second skin; the fresh, inky smell of new comics and/or the fresh, plasticky smell of new bubble-packed action figures, which envelops you every time you open a delivery box; Laura Stevens.

Okay, I lied. The other stuff I like in no particular order, but I deliberately left Laura till last because she's the best. She's been working at Planet X for six months now, and she's been my girlfriend for three. She's the coolest girl I've ever met, and the only one I know who can sit through my entire collection of Takashi Miike movies without throwing up or bursting into tears. Lately we've been talking about getting a place together. Trouble is, we've both got so many comics and stuff, it'd have to be a *big* place. Another problem is that our collections overlap in some areas and we're not sure what to do about that. We *could* sell the overlap on eBay and make some money, but I know she thinks the same as me on that subject, even though neither of us wants to say it: what would happen to our joint stuff if we split up?

But that's our problem. It's nothing to do with this story. I guess that started when Rik came out of the back office this morning and up to the counter, where I was talking to one of our regulars about the *Iron Man* movie.

"Hey, Als," Rik said, "there's a call for you. It's your mum."

"'Kay," I said, trying to sound casual, though to be honest I felt a bit embarrassed. Getting a call from your mum at work *always* makes it seem as if you're a mummy's boy, even when you're not. It gives people the idea that you still live at home, and that your mum's ringing to check you've brushed your teeth or are wearing clean underpants.

To be fair, Mum didn't ring me at work that often. In fact, I couldn't remember when she'd *ever* rung me at work before. I'd given her the number, but had issued strict instructions that she should use it only in an emergency. Because of this, I was feeling queasily nervous by the time I picked up the phone in the cluttered back office.

"Hi, Mum, what's up?" I said.

"It's your dad," she said, "he's had a heart attack."

There was an *Incredible Hulk* poster on the opposite wall. I wasn't looking at it as such, but it was in my eye-line, and as soon as Mum said those words the room seemed to stretch like elastic, then to shrink back again, and the acid green that was the predominant colour in that poster seemed to bleed out and engulf my senses, like a spreading ink stain on a sheet of blotting paper. And all at once I knew that whenever I saw the *Incredible Hulk* from now on it would remind me of this moment. I had a split-second to feel sad, and even a bit resentful, about that, and then without thinking I said, "Shit. Is he all right?"

I never swore in front of Mum. Never. I expected her to pull me up on it, but she said, "No, Alan, he isn't. He's very ill. The doctors say he might not last out the night. I think you should come..."

Her voice choked off, and suddenly I realised how hard this was for her, how desperately she was trying to hold herself together.

"'Course I'll come, Mum," I said. "I'll come straight away." And then I did that thing people always do in adversity, which is to try and sound cheerful. As if a bit of cheer can stave off the darkness somehow.

"You hang in there, Mum. And tell Dad he'd better do the same or he'll have me to deal with."

I set my face and went back out on to the shop floor. There must have been something about my expression, though, because Rik took one look at me and said, "You okay, dude?"

I told him what had happened, and asked if it was okay to have the rest of the day off. He pulled a doubtful expression, hissing through his teeth.

"I dunno, mate. We're expecting a big delivery of Manga later." Then he widened his eyes to show he was joking. "Well, *duh*, course it is. Take as much time as you need." I turned away and he too did that cheerful-in-adversity thing: "I doubt we'll even notice you're gone."

I went into the back office to grab my rucksack and get my head together. Five minutes ago I'd been looking forward to my lunchtime veggie pasty and tonight's episode of *Heroes*; now my whole world had been tipped on its head.

Laura came in just as I was shrugging my rucksack on to my back.

"Thought you'd try and sneak off without saying goodbye, did you?" she said.

I was too preoccupied to realise she was also joking. "No, I was just going to —" I began, but she put a hand on my arm. Her fingernails were painted green with little gold suns in the centre of each one.

"Rik told me what happened. Do you want me to come too? Offer a bit of support?"

I shook my head. "No, it's okay."

"I don't mind."

"It's probably not the best time to meet my parents."

It struck me that this might be Laura's *only* opportunity to meet my dad, but I didn't say it.

"You're probably right," she said. "But you drive carefully, okay? Keep yourself safe. I'll be watching over you from afar."

"I will." I kissed her, and she responded so tenderly that for a moment I wanted to cry.

Ten minutes later I was on the motorway.

My car's shit. It's a clapped-out, fifteen year-old Mazda 323, which could boast half a dozen reckless owners before me. The bodywork's dented, the front passenger side door won't shut properly, the interior lights flicker, the engine sounds like an asthmatic old man, and the radio reception gives the impression all stations are broadcasting from Siberia. But it's all I can afford, and at least it gets me from A-to-B *fairly* reliably. Laura calls it 'The Bastard', due to the fact that I encourage it with cries of, "Come on, you bastard!" whenever it's straining to get uphill.

Mum and Dad live in a little village not far from Cirencester in the Cotswolds. I live in Leeds, which is a couple of hundred miles away, give or take. It's a four-hour drive on a good day, and it had never struck me before what a fucking long way that is. Because when things are ticking along nicely, it's fine. I talk to Mum and Dad on the phone whenever I want, and when I go to see them (which admittedly isn't that often — maybe three or four times a year) it becomes a proper *event*, which I've always thought was quite nice. I've always liked the fact that seeing Mum and Dad is special, but at the same I'm glad that I don't see them that often.

I mean, don't get me wrong — I love my parents. But I also love the space and freedom to live my life as I *want* to live it, and I know that if I was nearer to them we'd end up falling out more. Dad always wanted me to be a solicitor or a doctor or something, and if I lived close to him he'd become more aware of my lifestyle, and would view it with disappointment and disapproval. I know he'd only do it out of concern and love, but that doesn't mean it wouldn't piss me off and lead to massive rows between us.

So yeah, I'd always been happy that I lived a couple of hundred miles away. I'd never seen it as a problem. But it was a problem now, now that the doctors had told Mum that Dad might not last out the night. I mean, what did that actually *mean*? That Dad had about twelve hours left before his ailing ticker finally wound down? Or that he might go at any moment? That he might die while I was half-way home, and I'd end up missing his last moments?

I'd never expected it to be like this. I know that sounds really naïve, but I'd honestly always thought that when it came to my parents' deaths, I'd get plenty of warning, plenty of time to prepare. Of course, I'm aware that people die 'suddenly' all the time. You see it in the obituary columns every day — 'Suddenly, at home' (and by the way, have you noticed how it never says, 'Suddenly — in a massage parlour...' or 'Suddenly — while out shopping at Sainsbury's...'?). Even so, I'd always envisaged Mum and Dad living to a grand old age, and ending their days fading away in a nice old peoples' home. I'd imagined I'd be there by their bedsides, holding their hands and listening to their peaceful breaths getting slower and slower. It had never occurred to me that Dad might wake up one day feeling fine, and be dead by teatime. Not that he *was* dead, of course, not yet — or at least, I hoped he wasn't — but you know what I mean.

Traffic on the motorway was slow. All stop/start, with lanes narrowing due to non-existent road works, and bloody bollards everywhere. And there were loads of lorries, and rain, and by the time I got off at the junction that would take me onto the A-road, that would then lead to several B-roads, and finally to the winding country lanes of my childhood, I was fraught and frazzled and calling God a twat for throwing a bunch of obstacles in my way just when I needed them least.

And *that* was when I hit the worst traffic of all. It was about 4 P.M. by this time, but because it was January, and a shitty day weather-wise, it was already starting to get dark. All the cars had their lights on, and all the lights, surrounded by misty haloes of rain, were reflected in jagged, gleaming strips on the wet road. It struck me that this was the perfect weather to die by — murky, cold and slipping towards premature darkness. It would have depressed me if I hadn't been so angry. What *made* me angry was seeing the stationary line of traffic ahead, just when I thought I'd finally managed to escape the worst of it. I slowed down and gave the top of the steering wheel a hefty whack with the flat of my palm.

"Fuck!" I shouted. "Fuck! Fuck! Fuck! This is *so* fucking unfair!"

Then it occurred to me that this might be God's punishment for calling him a twat, and so I apologised and promised never to do it again. But nothing happened, which I could only conclude meant that either he didn't exist or that he was still hacked off with me.

I sat there in traffic for the next fifteen minutes, my stomach tying itself into knots, and in that time the traffic crawled forward a grand total of fifty yards. The urge to throw open the door, jump out and run along the row of cars ahead of me, screaming that my dad was dying and that they all had to get out of my way, was superseded only by my natural reluctance to draw attention to myself. And so I just sat, listening to the windscreen wipers swishing back and forth, and thinking that that was probably what the respirator in my dad's hospital bedroom sounded like. I was so stressed that I thought if I didn't calm down soon, Dad wouldn't be the only member of the family having a heart attack that day.

Eventually I gritted my teeth and turned on the radio. I tried to do this as little as possible, because no matter how low the volume, the surges of static you'd get whenever you tried to tune the damn thing in were so sudden and loud that they'd sometimes make your fillings ache.

Sure enough, as soon as I clicked the dial to 'on' I was met with a rush of white noise akin to being engulfed in an avalanche of gravel.

"Fuck off!" I screamed in such a hysterical voice that I frightened myself. Squinting and clenching my teeth, I began to twist the dial, searching for a local station that might have some traffic news. It took a while, but eventually, through the mess of interference, I heard a female voice say, "...local...affic..."

I listened closer and heard: "...outhbound A...oad closed...van fire...police...ternative route...lays are expec..."

There wasn't much else. Or at least, I could only pick out the odd meaningless word. Then eventually some music started, which — because of the crap reception —took me a good thirty seconds to recognise as a little-remembered 80s hit by the little-remembered JoBoxers.

I switched the radio off. I didn't even know if what I'd heard applied to the queue I was in, but I assumed it did, simply because I had nothing better to go on. It sounded as if a van had caught fire (how, in this weather, I had no idea, but no doubt it had done it just to spite me) and police had closed off the road and were now encouraging motorists to find an alternative route. Which was all well and good, but how could you find an alternative route when you were stuck in a fucking gridlock? I had a good mind to drive up the embankment, smash through the fence at the top and career across a farmer's field simply to prove my point.

But I didn't.

Instead I got my map book out and considered the alternatives. I wished I could call Mum to let her know what was happening, but of course neither she nor Dad had mobiles. They had always been proud of this fact, just as they were proud that they had neither internet access nor SKY TV. Before today I'd found their attitude towards the modern world partly irritating and partly endearing, but right at this moment I found it wholly irritating. With a capital I.

I tried to stay calm and saw that if I got off at the next junction and took the first exit at the roundabout I could work my way home *via* the back roads. It was a circuitous route, and would add a good forty minutes to my journey, but it was better than sitting in traffic for the next hundred years.

By the time I finally reached the junction, I'd been on the road nearly six hours. It was after 5 P.M., but it was so dark it might as well have been midnight. No doubt Mum would be wondering where I was by now. I just hoped she wasn't in a private hospital room, sobbing over the death of the man she had spent most of her life with and thinking that everyone had abandoned her. I wondered whether my sister, Josie, was on her way up from London, and whether she was having as horrendous a time of it as I was.

When I got to the top of the slip road I saw that the police had closed off the exit I wanted to take. There were red plastic barriers stretched across the road, cutting it off completely, and a police car parked on the verge, presumably to prevent desperate fuckers like me from lifting the barriers aside and driving through. As I gaped at the barriers in disbelief, the two police officers sitting in the car stared back at me implacably. I thought about stopping and asking them what was going on, but I was flustered, and I always feel a bit nervous around authority figures. Besides which, I didn't want them looking too closely at the Bastard. I had a suspicion that it was probably un-roadworthy in several different ways.

So I drove on and got off at the next exit. As soon as I spotted a lay-by I pulled over and consulted the map book again. I saw that if I drove up this way for a bit, then turned left, and left again, I could still work my way back to where I wanted to go. I felt as if I was in a maze by now, trying to reach the tower in the centre, but being forced further and further afield by dead ends.

At least there wasn't much traffic on this road, though as I sat there in the lay-by with the windscreen wipers swiping back and forth and the heater struggling manfully to keep the temperature above zero, I was vaguely aware of a silver Maserati cruising gracefully by. I probably wouldn't have registered it if I hadn't seen the same car coming back in the opposite direction a few minutes later. The driver, a shaven-headed guy in a black suit who looked like a nightclub bouncer, was scowling. Alarm bells immediately started ringing in my head.

Sure enough, I rounded a corner a couple of minutes later to find another police barrier. As I slowed down, staring at it in despair, a policeman got out of a panda car parked on the verge, put his hat on (probably just to protect himself from the rain, though it made me think of a judge putting his wig on to pass sentence) and strolled over to me.

I didn't particularly want to speak to him, but I couldn't just drive away. So I wound down my window and said, "Hi."

The policeman was young, probably even younger than me, which reassured me a bit. He talked just like any other policeman, though. "I'm afraid the road ahead is closed, Sir."

"Yeah, so I see," I said. "What's going on?"

"There's been an incident, Sir," he said, in a way which suggested either that he didn't know or that he wasn't allowed to say.

"Right," I said, and wondered whether I should ask him what sort of incident. Instead I said, "Any idea how I can get to Melcham?"

Stony-faced, the policeman said, "You'll have to find an alternative route, sir."

"This *was* my alternative route," I said, trying to sound light-hearted rather than confrontational.

"Sorry, sir," he said bluntly.

I got the feeling he wanted me to finish the conversation there, to say something like, 'Oh well, can't be helped', and then to turn round and drive away. But instead I said, "The thing is, my dad's had a serious heart attack and I really need to get home. I might already be too late."

I don't honestly know what I expected him to do. Open up the barrier and let me through? Escort me to the hospital? Call up a police helicopter and have me airlifted in? He didn't do any of these things. Instead he just adopted a slightly more sympathetic look than before, and said, "Very sorry to hear that, Sir, but these restrictions are in place for your own safety. I'm afraid I can't make any exceptions."

Anger rose in me suddenly, which surprised me a bit. It wasn't directed at the policeman, but simply born of frustration. Even so, I had to bite back a sarcastic retort. I took a deep breath and felt my head sink. For a moment I felt dizzy and tired; I just wanted to give up, go home, go to sleep. I heard the policeman say, "I hope you manage to get where you want to go, sir. And I hope your dad's okay."

I looked up at him, and suddenly I saw his youth and inexperience and humanity. I nodded. "Cheers." Then I wound up my window, turned the Bastard round on the wet road, and drove back the way I had come.

Looking back, I feel as though I didn't know what I was going to do until I actually did it, that it was just a spur of the moment thing. I drove back down the road for a mile or so until I reached the lay-by on the opposite verge where I had stopped earlier, and without even pausing to think I pulled over and cut the engine.

For a minute I sat there, looking at the rain slithering down the windows and at the black fields over the low hedge to my left. Then I grabbed my rucksack and got out of the car. I walked round to the back and opened the boot, hoping that my memory wasn't cheating me. It wasn't. There was a dusty, crumpled-up cagoule squashed into the back corner, next to my hiking boots, left there from the last time I had gone walking.

I pulled the cagoule over my head, flipped up the hood and put my boots on. Rain pattered on the plastic hood as I hunched over to tie my laces. It was a soothing sound. It made me think of camping trips as a kid, curled up warm and snug in my sleeping bag while it pissed it down outside. On one trip Dad and I had gone fishing, and a duckling had somehow got a fishhook stuck in its throat. I have no idea how Dad caught the duckling (did he reel it in like a fish?), but I have a vivid memory of him tenderly and painstakingly removing the hook before placing the tiny bird carefully back into the river, whereupon it swam happily away, seemingly none the worse for its ordeal.

The memory abruptly made me well up. Stupid, I thought, swiping at my eyes. What I was planning was probably stupid too, but I couldn't see any alternative. If I was going to have any chance of seeing my parents today, I had to strike out on foot, head back home across the fields, in the dark and the rain.

I thought about calling Laura, just to let her know what was happening, but decided not to. She'd only persuade me it was a really dumb idea and then I'd be stuck, not knowing what to do. I wasn't exactly looking forward to tramping through the pitch black, and knew that sooner or later I'd almost certainly freak out and start imagining all sorts of creepy stuff. But what was *really* the worst that could happen, I asked myself. This was rural England, not some freaky American backwoods, full of grizzly bears and inbred cannibals. Probably the scariest thing I'd come across would be a stray sheep, looming out of the darkness like a dozy-looking ghost. Just the same, I could have done with a map of the local area and a torch to light my way. But I had neither. I hadn't exactly envisaged this little jaunt when I set out earlier.

I climbed over a rickety stile which led in to the field behind the hedge and started walking away from my car, boots squelching through the waterlogged grass. After twenty yards or so I felt as if I had already left civilisation behind. Despite everything, my thoughts were more active in the darkness than I would have liked. It wasn't long before I was imagining a newspaper bearing the headline: CAR OF MISSING MAN FOUND. Then I found myself picturing another, and on the front page of this one the headline read: MUTILATED REMAINS DISCOVERED IN WOODS. It would be a dog-walker, I thought. That or children playing. It was *always* either one or the other. I saw the story spooling out before me, almost as though it was written on the rain-lashed darkness: *A dog walker today made a grim discovery in woods close to the village of Melcham, near Cirencester. The dismembered remains of a man were found in a shallow grave, not far from the spot where the car of missing Leeds man, Alan —*

Stop it, I told myself firmly. Stop it *now*.

I wished I had a better sense of direction, but I was rubbish when it came to instinctively knowing which way to go. I can read maps okay, but put me down in the middle of somewhere without one and I'm fucked. My mum says that you're either born with a pigeon in your head or you're not, and I guess I'm one of those people who's not. Oh well, at least that means I don't have to put up with a crap-eating winged rodent in my skull, fluttering about and shitting everywhere (*har-de-har-har*).

The thing is, I didn't have much of an idea where Melcham was from here, but I knew it couldn't be more than about five miles away. I reckoned all I had to do was keep walking, and eventually I'd come to a road within the cordoned-off area, where there'd be signposts.

As I walked it struck me for the first time how odd it was that the police had closed off all these roads just because a van had caught fire. You could understand one or two roads being out of action, but a simple vehicle fire couldn't be causing this much disruption, surely? I started to wonder whether something else was going on. Maybe terrorists were using germ warfare, and had decided to test it out on this sleepy little corner of the Cotswolds. This whole scenario reminded me of that film, *Village of the Damned*, where everyone within a certain area fell asleep for twenty-four hours, and everyone who went into that area instantly fell asleep too, and in the end the police and the army put a cordon around the place, until eventually, a day later, everyone magically woke up again, only to find that all the women were pregnant.

It took me about ten minutes to walk across the field, my feet squelching and the rain drumming on my hood all the way. At last I came to a tough, prickly hedge. I walked along it for a couple of hundred yards until I arrived at a gate. The mud around the gate oozed up over my boots, and each step I took made a sound like a sink plunger unlocking a toilet, but at least my feet stayed dry.

I was half-way across the next field, with the black bulk of the woods looming up, several hundred yards in front of me, when I saw the lights.

They were over to my right, a string of bobbing yellow circles, maybe a dozen or more. In the dark it was hard to judge how far away they were, but I'd say about half a mile, maybe less. My initial, ridiculous thought was that they were fireflies; then I realised, a split-second later, that they were the beams of torches. As far as I could see, that could mean only one of two things.

Either this was a group of boy scouts out on a camping trip, or it was a police search.

But if the latter, what were they searching for? A missing child? An escaped criminal? And what would they do if they found *me*? Before I could help myself, I was picturing a frenzied mob from an old Frankenstein film, so fuelled by anger and alcohol that they would shoot first and ask questions later.

Whoever the torch-bearers were, I decided that I wanted to avoid them. So I veered off to my left, in a direction that would take me away from the search party, but towards the thickest part of the wood.

I wasn't exactly scared, but I was a bit nervous, and anxious to press on, to put this awful day behind me, despite what would be waiting for me at home. I reached the edge of the wood and plunged into it without hesitation, the trees and bushes around me coalescing into an impenetrable tangle of blackness. However, even at this point I didn't feel any fear — at least, not until I heard the growling.

It came from somewhere ahead of me and to my right, and it immediately stopped me dead. Coldness washed over me that had nothing to do with the rain. Feeling constricted within my hood, I pulled it down, and at once several fat drips of rain splatted on my head as if they had been waiting for just this opportunity. In the wood the rain was a soft sound, like the distant drumming of tiny hoof beats.

Had I really heard something growling? Maybe it was what the police were looking for — a savage dog, or a big cat, like a puma or a panther. Maybe the animal had already attacked and killed several people. Surely I wasn't about to become a 'shreddie', the real-life equivalent of one of those unnamed victims from a million horror movies?

The experts say that if you're ever confronted by a large predator you should stay still — but I was fucked if I was going to stand around here all night. So I started walking, slowly and deliberately, feeling my way ahead with the toes of my boots, alert for the slightest sound or movement. I suppose I must have taken around a couple of dozen steps when I heard the growling again.

It was behind me this time, and it almost made me piss my pants. 'Fuck', I muttered in a rusty croak, 'fuck, fuck, fuck.' As potential last words go, they weren't exactly earth-shattering, but as there was no one around to hear them, I guess it didn't much matter.

I think it was at this point that I came to the conclusion I had watched too many movies. I could almost picture the scene shot for shot: close-up on my face, eyes widening, as the 'beast' slowly rises, slightly out of focus, over my right shoulder; slow camera pan, the tension building, as I turn to confront whatever is behind me; brief, almost subliminal, close-up of burning red eyes and slavering jaws full of long sharp teeth; and then...

I whirled round, unable to prevent air escaping my throat in a thin squeal.

There was nothing there.

Except there was. It may not have been *right* behind me, but it was there somewhere, in the darkness. Watching me. Stalking me.

'Fuck,' I whispered again, and resumed walking. It was all I could do. Put one foot in front of the other, and tell myself that each step was a step closer to safety.

My legs felt tight and I could feel my muscles bunching in my back. I walked in a semi-stoop, head hunched into my shoulders. I felt flimsy and vulnerable, my body a fragile cage around my pummelling heart. I considered dialling 999, but then thought that if the animal heard how scared I was, it might just gain the extra bit of encouragement it needed to attack. I clung to the hope that at present it was still sizing me up, wary of tangling with such a sizeable opponent. Maybe the rain was damping down my terror, which I guessed must be pulsing from my body like radio waves.

The next ten minutes were the longest of my life. I just kept walking, all the time imagining that something large and fast, with hooked claws and pointed teeth, was about to leap out of the darkness. I saw it a dozen times out of the corner of my eye — a sudden flash of movement — but whenever I whirled to confront it, there was never anything there.

At last I realised I was nearing the other side of the wood. The mass of blackness began to break apart into the jagged, though blurry shapes of individual tree branches, through which I could see darkness that wasn't *quite* as dark as the darkness in the wood — if that makes any sense. What I mean is, by any normal definition the darkness was still dark, but it was no longer *black*. The sky was full of deep blues and dense greys, which meant that the land visible beyond the trees had a kind of murky definition. I could certainly see enough to tell that there was another field ahead of me, bordered on the far side by a black thread that must have been a stone wall. And just beyond that was a straight-angled block of blackness that could only have been a building.

I trudged on, the sound of rain becoming harder as I moved out from under the cover of the trees. I hadn't heard the growling since it had seemed to be right behind me, ten or fifteen minutes earlier. I didn't know whether to feel encouraged by that or apprehensive. One thing I definitely wasn't was complacent. I decided that the building was a good place to head for, and that once I got there (*if* I got there) I would re-assess my situation.

I wondered what I'd do if I saw the bobbing lights of the search party again now, and thought that I'd almost certainly decide there was safety in numbers and head straight for them. Hearing the growling had put a whole new complexion on things. Suddenly the chance of speaking to other human beings was something I'd welcome with open arms. But the string of torch lights was now nowhere to be seen. I, and possibly the creature that the searchers were looking for, seemed, without too much difficulty, to have slipped through the net.

Since I'd started walking again after my last scare I hadn't looked behind me. Partly that was because I hadn't *heard* anything behind me, and partly it was because a kind of fatalism had set in. Terrified though I still was, I'd decided that if the thing was going to attack it was going to attack, and there would be nothing I could do about it. However, once I left the oppressiveness of the wood, with its many potential hiding places, and started trudging across open ground again, I started to think differently. Suddenly I *wanted* to turn round, if only to reassure myself that the animal wasn't right behind me. If I could get half-way across the field, and turn in a circle to see nothing but open ground around me, then I might allow myself to start believing that things would turn out okay after all.

And so I turned round.

And there it was.

It was standing at the edge of the trees, almost but not quite blending into them. It was as big as a Great Dane, but shaggier, with a pointed snout.

Wolf, I thought. *It's a fucking wolf.* And it wasn't *just* a wolf, it was a *big* wolf, its head almost on a level with mine.

I started to back away slowly. The wolf padded forward, keeping pace with me. It looked relaxed and casual, but I couldn't help thinking it was letting me know that it could close the distance between us in a matter of seconds if it wanted to. Even though the creature showed no immediate signs of attacking, I honestly don't think I could have been more terrified than I was at that moment. I was out in the open with a wild animal, for fuck's sake! People generally think of wolves as being like big dogs, but I was so scared that as far as I was concerned, it might as well have been a tiger or a grizzly bear standing by the trees. I might as well have been treading water with a Great White Shark circling me.

I'd like to say that I acted sensibly, that I carefully assessed the situation and how best to handle it. But that's not what happened. *Some* people might have had the presence of mind to think things through, but all that happened with me was that my brain locked, and my body responded by doing exactly what every instinct was screaming at it to do, which was to turn and run like hell.

It's weird. Even as my body chose the flight over fight option, even though my thoughts felt frozen with terror, there was a part of me that knew I was doing a very, very stupid thing. More than that, there was a part of me that was comparing my actions to the movies once again, even to the point of callously informing me that if I was a character in a film, then I'd *deserve* to die, simply for being such a moron.

Something else: I was dream running. Or at least, that was what it felt like. You know in dreams, when you're trying to get away from something and you feel as though you're wading through sludge? Well, all I was aware of as I fled was how stiff and heavy and slow I was, and of how the mud and grass absorbed my footsteps, draining my energy and making me feel as though I was about to stumble and pitch headlong any moment.

And yet I made it. It sounds impossible, I know, but I did. Don't get me wrong: I don't for a second think I *outran* the wolf. If it had wanted to catch me, it would have done so, no problem. All I can tell you is that I ran and ran and kept on running. I reached the wall and scrambled over it, and then thirty seconds later I reached the building, which I could now see was a rickety and abandoned old barn. I threw myself against the door, desperate for some kind of sanctuary, however flimsy. I had a horrible few seconds when I realised that the door opened outwards, and that it was stuck through lack of use. I hauled on the edge of it, screaming and swearing, and at last it gave a little, creating just enough of a gap for me to slip inside. Once there, I curled my wet fingers around the saturated wood and yanked the door shut again. It was a big door, warped and spongy, and there was no way of locking it. All I could hope was that the wolf, unable to find a gap big enough to fit through, would lose whatever interest it had in me and bugger off.

Once I was inside and had shut the door, I assessed my surroundings. Not that there was much *to* assess, to be honest. The barn was old and empty, and obviously hadn't been used for some time. It smelled of manure and wet mould, and it was so dark that I couldn't even see the ceiling above me. I had a quick scout around, mainly to check the walls, and realised — because I kept walking through the bloody things — that the place was full of spider webs. At one point, after the sticky strands of a web had stretched across my face, I'm sure I felt its owner scuttle across my cheek and through my hair. That was only slightly less alarming than stumbling across what I at first thought was a slumped body, only to realise that it was a heap of old sacking.

By this time my ordeal was catching up with me. I was starting to feel weak, sick and shaky, and all at once I had a desperate need to sit down. I stumbled over to what I thought was roughly the middle of the floor and sank into a cross-legged squat, my upper body slumping forward. I was aching and exhausted, and soaked with rain and sweat. I was starting to shake badly now with cold and reaction; I felt as though I was coming down with flu. Suddenly even sitting down wasn't enough. I needed to *lie* down. The ground was damp and earthy, but at that moment I didn't care. I stretched out, put my wet rucksack beneath my head as a pillow, and closed my eyes.

I had never felt so lonely, so scared and so far from civilisation. I couldn't believe that an hour ago I had been in my car on the motorway. The rain continued to patter down outside, like an echo of my chattering teeth. I felt my thoughts breaking up, drifting away. For a few seconds I resisted, thinking that I ought to stay awake and alert, be ready to run or fight. Then I thought: fuck it. And I allowed sleep to take me.

I have no idea how long I was out for. It could have been a couple of minutes or a couple of hours. However long it was, the sleep I had was deep and black and total. Being jerked out of it felt like being born, propelled into a world of stress and clamour. I experienced an instant of profound and heartfelt regret before realising that someone was hammering on the barn door.

Feeling like an old man, I unfolded myself into a sitting position and stared in the direction of the banging. For a few seconds I didn't speak or do anything. All I could think was that this was it, that the wolf had finally decided it was hungry and was coming to get me. In my confused state of mind, it didn't occur to me that wolves didn't tend to knock on doors — except maybe in fairy tales. It was only when I heard a girl's voice shouting, "Help me, please!" that my thoughts snapped fully back to reality.

Pushing myself to my feet, I walked on shaky legs to the door. I was almost there when the banging came again, accompanied by the girl's voice, which was even more desperate this time. "Is there anyone in there? Oh God, please help me! *Please!*"

"Hello?" I said, too dozy to think of anything *else* to say.

"Oh, thank God," said the girl. "Please, will you let me in? There's something out here."

"The door's not locked," I said.

"I can't open it," she said. "Can you do it for me?"

So I shoved the door, which opened with a wet, gritty scrape. The girl bobbed into view, and even in the darkness I saw that she was pretty and blonde and terrified. She looked behind her, and then at me.

"There's something out here," she said. "It's been following me."

"I think it's a wolf," I said. "It followed me too."

"Can I come in?" she asked.

"Yeah, course you can," I said.

So she slipped through the gap and I closed the door behind her.

"Sorry it's so dark," I said. "I haven't got a torch."

"That's all right," she said from about twelve feet away. "I've got some candles. Hang on."

I heard some rummaging about, then the scrape of a match, and suddenly we had light. The girl had lit a fat white candle, which was standing in a copper candle-holder on the floor. As our grungy, cobwebby surroundings came alive, the rotting and rain-sodden wooden walls lapped by warm, buttery light, the girl moved across to another white candle in another candle-holder a few metres away and lit that too. Now the light was quite homely. Or spooky, depending on how you looked at it.

The girl looked at me and gave me a smile that, if I didn't know any better, I'd say was a bit seductive. "Thanks for inviting me in," she said.

"That's all right," I said, though I have to admit I felt slightly nervous. The girl was really pretty, and I'd been desperate for someone to talk to, but all the same I couldn't help feeling that something was… well, *wrong* somehow.

It was the girl's manner for one thing, the way she had gone from terrified to flirty in a matter of seconds. And another thing was that she wasn't really dressed for a night-time trudge through the countryside in the rain. She was wearing a thin sweater — a *tight*, thin sweater, which proudly showed off her considerable attributes — a pair of jeans, a pair of trainers, and that was it. Her clothes were drenched and her blonde hair hung down her back in dripping wet ropes, but she didn't seem to care.

"Were you with the search party?" I asked.

She shook her head, as if she was amused by the question.

"Where've you come from then?" I persisted.

She walked towards me, light and lithe like a ballet dancer, water dripping off her. She stopped a metre or so away and tilted her head slightly, looking at me as if I was something new and interesting.

"Do you know what the search party were looking for?" she said.

I shook my head. Then I said, "The wolf, I suppose."

She laughed and the sound was disturbingly deep and guttural. "I suppose..." she murmured, as if mimicking me. Then she looked at me again, *examined* me again. "Have you really not heard the rumours? The *silly* rumours? They've been on the local radio all day."

"I've been busy," I said. "I'm not from around here."

I took a step back as she took another step towards me. She was close enough to kiss.

"When sheep are found with their throats torn out," she said, "folk don't pay much attention. But when a *person* is found in the same condition..."

She grinned, showing all her teeth, revealing long pointed canines.

And suddenly I thought back to that radio broadcast I'd only partly heard in the car, and it struck me that maybe the newsreader hadn't been saying 'van fire', after all.

I'd like to say I fought bravely, but the truth is, she was so fast I didn't even have time to blink.

When I woke up, she was gone, leaving nothing but the still-burning candles to show she had ever been there. I sat bolt upright and then leaped to my feet, feeling stronger, faster and more alert than I had ever felt when I was alive.

I knew what I was, of course. I knew it immediately and instinctively. I thought of Mum and Dad and Laura.

I had such a gift to bestow upon them.

And I had such a *thirst*.

ABOUT THE AUTHOR

MARK MORRIS BECAME a full-time writer in 1988 on the Enterprise Allowance Scheme, and a year later saw the release of his first novel, *Toady*. He has since published a further thirteen novels, among which are *Stitch*, *The Immaculate*, *The Secret of Anatomy*, *Mr. Bad Face*, *Fiddleback* and *Nowhere Near an Angel*. His short stories, novellas, articles and reviews have appeared in a wide variety of anthologies and magazines, and he is editor of the highly-acclaimed *Cinema Macabre*, a book of fifty horror movie essays by genre luminaries, for which he won a British Fantasy Award in 2007. His latest novels are *Doctor Who – Forever Autumn*, which was voted "Best Doctor Who Book of 2007" by readers of *Doctor Who Magazine*, and *The Deluge*, published by Leisure Books in the USA. Forthcoming work includes a novella entitled *It Sustains*, a "Hellboy" novel entitled *The All-Seeing Eye* and another book in the immensely popular "Doctor Who" range, *Ghosts of India*.

www.markmorriswriter.com
www.humdrumming.co.uk

HUMDRUMMING TITLES BY MARK MORRIS:

Toady [JACKET-LESS HARDBACK EDITION]
Stitch [JACKET-LESS HARDBACK EDITION]
Long Shadows, Nightmare Light [COLLECTION, FORTHCOMING]
The First Humdrumming Book of Horror Stories [INTRODUCTION]
World Wide Web (and Other Lovecraftian Upgrades) [INTRODUCTION]

WARY BE THE TRAVELLER

CAROL WEEKES

THE EVENING WAS cold with a high wind which swept along gutters, forced draughts beneath doors and branches to bend, and sent gusts of fallen leaves into dervishes near the curb. It was late October, the night creating a bitter-sweet tinge of decaying gardens. All Hallows waited three days away, lending a gothic atmosphere to the evening and what they were about to incur. MacNaughton felt exhilarated. He twisted the collar of his tweed coat higher up along his neck and tucked his chin into the fabric to ward off the bite of frost nipping at his face. He hurried toward the Tinsdale residence, a three story Victorian, newly renovated and recently purchased near the edge of the dark St. Lawrence River. He'd met the Tinsdales on a train trip out west and their combined interest in things metaphysical appealed immediately. They'd decided to keep in touch with the exchange of business cards and phone numbers. They were much older — MacNaughton guessed in their early to mid-'80s and remarkably youthful despite their time — with an air of wisdom and knowledge that encompassed them both, like a fine veil of energetic silk about their person. As luck, in MacNaughton's philosophy would have it, it turned out that the Tinsdales lived a mere two miles up the road from where he kept a small, but cozy apartment. Here he'd been close to folks of common interest for over a year and had not known it until a month ago. This would be their first meeting since their trip.

He'd been reading about penetrating the spiritual realms for a considerable while now, but to date, had had little luck in experiencing anything beyond what he considered to be an over-active imagination during his solo quests. He hoped that the combined energies of Margot and Sanderson Tinsdale, both experienced practitioners of the psychic and other-worldly realms would increase his chances of actually making 'contact' with something beyond the mortal world. An academic by trade (MacNaughton taught mathematics within the sterile capacity of the college classroom), he longed for elements that moved beyond the black and white of numeric computations, predicted resolutions, and anticipated outcomes. He wanted more out of life, more beyond going to work, paying bills, watching conventional television, reading the standard fare within the covers of far too many books. He wanted something beyond all of that.

The Tinsdales' residence loomed up suddenly, the bulk of its windows dark, other than those which appeared to contain the formal décor of a parlour that sat at the front of the large house. Its windows were heavy, antiquated and rippled in effect, their patterns consisting of stained glass leaves, twisting vines, and blood-red roses. Glow from an interior lamp threw a band of gold across the ground. The Tinsdales had set pumpkins and gourds upon the step and above that, a whirling ghost consisting of swatches of grey-white fabric which resembled cheesecloth. A plastic face that looked far too much like actual bone — its eye sockets dark holes above a grin consisting of realistic teeth aligned in a death-leer — spun to regard MacNaughton as he mounted the steps.

"Good evening, old chap," MacNaughton said with an air of frivolousness. "Think you're scary, do you? I'm sure the young ones will a few evenings from now." He pushed past the decoration and, as he did so, detected a faint bouquet of something rank. He paused for a moment, sniffing. It seemed to come from the gruesome adornment. MacNaughton took a tentative step toward the thing, inhaled and noted the scents of old fabric, past rains and winds, something spicy...when the door to the house opened and Margot Tinsdale, resplendent in a midnight blue silk gown with matching trousers, heralded his arrival.

"How wonderful that you still decided to come," she said, ushering him into the warm house and shutting the door behind him.

"Interesting artefact you have," he said, using his chin to motion toward the porch and the now invisible decoration. "It disturbed me. No doubt, it'll have a positive effect on All Hallows. Odd scent about it."

Margot, her eyes deep and a clear, dark blue, regarded him. "Ah, yes, the ghoul. We call him Masterson. We kept the decorations in the basement until this year when we discovered that a mould had invaded the boxes. We're hoping the wind eliminates some of the… miasma. Do come in. Sherry or scotch?"

"Scotch, thanks, on the rocks."

It was done. Margot led the way along a shadowed corridor, past a sweeping stairwell and directed MacNaughton into the parlour where Sanderson Tinsdale sat in a large armchair before a colossal fireplace. A fire had been well-lit for a while now, its flames dancing and flickering a good two feet high within the hearth, casting a welcome glow and warmth into the room. Sanderson glanced up from reading a book poised upon his lap to greet MacNaughton.

"Good man!" Sanderson proclaimed. "I wondered if you'd come out tonight. Vile drop in temperature, if you ask me. Did you walk?"

"I'm grateful to be inside, and yes, I arrived by foot."

Sanderson's face, etched in golds and russet from the flames, regarded him with a mixture of amusement and earnest. "I trust that Margot is looking after your needs?"

"Scotch, yes, thanks."

"Good. Good. It's the perfect evening to undertake what we're about to do."

"I agree," MacNaughton chose a similar chair of three which had been placed in a half circle before the grate. "Although, I must admit that, as much as I anticipate my first *bona fide*… ghostly experience… a small part of me feels some trepidation. This is new to me, beyond my mere readings, of course."

At the mention of 'ghost', Sanderson Tinsdale guffawed in laughter. "Oh, my dear friend, let your doubts rest, for, as the old philosophy states, there is nothing to fear but fear itself. We hesitate with what we don't understand. Knowledge is power. Ah, here's your Scotch and with it, some hot *canapés*."

Margot swept into the room then, carrying a matte silver tray in both hands upon which sat two tumblers of amber liquid, the ice tinkling against glass, and a plate which contained an aromatic display of fine water crackers upon which she'd placed such delicacies as finely shaved cucumber, smoked salmon with fresh dill, and a *piquant* creamed cheese. On another plate heavy crusted bread and chunks of what appeared to be a bowl of spiced liverwurst, much of the fare consisting of MacNaughton's favourites. It was as if they'd read his mind. Although he'd partaken in a bowl of thick soup with crackers before his departure, he became aware that his appetite had since been whetted by the weather, as well as a sudden burst of adrenaline coursing through him. He was excited (and yes, a bit nervous) to be here. He was, after all, still new to the demeanour of the Tinsdales.

"I am your student, grateful for your hospitality and wisdom this evening," he said. "I shall return the favour during the following week. My place; dinner, atmosphere, albeit not quite to the splendour of this..." and here he gesticulated around the room with its high ceilings, its fine crystal chandelier, its thick oak boards and ancient plaster walls.

He took the scotch, something with a hint of smoke to its flavour, and helped himself to two of the *canapés* and a chunk of the bread which he spread liberally with the liverwurst. It was homemade and balanced nicely with a hint of garlic and something else; something for which MacNaughton couldn't define with any exactitude, but which rang a note of familiarity within him. He reserved the thought that he'd come back to this later, much like a need to identify a sought yet evasive word dangling on the tip of one's tongue.

"Eat, and then we'll begin," Margot said. "So; you wish to discover if realms beyond our mortal world exist. Indeed, they do. Sanderson and I have been investigating and partaking in these... ethereal layers, if you will... for many years. Ah, the fire is splendid." She leaned forward and warmed her hands, thin yet strong with fine blue veins that criss-crossed her skin, and yet without the usual spotty blemishes of an octogenarian.

A few minutes later, when they'd exhausted their appetites for the time, they settled down to begin the purpose of their business.

"You said upon the train that you wish to know for a fact if there is existence beyond what we call the 'mortal' realm. Is that correct?" Sanderson Tinsdale regarded him with an expression of inquisitiveness.

"Yes," MacNaughton said with a hint of reservation. "Isn't it a question every man and woman asks themselves at some point in their life upon this earth? Do we go on? What lies beyond the grave? Surely, what we know upon this earth cannot be it. Therefore, I would like to know where something else awaits us. Where indeed?"

"You can find other realms within the confines or your own living room; or ours, for that matter. It is a matter of mindset, young MacNaughton. Mind over matter. Our bodies are mere vehicles through which we conduct our earthly business. You must learn to concentrate. Concentrate with care and ask but a wish. What do you wish to know for certain? Pose your question."

MacNaughton felt the weight of the moment upon him. He licked his lips, the aftertaste of the food lingering in his mouth, and took a long sip of the quality scotch to abate it. "I want to ask if I can survive the physicality of my body. I want to know that I can overstep death. I want more excitement than the monotony of ordinary life as we know it."

"And what is 'death' in your current opinion?" Margot asked, her voice barely above a whisper. The wind gusted at once, throwing its force along the chimney suit and sending the flames into an erratic dance.

"The end," MacNaughton stated. "The unknown. Darkness. The confines of a casket below the ground, reeking of earth's mildew and penetrated by worms and insects. The decaying of the flesh. The end of everything." A shiver crossed his skin and that need to capture something evasive — like some reclusive tidbit of information yearned for — floated back to him.

"Well, my dear friend, you are wrong," Sanderson told him. "A casket is but a box enclosing the mere shards of what once was; a closet containing the clothing of that which no longer houses a body. There is something more, believe me."

"How do you know for a fact?" MacNaughton leaned forward, piqued, his elbows resting on his knees. The scotch was smooth and warmed him deep into his gut. "Is this place haunted? Do you believe in ghosts and all things that go bump, bang, and clang in the night? Or evil?"

Sanderson sniggered a little. "Evil," he said, "is what you want to make of it."

"I don't follow."

"No matter. We won't go there. Instead, let us take you into a most wonderful realm above and beyond the ordinary of anything you've ever before experienced."

"Yes, let us show you," Margot said. She held her glass up to the two men. "Cheers!"

"Cheers," MacNaughton echoed, eager but suddenly nervous. "What do you plan to do?"

"That is for us to know and for you to realize. Let us begin."

MacNaughton placed his drink upon the serving tray and clasped his hands.

"Shut your eyes and begin to breathe deeply," Sanderson told him. "Count with me… one, two, three. Deep breaths. In, out, in… do you feel yourself getting lighter? A kind of drifting sensation?"

MacNaughton did as he was instructed for he'd spent years in school and followed directives with ease. He inhaled and exhaled, smelling the aromatic nature of the wood smoke and listening to the fire crackle. Every now and then a knot in the wood would pop, causing him to jump. He wasn't sure what to expect and, now that he was here, wasn't as comfortable as he thought he'd be. What did he expect? That a bogie man might leap from the shadows in a corner to encompass him in its shadowy fists?

"We are on a journey," Sanderson continued. "A special journey that will take you beyond this world; keep in step with us. Do not allow your mind to wander. Concentrate. Your eyes must remain shut at all times — do you understand me, for your own safety!"

MacNaughton shivered a little despite the fire and the liquor. "I'm a tad uneasy by your words, if I do say so myself. Pray tell, what do you mean by my own safety? What *could* possibly happen? I mean, we're talking about non-material worlds and things, aren't we? It's not as though something tangible is going to latch on and –"

"Never doubt what you're about to get into," Sanderson spoke in a terse tone.

MacNaughton's eyes popped open. Both men stared at each other, Sanderson's gaze one of consternation and MacNaughton's one of frightened dubiousness.

"I-I'm unsure..." MacNaugton began.

"Do you want to do this? You must be clear," Sanderson said, "or speak now lest you set out on a journey for which you are not prepared to see what may come."

MacNaughton wavered and his lower lip shook a little. He thought of the decoration twirling and whipping about on the end of its tattered rope, the face looking a trifle too bone-like, the odd smell... he made a mental note to feel it when he left, as much as the idea of it made his skin crawl. He could tell real bone if he touched it.

"All right," MacNaughton said, frightened, yet determined not to show it. He had, after all, asked these people about their abilities while travelling with them and had, through his own workings, arranged for this private appointment, for neither offered their services openly. The conversation about metaphysics and worlds beyond had come up as if it had been meant to be a synchronicity of sorts. His curiosity bade him to see this through, a little further, at least. He told himself that should anything feel suddenly, undeniably uncomfortable, he would halt the proceedings immediately and extend a good night. He would be on his way; collar re-established against his neck, hea`d bent into the wind as he headed back toward his apartment. It would be as simple as that.

The Tinsdales readjusted themselves in their seats. "You must understand that by learning how to still ones mind one opens oneself to a variety of possibilities," Margot said. "If at any moment you should feel uncomfortable, simply clap your hands together and end the session. You are always in control. A brief clap-clap and you'll return right where you are, safe and sound in your chair. Understood?"

MacNaughton nodded. "Understood. Let's try this again, then?"

They all shut their eyes and Sanderson began his dialogue again. They breathed in deeply, listening to the tick of the wind and rain against the windows, listening to the occasional creak of a board or shutter somewhere off in the house, listening to the beating of their combined hearts.

Within minutes, MacNaughton felt somewhat light-headed and drifted off into a somewhat pleasant state that consisted of fragment-puffs of various mind imagery; he imagined clouds rolling and tumbling across a blue sky; he imagined the sound of waves hitting a shore; he imagined –

...the thing called Masterson circling and spinning, its eye sockets dark and yet full of life somehow like something caught within a cage. Like...

Something cool and sudden touched MacNaughton against a shoulder. He cried out and his eyes shot open. He continued to feel a little dozy, even as he willed himself back to full consciousness. He clapped his hands for effect but nothing changed. He noted Margot and Sanderson, still seated but watching him. Watching him as if their eyes had never been shut the whole while; as if he'd become an obstacle of observation. MacNaughton felt suddenly vulnerable here. His gut instinct told him to call this off; it had been a mistake. They could offer him nothing that he wanted any longer, no matter what it might be and a tingling sensation in his innards told him that this was nothing good, nothing right.

"Is something the matter?" Sanderson asked too brusquely. "We told you to keep on track with us and not vary from the directions."

"A sudden thought occurred to me," MacNaughton replied, standing up and pulling his coat to him. He thrust first one arm into a sleeve, then the other. "I just recalled a meeting I have tomorrow morning. I've had a lot on my plate lately," he continued to fib, not caring, yet feeling as if they knew of his deception. "I'd clean forgotten about it. I'd best be going, given it will be an early start tomorrow."

Margot looked more annoyed than disappointed. Yes, she'd gone to the trouble of food and all but MacNaughton sensed that her angst stemmed from something much deeper, something for which he couldn't place a finger upon.

"We've just begun," she blurted. "You haven't given it a chance."

"I think the timing is incorrect," MacNaughton said. "I apologize profusely for having taken up part of your evening and for this unexpected disappointment. I thank you in earnest for your willing hospitality."

"I can give you a lift," Sanderson told him.

This made MacNaughton start. "No thank you. I enjoy walking outdoors."

"The evening is getting worse; look, it's starting to snow."

MacNaughton looked and saw that, indeed, the rain had turned to sleet. Still, something told him to go, now. Just leave and walk, no matter the clime.

"Thank you anyway, but I'll be on my way," he said.

As he made his way toward the front corridor bathed in full shadow now, he heard them step up behind him and Margot clearly say "Get his wallet." At the same instant, he saw the thing called Masterson twirl and leap on the end of its rope and knew, without a doubt now, that it would be real bone and that the odd aroma he'd detected earlier was one of doom settling into his heart. As he began to twirl, he saw the fire iron coming swiftly toward the centre of his forehead before it connected and all went dark.

* * *

The Tinsdales were correct. Perception *was* different from this place. MacNaughton acknowledged that he was dead; whatever dead meant and he knew that, somehow, he'd been duped out of a proper death by the Tinsdales powers, all for the price of a wallet. He'd carried two hundred dollars and two credit cards which they'd run to the hilt over the past two days. He knew. He heard them discussing him, but he couldn't even haunt for he was stuck inside a thing which looked like a ventriloquist's doll; a natty thing with checker trousers and a little tweed jacket, its painted grin too red around its painted wooden white teeth. They sat him — inside the doll, its eyes made of glass and providing a rather milky version of the world to MacNaughton — on the lowest step of the house, just below Masterson who blew and spun about him. At night, when no one was around and things grew unnaturally quiet, MacNaughton heard the skeleton speak in a disembodied voice that sounded a little too much like moaning wind; or perhaps it was like him caught inside this doll — shattered voices captured like fireflies inside a jar. Somehow the Tinsdales had sealed them both in. He'd had time to think about the name 'Masterson' and thought he recalled, rather vaguely, a missing person article in the local paper a few weeks back; something about a car found in the lake without an occupant, the case still open; as fresh as footsteps might be in new snow circling around about the house where the Tinsdales kept a smoke house which burned for many hours each day. A most unique flavour to the liverwurst.

He hated the taste of the wood inside the doll's mouth and the way the glassy eyes distracted from the view of the distant water. Children would come for treats this evening and step past both him and Masterson to ring the doorbell. He wanted to warn them to run, go, do not approach the house, but Tinsdale had rendered him speechless unless Tindsdale wished him to do so. Tinsdale would approach the doll and, lifting it up upon his arm, ask "So, how are we today, MacNaughton? Pity you missed your meeting. I'm sure they'll reschedule." Then, he'd screw his face up and reply, in a falsetto voice with lips barely moving: "Oh, no problem, Master. I have forever to make it up, don't I?" He'd laugh to himself, give MacNaughton's wooden body a pat, and set him back down on the step amid the leaves and dampness.

"Don't worry about the children," Tinsdale told him, "for they carry naught but pennies and other low coinage among them; certainly nothing worth any trouble. Quite the savings you had in your account, my good man! Saving up for a rainy day, were you?"

A rainy day, indeed; one where a large fire waited beyond the shadows of a spinning ornament with an odd, displacing odour. Tinsdale walked back inside and shut the door on the two of them.

As Peterson skulked away, Thrummond mentally cursed him, and momentarily wished he'd had a brick handy to smash into the back of Peterson's head. He pictured Peterson's hair matted with thick blood, imagined the surprised 'O' of his mouth.

* * *

Rain. Thrummond had forgotten his umbrella. A sodden newspaper over his head, he'd dashed to the bus stop just in time. It was past supper time but not yet dark when Thrummond climbed aboard the №102 and sat heavily in a ratty seat near the back, its vinyl scabrous and torn. Chelsea wouldn't be pleased. He was late again. And she'd be further displeased to know it was his weekend with Timothy, his son. But he only had visitation rights alternating weekends, and he'd be damned if he was going to give that up, even if Timothy mostly ignored him and moped sullenly.

The rain turned to drizzle. A fine mist coated the bus windows which, combined with the wan sunlight reflecting off storefront windows, created a strange transparent watercolour, a slow-motion blur as the bus bumped along the streets, Thrummond staring out its window. When the bus jolted to a stop at a pedestrian crossing, Thrummond saw a small dark figure with a white hat looking at him from a dark storefront. He couldn't be sure, but the man seemed to be smiling unpleasantly, momentarily vacillating between a bright pleasure and black torment.

* * *

Thrummond stared at her, trying to read her mood. Chelsea was on the chesterfield, painting her toenails a fluorescent pink. She didn't glance up. Had barely said a word to him when he'd come in. The television was on, static flickering across the screen.

He rubbed his chin. "What say we go out for a drink? The rest of the weekend is shot."

Her eyes flicked up. Sullen and bored. Face slack. "I've other plans," she said. She turned back to her toes. "Go on without me. Besides," she added, "the weekends are always shot. You're always off somewhere else."

He grimaced. It wasn't fair. She didn't understand about Tim. She never would. And Tim wouldn't understand about Chelsea.

Thrummond sighed. This was the moment he'd been avoiding. This moment of anguish. "What is it?" he asked. "What's wrong?"

Chelsea glanced up, her face grim. "I don't want to talk right now."

"I see," Thrummond said. He pressed on. "Don't I make you happy?"

"Not now," she repeated, her mouth rigid.

He stared at her features, set like cracked ancient stone. "You never smile anymore," Thrummond said. And it was true. Lately, whenever Thrummond spoke to her, all he got back in response was a stunned look of surprise, as if all the air had gone out of her.

"Go on," Chelsea said, rising from the chesterfield. "Go for your drink." She brushed past him, the smell of toenail polish thick in the air. She stopped at the bedroom, turned. "That's all you really want, isn't it?" she said. "A crappy job that pays just enough for a drink or two; a girlfriend you can fuck whenever you want; nothing more, no responsibilities." She paused, caught her breath, and when she spoke again Thrummond heard a terrible sadness in her voice. "Everything carefree. You don't want to reach higher. You never will." She stepped into the bedroom, closed the door.

Thrummond tottered forward, stopped. "I just want to see you smile again," he said, hating the pleading sound of his voice. "That's all."

He returned to the couch to sit and stare at the flickering static of the television.

* * *

Aside from a small group in the far corner holding some kind of celebration, there was no one else in the park but Thrummond and Tim. Dead leaves scuttled along the hard-packed ground and the sky shone dully like a tarnished nickel. He wondered why anyone would want to hold a party in a park on a day like this.

He watched Tim move from the swing-set to the rocking horse. The rocking horse balanced on a large metal coil, and seemed to lean toward Thrummond, a knowing conspirator. The horse's face held a crudely painted leer. He stared at the head as it moved up and down to the rhythm of Tim's rocking. As the rocking horse moved, its grin seemed to grow ever wider.

The sound of a child's cry brought him back to his senses. It took him a moment to realise that it was Tim crying. The boy lay on the dirty ground, beneath the still moving rocking horse, clutching his arm.

Thrummond rushed to Tim's side, scooped him up, patted his head and cooed placating words. He was good at calming words; it always seemed to soothe Chelsea. Tim's cries eased to a low whimper.

"Let's have a look at that," he said, moving Tim's hand aside to get a look at the arm. The nylon jacket had torn through and he could see a deep, bloody scrape on the arm. It was a nasty abrasion and if he didn't take good care of the wound it would mark Tim's perfect skin.

The boy had settled some and Thrummond helped him to his feet. "Come," he said, "we'll need to take care of that."

Tim looked up, hopeful. "Are we going to your apartment?" he asked.

He gaped at his son. Chelsea was at the apartment: he couldn't chance it. "No," he answered. "We'll need to take care of this quick. We'll go to the clinic or the pharmacy. Then we'll get an ice cream before we have to get you back."

He pulled Tim along, herding him toward the exit. They passed the small group in the corner. The party was in full swing. It was a child's birthday party by the looks of it; cake, ice cream, music, laughter, streamers and balloons. Thrummond stopped.

The bright balloons were tethered to the corners of a picnic table by means of long pieces of colourful string. They danced and bobbed in the afternoon wind, jostling and bumping into each other as if choreographed. Thrummond stared. His body began to vibrate, and he felt like a string on a guitar that had just been plucked out of tune, all out of sorts.

There was another party, Thrummond recalled, many, many years ago. He was but a child, maybe Tim's current age, and he'd been invited to a classmate's birthday party. He hadn't wanted to go the party, he remembered, it was a Saturday afternoon and the Orioles and Yankees were on the television, and his classmates didn't like him anyway. But his mom had admonished him and shooed him out the door, so on a grey day with greyer thoughts he'd trudged to the party, token gift in hand.

As usual, they ignored him, shooting strange glances his way. He stood alone in a corner, playing with a bouquet of colourful balloons taped to a wall, batting at them feebly, whilst the others played Pin-the-Tail or Musical Chairs. The birthday boy, a chubby penguin-like child wearing a jaunty sailor's cap, an insincere smile, and cake-stained cheeks, remarkably won each challenge. A red balloon had come loose from the wall and floated to the floor. Thrummond grabbed the balloon with the intention of trying to affix it back to the wall. He clasped two chubby hands around the sphere and lifted it to eye-level. He could see through the thin membranous material, and everything was distorted, pulled at the edges, and bathed in a weak red light. The plastic material felt good in Thrummond's hands. His body tingled. He held tight to the balloon, rubbed it with a trembling hand, then brought it up to his face and moved it jerkily along his cheeks. A hard knot of pleasure emanated from his lower belly and grew. He closed his eyes, rocked slowly, and rubbed the balloon faster. The pleasure grew, his body quivered. Then a small sound, a child's cruel laughter, and Thrummond went rigid, his eyes snapping open. Through the balloon he saw the birthday boy's grinning face, fuzzy and taffy-pulled, awash in red. Thrummond felt as if he were wearing a mask, as if he were someone else altogether. He blinked. The boy mouthed something like "Boo," and Thrummond started. He reached up, extended a finger and poked the balloon.

Pop! The balloon exploded in Thrummond's face, and that firm lump of pleasure released. The party had stopped. His classmates stared at Thrummond, silent as new ghosts. Then they grinned as one and a chorus of laughter echoed all around him. Thrummond bolted from the room, from the party, from everything; down the red twisting streets that seemed sticky and unreal, to his house, to his room, to his bed, where he discovered he'd soiled his pants.

The sound of a child's whimper brought Thrummond back to reality. Tim was crying again, staring up at him red-faced. The party had stopped, and everyone was silent, frozen in some sort of Dali tableaux, staring at them. And before they could grin and laugh, Thrummond jerked Tim's arm, pulled him along the path and out of the park.

* * *

It was growing dark outside, the mottled sun setting, a deepening twilight colouring the streets orangey-green. The roadways were slick with water, pooling in choked gutters, coating the brick in a wet, dripping covering. Thin dark clouds massed in an equally thin pale milk sky. Twilight. Thrummond's favourite time of day.

Hands jammed in pockets, Thrummond cruised along the mid-town sidewalks, crumbled glass crunching under foot. Street lights winked on as if the city were a slumbering beast just now waking. He kept walking east, through mid-town, toward the docks where the sidewalks began to heave up, where the streets were little more than narrow, wet, dimly lit alleys. And where the air smelled of brine and fire and semen. The sullen city suited his sullen mood.

At the next corner lurked a man on a concrete stoop. He stepped off the stairs, blocked Thrummond's way. The man wore a tattered black trench coat, the torn ends flapping uselessly like mutilated crows wings. An old Captain's hat the colour of dirty dishwater leaned precariously on his head. To Thrummond, there was something vaguely familiar about the man.

"Fancy a little something?" said the man.

Thrummond thought he heard sobbing. Nothing unusual in this part of town, he reasoned. He glanced up, saw movement in a dark window. A blur of a pale face, perhaps. Elsewhere he heard a dog barking, then a strange yelp, and he winced.

"I know my way around," he said, and pushed past the man.

"Suit yourself," said the man. He called after Thrummond. "There's a new game in town, mate. Come see the Captain when you get bored."

Thrummond turned down a dark alleyway. Something scurried out of a trash pile and ran across his foot. Another sob reached his ears, then whimpering. A red scream. He looked up again, saw ghostly hands on a window. He turned away, continued down the alley, splashing through greasy puddles.

The alleyway opened onto a small side street. People moved about in the dim shadows. He sauntered down the street, peering into the gloom. Boys and girls, thin and restless, called after him from dark doorways. He studied some of them, then moved on. All he wanted was a drink.

Almost near the docks now, and the water smashing into the wharfs was a hypnotic beat, a lulling rhythm that kept his legs moving. Movement to his right and a wan visage leered out from a smudged ground-level window; a wide, livid, forlorn smile stamped into a fuzzy face. He stopped, stared. Through the grime he couldn't tell if the person was male or female. The smile didn't waver. The face slowly receded, as if it were swallowed up by dark waters, leaving an empty, murky window.

He shuddered, stepped back. The pub was half a block away. Eyes fixed to the dark window, he back-pedaled most of the way there.

It wasn't much of a pub. A large, dark, smoky room with a long L-shaped bar and wobbly, skeletal tables shoved against the walls and wedged into the dim back corners. The seats were torn, the tabletops and walls scarred. The beer was cheap, though, and the atmosphere suited Thrummond fine.

Debbie, the bar maid, placed a pint of bitters on Thrummond's table. She glanced up, frowned, then smirked. "Try a smile once in a while," she said. "It won't kill you. What happened to you?"

Thrummond shrugged, sipped his beer. Debbie disappeared. "Things change," he said to himself, quaffing half the pint.

Debbie was back, placing another pint beside Thrummond's half-empty glass. "How's the love life?" Debbie asked.

Thrummond blinked. Debbie's face was pitted, acne-scarred, not smooth and clear like Chelsea's skin. He felt queasy. He must have looked queerly at Debbie, as she folded her hands in her apron and bunched it tightly.

"Fine," Thrummond announced, proud that his voice wavered only slightly.

Debbie unfolded her hands from the tangled apron, drew a rag from a pocket and wiped the table. "Okay, didn't mean to pry," she said, and bustled off.

Now that it had been brought up, his thoughts turned to Chelsea. He knew, for once, that it wasn't his fault. Not all of it, anyway. Usually he cocked up every relationship. He grew easily bored. But Chelsea was different. There'd always been a feral air about her. It was she who had grown bored of him. Truth was, he really didn't know where she was right now. "I've got other plans..." Out with her mates. Or, as he suspected, with another man. He couldn't give her what she wanted anymore. Whatever that was.

He finished his first pint, started on the second. Through the greasy pub window, Thrummond imagined he saw Chelsea outside on the sidewalk, peering in, her smile wide and infectious; he knew that was impossible. But there *was* someone out there, gazing in at him: The Captain. Thrummond could just make out the hat.

The Captain moved up to the window, pressed his face and hands against the dirty glass. His features seemed bloated, distended, as if viewed through a fish bowl. He stared at him, smiled. And that's why he'd seemed familiar to Thrummond. While he was on a city bus earlier in the week, the Captain had leered from a doorway and smiled in much the same manner. A smile for Thrummond alone.

Thrummond fished some money from a pocket, deposited it on the table. He went out the front door and confronted the Captain.

"What do you want?" Thrummond said. "Why are you following me?"

"I can get what you want," the Captain said. "Whatever you need. Anything."

Thrummond was inches from the Captain's face. The Captain's breath was rank, and Thrummond shrank back. "Do I look like I need anything?" Thrummond asked.

Another queer smile from the Captain. He pushed his hat up on his head, nodded. "Yes, you do. We all need something, don't we?"

It seemed to Thrummond that the Captain was reciting a script, that this was his stock conversation with everyone. Thrummond decided to play along. "Where?" he asked.

"Follow me," the Captain said, turning and scurrying off.

Thrummond hurried to catch up. He told himself he'd humour the old bastard for a bit. After all, he had nothing better to do. Nowhere else to go. Nothing to get back to.

The Captain moved with surprising grace, disappearing in and out of the dark shadows that pooled along the sidewalk, winking in and out of existence. One moment he was just ahead of Thrummond, then the next he was gone, swallowed up by darkness, as if he were never there. But he'd always reappear, never looking back. And Thrummond thought he could hear The Captain whistling some strange, tuneless melody.

They walked through the dark twisting streets for several minutes, seemingly turning down alleys at random. This was unfamiliar territory for Thrummond. He felt like a stranger in a strange city; a blind rat in labyrinthine passageways. Behind him the streets hissed wetly as small, dark cars scuttled roach-like about. He heard a howl, then another, and another, as if a pack of wild dogs were conducting some strange canine chorus. He shuddered, wondering where the dogs congregated, and whether he could avoid them.

He was about to quit the journey, when the Captain suddenly darted down a dim laneway and announced with dramatic flourish, "Here we are, mate."

Glancing to where The Captain pointed, Thrummond saw a small recessed alcove with a green door. The Captain produced a skeleton key, unlocked the door and pulled it wide. "In you go," the Captain said, giving him a nudge.

"How much?" Thrummond asked.

The Captain smiled. "First one is on the house. You'll be back. They always come back. And you'll pay dearly next time."

He passed through the door into a long narrow hallway lit by intermittent bare bulbs. The bulbs swayed in a faint breeze, throwing wan pools of light across the floor, making Thrummond lose his equilibrium. He threw a hand out and braced himself against the wall.

Behind him the door clicked shut. He turned at the sound, and found he was alone. The brief moment of panic passed when he pulled on the door and found it unlocked. He let the door close then turned and walked down the dim hallway.

At the end of the hallway, he discovered another unmarked green door. He opened the door and stepped into a small room with pale light the color of thin watery blood. A wide glass partition stretched across the back of the room. A lone metal chair sat in front of the frameless window. Beyond the glass, Thrummond thought he glimpsed movement. Checking that this door also would not lock behind him, he walked over to the chair and sat down.

A soft electric hiss, like the sound of a television left tuned to a channel that has gone off the air for the night, droned through the walls of the room. Slowly, as his eyes adjusted to the pallid light, Thrummond thought he saw figures beyond the glass. Blinking, he leaned forward and licked his lips.

He could just make out what appeared to be thin, nude, sexless, ghost-pale people with long, luminous limbs moving about in the ashen light. Their movements were languorous, somewhat sensual, as they danced and stroked each other, their heads rhomboids. Each person wore a white-white mask with crude vertical lines drawn in charcoal or magic marker under the eyes, as if they were crying black tears. A horizontal slit for a mouth, with the ends slightly curving upwards, gave the impression of a cruel smile. Thrummond gazed at the strange montage. Performance art, he thought. Some strange pantomime.

The figures moved as one languid entity around a table upon which lay a naked, hairy male. They stroked the prone man and he squirmed. The man's penis twitched, then grew rigid; as did Thrummond's. The ghost-pale creatures moved deliberately, their long fingers caressing, kneading, gently tugging; they dipped their heads and rubbed their masks along every inch of the man's body. Thrummond noticed one of the masks slip off, and briefly, before the performer could reattach it, Thrummond caught a glimpse of a rubbery, bloated balloon face with black dots for eyes and a thin eager mouth.

The man on the table writhed. And Thrummond spotted the leather restraints binding the ankles and wrists to the table. A soft moan — whether pleasure or anguish, Thrummond couldn't distinguish — emanated from the man. The dancers swirled around the table, bending their faces to the hairy man as if planting delicate plastic kisses. The man screamed, thrashed. Thrummond started, pulled back, and then leaned in closer. The faces circled, dipped, and caressed the man with their magic-marker grins. Thrummond remembered how Chelsea used to shower him with smiles and kisses.

Another shriek and the man's head snapped towards the glass partition. He seemed to be staring straight at Thrummond. His eyes were wild and so was his grin. The performers had stopped. They were still and silent and they stared at Thrummond with their dispassionate smiles. Smiles, Thrummond knew, directed at him and him alone. And Thrummond smiled back. Then the lights went out and there was another sound …

… *pop pop pop* …

… then a muffled scream.

* * *

It was late when Thrummond returned. Somehow, he'd managed to find his way through the numerous meandering dark alleys and locate his apartment building. He stepped into the dim apartment. From the entryway he noticed the television flickering, throwing harsh black and white static across the living room, a swirling chiaroscuro.

Thrummond hoped Chelsea wasn't waiting up for him. He called out softly, above the hiss of the television. "Hello." He stepped into the room. A figure sat on the loveseat, awash in the grey-blue glow of the television, still, unmoving. "Chelsea?" He moved closer. She slouched awkwardly, her head lolling to the side, asleep. Thrummond bent, reached under her and lifted. Chelsea had always been very light. And pliable, Thrummond thought, a salacious notion entering his mind.

He shook off his inopportune thoughts and carried Chelsea to the bedroom, where he lay her down and made her comfortable. Thrummond quietly moved back to the living room and sat down in front of the television. He stared at the grey screen, watched the flickering static. It bathed him in a cold antiseptic light. After a while it seemed Thrummond could see shapes and patterns emerging from the screen; black and white and grey forming images of grinning, leering faces; faces with strange mouths that tried to communicate with him, attempting to deliver some vital message that Thrummond couldn't hear above the terrible hiss of the static.

* * *

Thrummond was opening the days' end correspondence when Peterson leaned over the cheap office cubicle and glared at him.

"Still here?" Peterson asked. "Not finished?" His breath stank of cheap whisky and his face was red and expanding.

"Almost done," Thrummond remarked. "That last pile you gave me was quite large."

Peterson smirked unpleasantly, then belched. "You're slow, Thrummond. Slow." His head pulsed, bulged, grew outward. "I dropped in to pick up some supplies." He winked at Thrummond. "Kids have homework, you know. This place is a veritable Office Depot." His face stretched. "Perk of the job, you know." He grew serious, leaned closer to Thrummond. "But don't tell anyone."

Peterson's skin stretched like elastic. To Thrummond, it was a pulsing, infected boil. He reached out with the letter opener and poked it. There was a small "ow," and a *pop*, and he poked it again, then again, and again.

* * *

The Captain was smiling. Thrummond, shaking, handed the money to the Captain. The Captain made a great show of counting out the bills. He said, "Told you you would pay dearly next time." Thrummond nodded.

The Captain gestured to the green door. "Off you go, then."

Thrummond went through the doorway and walked down the long, dimly-lit hallway; opened the second green door and went into the spartan room. The glass partition was gone. There was just the table — really no more than a stretcher with restraints — and the masked balloon people. The masks turned in Thrummond's direction, glared impassively at him as if he'd interrupted their party. But that was impossible. They couldn't have started without him, he was the guest of honour.

He tottered forward and climbed up on the table. The party people lashed his ankles and wrists to the table legs. Then they began to move, bumping and gyrating.

The party people danced, circled slowly and leaned in. As their wiry limbs reached for Thrummond and their pale, mask-draped, stretched-balloon faces loomed above him, he noticed their grins, how wide they were, how cruel, and how terribly hungry.

Pop!

ABOUT THE AUTHOR

MICHAEL KELLY'S FICTION has appeared in several journals, magazines, and anthologies, including *All Hallows*, *Alone on the Darkside* (Roc), *City Slab*, *Dark Arts* (Cemetery Dance), *Flesh & Blood*, *Space & Time*, and *The Book of Dark Wisdom*.

In 2002, Michael edited a book of ghost stories, *Songs From Dead Singers* (Catalyst Press). His first collection of short fiction, *Scratching the Surface* (Crowswing Books), was published last year. *Ouroboros*, a novel co-written with Carol Weekes, is forthcoming later this year.

livejournal.com/users/lonesome_crow/
www.humdrumming.co.uk

HUMDRUMMING TITLES BY MICHAEL KELLY:
The First Humdrumming Book of Horror Stories [CONTRIBUTION]
Ouroboros [CO-AUTHORED WITH CAROL WEEKES]

MARYLAND

DAVIN IRELAND

THE FEDERAL SURVEILLANCE 'copter struggled through a shelf of low-lying autumn fog like a mosquito trapped in campfire smoke. Deputy Ryan Gatlin watched it touch down in the leaf-strewn clearing at the bottom of the slope and disgorge its lone passenger without incident. A man with sunglasses and a hardshell briefcase strode from beneath the churning rotors, face like a woodcut. With a deepening sense of unease, Gatlin took a last drag on his Kent, stubbed it on the gatepost, and slipped the charred butt into his pocket. Didn't want forensics flagging him up as a suspect.

"You Deputy Gatlin?" The man with the briefcase started up the shallow incline between them in a way that suggested a military record. Stiff, upright, metronomic gait. That figured. "I'm Special Agent Miller," the man added, and extended a hand.

"Welcome to Howard County, Agent Miller. Good trip?"

They shook, broke, and Miller swung about to face a ragged grove of trees that crawled up to the edge of the field like onlookers at the scene of an accident. The trees were white oaks mostly, with a few dogwoods and maples thrown in for good measure. But something about them didn't look right. Gatlin had noticed it himself earlier in the day but had blamed the perceived change on nerves. Now he wasn't so sure. Many of the low-hanging branches rested on the perimeter fence in a way that struck him as vaguely menacing, and the soughing of the wind in the canopy sounded almost as if the forest were shushing him to secrecy. Miller seemed more interested in the fog. As it crept over the forest floor, it angled towards them only gradually, as if reluctant to reveal the nature of its intent. "Fall is undoubtedly the prettiest season to view the world from the passenger seat of a chopper," the FBI man observed. "Unfortunately, it is also the most treacherous. Is the site over that way?"

Gatlin said that it was. "Where are the others?"

"Others?" Miller pulled off his sunglasses and folded the bows. "My team will be here in good time, Deputy Gatlin. The accident investigators will take a little longer. They're flying direct from D.C."

"Accident investigators?" Gatlin hooked his thumbs into his belt and wondered if he was hearing this right. "Agent Miller," he said, "I've been standing here waiting for you people since four o'clock this morning but I've been up most of the night. Believe me, if this was an accident I'd still be in bed."

"Now why doesn't that surprise me?" Miller slipped his sunglasses into the breast pocket of his jacket and smiled unctuously. "Didn't you used to be the Sheriff around these parts?"

Gatlin ignored the implied criticism. "Eleven years, all told. That was before my boy got sick."

"So where's this new boss of yours got to?"

"If you're talking about the sheriff," Gatlin told him, "he's sick too. Plain old influenza, I'm happy to report. We had him checked out this morning, right after the site was secured."

"Hmm. He'll need to be quarantined all the same. We can't afford any risks." Miller continued to watch the creeping carpet of fog, but every now and again his eyes were drawn to the trees and the way they strained against the fence. Almost as an afterthought, he asked: "How is your boy these days?"

Ryan Gatlin felt a twinge of sadness but no real pain. With a few well-practiced words he explained that Andy had never fully recovered from the sickness and had succumbed back in '94. Miller nodded and expressed nominal sympathy. But his eyes said something else. *You may have scored a point there, Deputy, but you know the game is mine.* Such were relations between FBI and local law enforcement at the time of the discovery.

II

The backwoods road was typical of its kind: narrow hardpan fractured in places by frost and the passage of time. The two men approached the clearing from the south, caught sight of the Ford Explorer trunk-end first, then gasped in unison. After a beat, Miller circled to the right until he gained a broadside view of the wreckage.

"Good God Almighty, man," he breathed, and let go of the case. It hit the ground with a thump. A pair of crows lifted from the tree-tops and flapped eastwards beneath the desolate sky. "Tell me the registration checks out."

When Gatlin told him it didn't, Miller took a tentative step towards the remains of the Explorer. The transformation was remarkable. The tires had melted completely, but not in any conventional sense. In defiance of gravity, the liquefied rubber had crept up across the rocker panels and hood in ugly black rivulets until it clung to the paintwork like a many-fingered hand clutching a prized possession. Had the fire occurred in a force nine gale, such an outcome might have been feasible. But the day was fog-bound and so perfectly wind-still that Gatlin had barely needed to shelter his match when lighting his smoke.

The tires paled into insignificance beside the rest of the vehicle, however. Miller squinted at the windshield as he continued to skirt the twisted pile of metal and glass. It was a reaction Gatlin recognized only too well. Strictly speaking, the windshield was still intact, but it had melted instead of shattering and now floated above the hood as if it had been collected in a bucket and hurled into the air from the driver's seat. Stringy ribbons of it still clung to the seals at the edge of the frame. The rest looked like a giant gob of saliva drifting on the foggy air, its murky comet-tail motionless before them.

Both men knew a single blow would shatter it into a billion pieces that would disperse like fungal spores, once again sowing the Eastern Seaboard with anarchy and misrule.

"It's them, ain't it?" Gatlin immediately regretted the outburst, both for the lack of control it demonstrated and — much worse, in the Deputy's opinion — for expressing himself in what his mother had always referred to as 'chicken-shit grammar'. "Don't mind me," he muttered, "this is the first time I've been here since sunup. Last I was here, the shadows were so heavy we didn't get this good of an over-view."

But Miller had issues of his own to contend with. Slowly, without diverting his attention from the scorched vehicle, the Fed withdrew his cell and thumbed the speed-dial button. It was answered on the first ring. "Truckle? It's me." It was pretty obvious the ensuing coded message involved the cancellation of the accident investigation team and the sanctioning of a more aggressive response. He put the phone away.

"Uh, excellent work, Deputy," he said, and then seemed to slowly lose the connection to what he was thinking. He wagged his finger at the vehicle a few times in silent admonition, but nothing would come. Then he caught sight of his briefcase sitting all alone on a bed of leaves, and the thought returned. "Exactly how secure is the area?" he asked.

Gatlin had been anticipating the question and wasn't about to make excuses. "About as secure as it's gonna get," he replied, "given the limited resources at our disposal. There are roadblocks set up east and west, and I've got a dozen armed men salted through the woods."

"Uniforms?"

"Some of 'em. We're a small community, Agent Miller. We make do with what we've got."

Miller didn't like that. "I appreciate your candidness," he said. It sounded like something you'd recite from a manual. Perspiring lightly, he withdrew a small Dictaphone from an inside pocket and resumed walking. "Subject is a large off-road vehicle, make and model commensurate with a Ford Explorer. Fire damage extensive, secondary damage typical of a visitation. Presence of a coven in Howard County now a foregone conclusion."

Miller stopped walking and pointed.

"What's that? Over there by the tree?"

The Deputy retrieved the item in question and set it down beside the scorched wreckage. "Milt Dawkins's stepladder," he explained. "You might want to take a look at the roof."

Miller agreed that he did. Gatlin turned away. He knew what awaited the Federal Agent and didn't envy him the experience one bit. The ribbed, uneven edge of the roof was not the result of heat distortion, as he had first assumed. Something far more sinister was at work here. When he and Milt had gone over the place shortly before dawn, the early morning sun had struck elongated shadows from the terrifying shapes that struggled up from the melted surface of the roof. Shapes uncomfortably reminiscent of tortured human faces — mouths frozen in jaw-cracking screams, features rendered in grotesque profile, hands clawing at a barrier pliable but ultimately unyielding. It was as if the occupants of the ruined 4x4 had attempted to effect their exit directly through the roof. Except there hadn't *been* any occupants, as witnessed by the lack of tire tracks. The vehicle had literally appeared from nowhere, as empty and abandoned as it was now. That's what Ryan Gatlin told himself, anyway. It was proving impossible to erase the motionless sea of limbs and faces from his mind, and thinking of those twisted aberrations as real people — or worse still, the souls of the departed — was simply too much to bear.

Agent Miller seemed to be experiencing a similar problem. He dropped to the grass and retreated a few steps, face draining of colour. He tried to speak, but when no words came simply beckoned the other man over. "Deputy Gatlin, have there been any" — he rationed his breath — "any similar incidents in recent weeks?"

"We had a couple of horses mutilated a month or two ago, but we figured –"

"Birth defects?"

"Come again?"

"Have any birth defects been reported in the last six months?"

"Well, no. Not as such."

Miller got a grip on himself. "'*Not as such*'? Deputy Gatlin, I'll be needing a good deal more accuracy than that. Were there or weren't there? And before you cover up for your drinking buddies, I suggest you think long and hard about your pension."

Gatlin was silent for a moment. The hell of it was, Miller's observation wasn't that wide of the mark. Very carefully, he said: "We had a little girl born a few weeks ago seems to be deaf. She exhibits no reaction to the Auditory Brain Stem Response test and it's pretty much the same on Otoacoustic Emissions. But that's it, I swear."

Miller nodded. He looked harried, dishevelled, and not a little panicked. But the most striking thing was the note of recrimination that had crept into his voice. "There hasn't been an active coven in this part of the state for nearly twelve years, Deputy. This particular county has scored a clean bill of health for over a decade. What the hell happened here?"

It was a good question. Right now, Ryan Gatlin didn't have an answer that made sense — but neither did he need one, for at that exact moment his cell twittered. The name on the display was 'Donald Boucher', a local mechanic presently on guard duty over at the Leyton farmhouse.

"Go ahead, Don."

"Ryan," Boucher yelled through a sea of static, "you'd better get up here right away. Something's gotten into the barn and it don't sound happy."

"On our way." Severing the connection, he led Miller off-road and into the woods.

III

Donald Boucher was a big man with a florid moon face and bright blue eyes. His colour was even higher than usual today, and when the two men arrived only slightly out of breath, he jumped to his feet and began pacing back and forth in a way that suggested they were just in time.

"Tell me where Hughie is," Gatlin said levelly. But before Boucher could respond, Patrolman Hughie Lang came hot-footing it around the side of the house with his gun drawn and an aggrieved look on his face. For a moment he didn't say anything, just looked at each of the men in turn. Then something in him seemed to unwind.

"The house is locked up front and back," he said, and neatly holstered his weapon. To his rear, little cyclones of autumn leaves corkscrewed into the limp air. "We searched the barn like you told us, barred the doors when we were done. Things weren't as straightforward when we investigated the surrounding area."

"That's right," Boucher confirmed. He scooped up a thermos flask that sat atop a nearby tree-stump and unscrewed the lid. "Crashin' and bangin' like you never heard before. I swear to God,

I even heard it cursin', but not with a... not with a *man*'s voice." He poured himself a cup of smoking black coffee and took a long pull. Grimaced.

Miller, who had re-activated the Dictaphone, held it beneath Boucher's ample chin. "Are you telling us the voice was female?"

"It wasn't human, is what I'm tellin' you." Boucher thumped the flask down but struggled for words. "If a bull could talk, that's what it would sound like. Only real angry; I mean pissed as hell."

The two newcomers exchanged a glance.

"I don't hear anything now," Miller ventured. "Is it just coffee in that thermos, son?"

Boucher looked at the 'Feeb' as if he were insane. "Mister, with my nerves the way they are right now –"

A resonating crash followed by a series of enraged grunts cut Donald Boucher's explanation short. He was right: it *did* sound as if a prize bull had been let loose in the barn, and for a moment Gatlin wondered if that might actually be the case. Then Agent Miller separated himself from the group for as long as it took to perform another of his speed-dialling tricks.

The three locals just stood around, questioningly looking at one another. *No, this was happening*, their faces rapidly agreed.

When Miller returned to the fold, his gun was drawn and face set. "The flares just went up in D.C. and Virginia," he announced, "but we have a chance to end this now, before it establishes itself. Deputy?"

Ryan Gatlin swept up the thermos, took an even bigger pull than his friend had, and shoved it at Hughie Lang. The liquor scorched the Deputy's throat, burned deep in his gut. "Just give me a minute here," he said, and strolled to the edge of the clearing. Andy's younger brother Brett was currently in his sophomore year up at Colombia, but was due back in Elkridge for Thanksgiving in two weeks' time. Gatlin intended to be waiting for him when he arrived. If a coven had resurfaced in this part of the world it needed to be dealt with and dealt hard, or there wouldn't *be* a Howard County to come home to. He rejoined the group, looked Boucher and Lang in the eye.

"You two fellas are strictly back-up, understood?"

Hughie nodded gratefully, frantically almost. Boucher merely checked the rounds in his revolver. "I'm scared shitless," he muttered, "I got a four-month-old back home and I can't –" He regarded them helplessly, as if unable to articulate his fear. It didn't matter: Gatlin was in no mood for speeches.

"What can we expect to find in there beside whatever's making that noise, Don?"

Boucher grazed his nose with the heel of his palm and sniffed. There was a quaver in his voice. "A couple hundred bales of hay, I guess. Ain't much else springs to mind." As soon as he said that, the side of the barn shuddered with the force of a terrible impact. The wooden planking bulged, a rain of dust and splinters pattering the dirt before them.

"It's getting stronger," Miller observed. His words were punctuated by a series of itinerant howls and crashes. They seemed to travel all the way up to the roof, where they rattled back and forth as if something big — something huge and manic and spoiling for a fight — were dancing between the rafters. Then the ground beneath their feet juddered with an impact of truly daunting proportions. The thing was growing.

All four men responded. Boucher and Lang bracketed the giant barn doors with weapons raised, the other two prepared themselves for entry. All about them, towers of dead leaves ascended skywards, rotating with excruciating underwater slowness. Agent Miller grabbed the crowbar securing the door and addressed them one last time. "If you're thinking about changing your minds, do it now."

As if in reply, the guttural curses and minotaur-like grunts from within escalated to a new level of belligerence. None of the men felt the need to comment or back down. Bracing himself, Miller lifted and hurled the crowbar aside, then grabbed the door handle.

IIII

Instant silence. Bars of dusty grey sunlight falling across a bare floor. The mute flutter of pigeon wings echoing among the rafters. Miller stepped gingerly over the threshold, the snout of his Glock waving like a nickel-plated viper. "Anybody home? Anybody here?" He lowered his gun, performed an almost comical double-take. Gatlin failed to see the funny side. Not only were there no capering demons in evidence, but not a single bale of hay remained.

Miller was completely nonplussed. "Where did it all go? *Where'd it go?*"

"There." Boucher pointed from the door.

The FBI man turned in the direction indicated. The hay was still there, every last blade. No longer in bales, it covered all of one wall, from the floor to the base of the A-frame in a layer as flat and pristine as a hotel lawn. *You couldn't have gotten it any flatter with a roller,* Gatlin thought. Don Boucher joined him a moment later. The mechanic reached out a hand and brushed the surface of the dry, grassy wall in a way that was almost affectionate. "Firm to the touch," he said wistfully. "It's packed real solid."

"You be careful," Gatlin whispered.

"Don't worry, I ain't about to –"

But that was as far as he got. One minute Donald Boucher was standing right beside them — palm laid flat against the prickly yellow strands, the armpits of his shirt dark with sweat — the next he was gone, yanked into whatever oblivion lay on the other side. It was then the remaining men realized the coven was not newly-formed at all, but old, sly, and loathsomely resourceful.

When Deputy Ryan Gatlin's senses returned, both he and Agent Miller were being pursued through the woods by the revolving columns of leaves and forest detritus that had formed over the course of their investigation. As he fled, the FBI man barked one word into his cell over and over again.

Abort. Abort. Abort.

V

Trees boomed and shook, the creeping fog cowered. They gained the sloping field shrieking like children, at which point the spinning pillars of leaves blew apart beneath the surveillance 'copter's downdraft. In the throes of take-off, it was already tilting forward, rotors thrashing against the soporific fog. Miller — briefcase, sunglasses, and Dictaphone forgotten — raced over the grass and threw himself head-first into the cockpit. A second later the craft slewed sideways across the tree-tops, engine screaming.

Gatlin howled in protest but his words were smothered by the churning rotorwash. What happened next was even more incredible. Bug-eyed and pale, Hughie Lang flailed from the undergrowth like something from a 1950s B-movie. His uniform was a latticework of slashes and bloody claw-marks, and his shoes looked as if they'd been forced through an industrial shredder. No sooner had he gained the clearing than he began shouting and pointing his finger as if it were a pistol and he were taking pot shots at the abomination that now confronted him. Ryan Gatlin felt his knees give way at the sight of it. The Clunky Bird was upon them. A foot tall and sporting a luminous orange beak, the most powerful demon in the universe resembled a cross between a toucan, a freeze-dried monk, and a clockwork sentry. It stumbled about the edge of the clearing like a mechanical toy... which many of the uninitiated believed it to be.

"Shoot it!" Lang begged, "shoot it before it makes us laugh! *Gatlin!*" Agonized tears of amusement already shone on his cheeks.

Gatlin didn't hesitate. Even as he unsheathed his service revolver the siren song of the woods — a sound he had once believed he would never hear again — resumed its plaintive, taunting cry.

Yoooooooooo-hoooooooooooo, called the otherworldly voices.

Cooooooooooo-eeeeeeeeeeee, replied their companions.

"Jam your fingers in your ears!" Gatlin screamed, "do it now!" But in that brief division of time, Lang's mind had popped like a bulb. He began capering around the clearing, raving and gibbering like a loon. Suppressing a chuckle of his own, the deputy took aim and fired. It was too late. The Clunky Bird had already broken into a shambling, comical run, the two halves of its huge orange beak clapping together like coconut halves, Gatlin felt the corners of his mouth turn up but fought the ecstatic bray of laughter that boiled in his throat like oxidizing agent bubbling in a drain.

Yoooooooooo-hoooooooooooo, came the familiar refrain.

Cooooooooooo-eeeeeeeeeeee, sounded the response.

The Clunky Bird was having a ball now. It flapped its flipper-like wings as it ambled along, jointless legs goose-stepping in awkward double-time. Just as Gatlin drew a bead on it, the creature span on its heel, performed a dainty little half-skip, and scuttled back the way it had come. Gatlin shot wide, a gout of turf leaping into the air. There was nothing for it now. Hoping for the best, he screwed his eyes shut and emptied the gun in the Clunky Bird's general direction. Miraculously, that ghastly emissary from the Underworld exploded in a rain of blood, clock-springs, and confetti, all of it mixed with a substance not dissimilar to ballistics gel. It rained down on the clearing as an insidious groaning noise filled the air. Perhaps eight or nine seconds had passed since the emergence of the Clunky Bird — not enough time for Agent Miller and his pilot to have cleared the scene entirely — and now the distant speck of the chopper was in trouble. Engine straining, rotors fighting a baleful wind, it vanished from the skyline.

For Gatlin it was as if the clouds had formed themselves into a giant hand that reached down and snatched the sputtering copter into oblivion. Teeth clenched, mind teetering on the brink of collapse, he fled back up the slope, groping blindly for Elkridge and temporary salvation. He had a wife and son there, he believed, although he could no longer recall their names or anything about them. The notion that he had all but forgotten the faces of his loved ones caused him to chuckle, then to giggle out loud. He clapped his hands over his ears and pressed on regardless.

Behind him, the voices still called and the stranded figure of Hughie Lang answered, wailing beneath the ghostly countenance of the daytime moon as the swirling leaves closed ranks.

Yoooooooooo-hoooooooooo.

Coooooooooo-eeeeeeeeeee.

Yoooooooooo-hoooooooooo.

Coooooooooo-eeeeeeeeeee.

Yoooooooooo-hoooooooooo.

Coooooooooo-eeeeeeeeeee.

ABOUT THE AUTHOR

DAVIN IRELAND WAS born and bred in the south of England, but currently resides in the Netherlands.

His fiction credits include stories published in a wide range of print magazines and anthologies on both sides of the Atlantic, including *Underworlds*, *The Horror Express*, *The First Humdrumming Book of Horror Stories*, *Zahir*, *Neo-Opsis*, *Rogue Worlds*, *Fusing Horizons*, *Storyteller Magazine* and *Albedo One*.

home.orange.nl/d.ireland/

www.humdrumming.co.uk

HUMDRUMMING TITLES BY DAVIN IRELAND:
The First Humdrumming Book of Horror Stories [CONTRIBUTION]
Slow-Motion Genocide [FORTHCOMING]

THE TOBACCONIST'S CONCESSION

JOHN TRAVIS

IT WAS THE end of the world again, which meant the hotel was busier than usual.

Not that it made any difference to Leo — the outside world could take care of itself; the hotel and the concession could not. They needed his careful attention, like they'd needed his father's before that. Leo had learned the basic workings of the place from him as a boy, on weekends when he should have been doing schoolwork — watching his father, he learned the art of how to deal with people, how to sell. Then, when his father died (his death was peaceful, for which Leo would always be grateful) and Leo took over the business, he knew that he had to learn how to deal with the other things too, because someone had to. This part wasn't always easy.

But, as his father had told him just before he died, he had been born to the job: Leo was a natural who took everything in his stride. Over the years he'd seen most things, standing behind the counter of that small and cramped kiosk — Births. Deaths. Marriages.

Giants covered in birdshit who looked like they'd just seen a ghost.

1.: The Abduction of the Penguin

"That's him." George said, squinting into the sunlight.

"You sure?"

"'Course I'm sure. Fancy dress. Take a look at him."

Artie did: Crisp white shirt, immaculately pressed black pants, liquorice black top hat, gleaming black cane. He looked down at his boss. "What's he come as?"

"The Penguin, how should I know? Who cares, it's fancy dress, right? The perfect cover."

The two men were parked at the side of the long, grassy road leading up to the hotel, its gleaming white castle-like structure a mile ahead. As the man, the Penguin, got closer to the car, Artie noticed the expression on the man's face, a mixture of anxiety and pain which he could empathise with. Suddenly, the man glanced up quickly at the car. Putting his head back down on his chest, he kept walking.

"What's he doing? George said, watching as the man walked past the side of the car.

And kept walking.

"Maybe he wants us to follow him." Artie suggested hopefully.

And walking.

"Why?" George snapped. "We're a good mile from the hotel here. Nobody's going to see us. What the hell's the matter with him?" with a grunt the little man got out of the vehicle, his short salt-and-pepper hair lifted into tufts by the stiff wind. "Hey!" he shouted to the retreating figure, "where do you think *you're* going?"

Stopping, the man turned on his heel. "Excuse me?"

"I said," George shouted, his voice now a sandpapery growl, "where do you think you're going?"

Pulling a face as though he couldn't hear for the wind, the man made his way back towards the car.

As he did George began tapping on its side. He was still tapping as Artie kicked his door open, its hinges groaning. With all the elegance of a giraffe exiting a photo booth, Artie prised his six feet eleven frame out from the tiny car's confines. As he unfolded himself back to his proper shape, the man in the costume spoke.

"I'm sorry, I couldn't hear what you said. What did –"

"Just hand it over, for Christ's sake," George said, a trace of disgust in his tone.

The Penguin looked perplexed. "I'm sorry, but I've no idea –"

"Artie," George said in a voice that was slowly losing patience, "If you'd be so kind...?" Rolling up his sleeves, Artie eyeballed the Penguin. In turn the Penguin began to nervously fiddle with his cane.

"Listen, I don't know what it is you think I've got, but –"

"Artie," George said quietly, "fetch."

Artie bent down and grabbed one of the man's ankles so quickly he didn't have time to protest. With barely a breath of effort, Artie upended him, holding him upside-down at arm's length as if he were contagious. Grabbing the man's other ankle, Artie shook him like a branch. Apart from a few coins and bills dropping to the ground, nothing much happened. Still holding the man upside down, Artie shrugged at his boss.

"Okay," George said. "Get him on his feet." The disoriented man was then placed right way up. Stepping forward, George stared up into his frightened eyes.

"Okay. Powder. *Now.*"

"I — I don't have any powder," he said, unable to back away with Artie standing behind him, "Listen, I don't know who you think I am, but — I'm at the hotel, and –"

Punching him in the gut, George expected him to fall to the floor, and he did; but he hadn't expected the man's chest to erupt in a wild bouquet of whirring feathers.

"What the –"

The ten seconds it took for all the terrified birds to fly past were among the longest in George's life — they flapped into him, into Artie, into each other — the air became unbreathable for feathers and birdshit. When he looked down at his suit, George saw it wasn't just salt-and-pepper hair he had any more; it was salt-and-pepper everything. Trying to maintain a semblance of dignity, he went over to the man clutching his belly on the ground.

"I don't have time to ask you what just happened there," George said, flicking at his suit, trying to keep as much dignity in his voice as he could, "I just want what's mine. Then we can –"

"Boss."

Following Artie's gaze he spotted the top hat and cane in the grass. Before he could issue the command, Artie brought them over.

"Nothing in the hat, Boss," he said, punching a hole through it.

Remembering the Penguin's nervous gesture earlier he instructed Artie to try the cane. Unscrewing it, he looked down its long thin barrel before tapping it with the flat of his hand. Finally he blew down it. "Nothing, boss."

George was fuming. "Put him in the trunk. We'll take him with us."

"Where we going?" Artie asked, bending down to pick up the Penguin. He knew damn well where they were going.

"The Sprawl. I knew that louse would welch on the deal. A few hours down there, this guy'll tell us anything."

When Artie opened the trunk the man began to scream. Knocking his head against the side of the car, the big man bundled the limp body into the trunk before folding himself back into the driver's seat. Taking a deep breath, he started the car and drove as slowly as possible. Artie didn't like the hotel.

From a distance it looked beautiful — a huge shining fairy tale castle perched on the Cliffside, its rock caressed by the foam of the North Atlantic far below, as white-breasted gulls painted invisible pictures in the air above. But Artie, who's mother had always told him he was a sensitive soul, saw how the view altered the closer you got; perhaps it was a trick of the light or something, or just his overly vivid imagination, but he always felt there was a moment when the glistening white structure ahead went from a fairy tale tower into something resembling an ugly, squat prison; a grey, flat-roofed monstrosity encircled not by a graceful parade of gulls, but by a vile squadron of vultures. As the car chugged forward he watched for it happening, as it always did, usually just before they reached the hotel's large sandy parking lot.

Suddenly a figure appeared to their left among the long grass, a young woman with a thick crop of shaggy hair, seemingly making her way towards the hotel. As Artie watched her, a solitary gull broke free from the others above the hotel and glided towards her, then around several times as if binding her with an invisible thread. Appearing to tire of her, it started to fly away, only to turn back suddenly and fly straight for her. Straight *at* her.

Straight *through* her.

Artie stamped on the brake pedal.

"Did — did you see that?" he said, trying to sound calm.

"I saw that." George tried to sound even calmer.

"But she's not there now. The gull — went straight through her, and she –"

"She vanished," George replied quietly, matter-of-factly, slowly removing a cigar from its wrapper, lighting it. "I know."

"Boss, she had –"

"Pink hair, I know." Puffing out thick cigar smoke helped to obscure his shaking hand. "Artie," George said, his voice not quite under control, "this is my last cigar. We'll have to go to the hotel and get some."

"Do we really have to go down there, boss?" Artie pleaded. "And the hotel as well? After *that?*" he pointed out of the window. George didn't answer.

Artie had quite forgotten about the view of the hotel as he pulled up among a hundred other cars in the quiet lot. Going round to the trunk he listened but heard nothing. With a sigh of relief he went to get George's cigars.

In the hotel's glass doors Artie saw his dishevelled reflection — a big man in a shabby suit splattered with bird droppings — he thought he looked like a ghost in waiting. He shuddered at the idea. Crossing the threshold into the hotel lobby he shuddered again, as he always did.

Seeing Leo at the kiosk didn't make him shudder, but it didn't make him feel any better either. He'd been buying George's cigars here for years, and despite Leo always being friendly and courteous towards him, there was something about the little man that always threw him a little off balance.

"Hello, Leo," he said glumly as Leo got the cigars.

"How are we today, Artie?"

As usual the big man felt that Leo was actually saying more than came out of his mouth. "Huh? Oh. Yeah. I'm er –" looking down at his bespattered suit, he waved a shovel-like hand at it, taking the cigars with the other. "Yeah. Fine. Er, I gotta go, we –"

Awkwardly, Artie spun himself round until he was roughly pointed at the exit. Before he got there he saw the damndest thing coming towards him. Moving away from the kiosk as quickly as he could, he decided today was going to be one of those days.

* * *

Watching Artie leave, Leo sensed the real reason behind his discomfort — it wasn't the fact his expensive suit was covered in filth, or the unusual costume of the man coming towards the kiosk. No, he knew what had turned the giant as white as a sheet: Things were about to change. Obvious.

As obvious in fact as his next customer's reason for buying Leo's most expensive penknife.

"Hotel's busy today," the man in the costume said breezily.

"Yes it is." Leo replied. "As well as the End of the World party there's a conjurer's convention on this weekend. Been booked for months. They decided to go ahead with it, end of the world or not. I mean, look at the number of times we've been told this time it was going to happen — it's like crying wolf, isn't it? Still, I suppose they've got to be right some time. And it's bound to be the end of the world for somebody today, right?"

As Leo smiled the man gave a small laugh, followed by a cough. "Well," he said, waving the penknife in reply to Leo's unwavering gaze, "I guess I'll go open that bottle of wine now."

"Yes," Leo said as the man headed for room 1127. "Yes. You do that, sir." He had no doubt that the man was going to 1127 — there was a thing about knives in that room. With a loud sigh he began to tidy his counter until the next customer came by.

2: A Rash of Stabbings

"There's a door at the door," the Devil said to the Insect on the bed.

"Tell it we've got one. Hasn't it got eyes?"

The Devil looked exasperated. "*It's a door!*" it said.

"Well," the Insect replied, scratching a mandible, "show it in."

With not inconsiderable difficulty the Door forced itself through the door. It spoke:

"What have you two come as?"

The Devil and the Insect cracked up.

"What have *we* come as?" the Insect laughed, pointing at the six-feet high oblong of cardboard in front of them. "Geez. Davy here's Lucifer and I'm a Locust. *It's an end of the world party.* Which begs the question," The Locust looked the cardboard figure up and down, frowning. "What the hell *have* you come as?"

The Door shook itself indignantly, like it was ruffling feathers. "I've come as The Door," it said huffily. "The one to *The Other Side?"* It glanced at the wall behind the Insect.

"Oh, well in that case," it said, "I hope you've brought something with you to help us get these beauties open."

With a papery rustle, the Locust, also known as Louis Sansano, got up off the bed and looked at the wall he'd been leaning against, slowly shaking his head in admiration.

"A masterstroke," he said to his two companions. "An absolute masterstroke."

For reasons unknown to most of the patrons of room 1127, twelve small and badly painted cupboard doors of varying sizes covered the entire space of one wall, with each cupboard door containing a small keyhole.

"If you ask at reception they'll tell you they're full of linen or cleaning equipment," Sansano told his colleagues, still admiring the wall. "An absolute masterstroke," he said again. "Okay," he turned to the Door. "What did you get?"

"This." Taking the penknife from one of its recesses the Door looked at each of them in turn. "Pretty inconspicuous, huh? The guy down there said it was the best penknife he had — it's got a corkscrew, half a dozen blades, toenail clippers –"

Sansano waved a pincer in the Door's general direction, a signal to stop.

"Oh — and while I was down there I saw Artie."

The heavy silence that followed was eventually broken by the Devil. "I told you we shouldn't have come here," he hissed.

Sansano turned to the Door. "Did he recognise you?"

"Not in this outfit. And there's –"

"Exactly." Sansano interrupted. "We're *all* dressed like this. All George knows is that we'll be here in fancy dress, with his merchandise. Only we have his money but don't *have* his merchandise and he's expecting us to meet him to complete the deal. But we can't. Luckily for us, by the time George realises we aren't coming and he's gone through the hundreds of people here in fancy dress trying to find us, we'll have got one of these doors open –" he pointed at the wall, "and be in The Sprawl. Which means that George and his oversized goon can't get at us."

"There's a magician's conference here this weekend too," the Door added. "The guy downstairs said so. They'll all be dressed up too."

The Devil thought about it. "What if George knows how to get down to The Sprawl?"

"He won't, he's too dumb." Sansano told him. "Snap that knife open and start opening doors."

The Door, bending over the bed, began trying various blades on the small cupboards. When the first door swung inward a stale blast of air rushed into the room.

"Nothing but pipes," the Door said, looking inside.

"Try the next."

It wasn't long before two more doors were open — one leading to a linen cupboard, the other into another maze of blackened piping. As the Door pried at the next cupboard, the Devil spoke.

"How do you know about this place?" he asked Sansano.

"From someone who used to work here. This place was built way back, when people lived in castles and were into hidden rooms and concealed entrances, that kind of stuff. In that it's like the Cliffside, which is supposed to be full of caves. But go far enough down and the whole cliff is hollow for miles and miles; it was used by smugglers at one time. Anyway, they built one of the rooms, *this* room, with a secret door so you could go right down there through all these secret passageways. The perfect place to hide."

The Devil stroked his chin. "And if the big one does go off in the next couple of days, we can escape the blast."

"Exactly. It's been used every time we've had a warning—people have died in fights to get down there. Remember that Nuclear Crisis a few years ago? Two parties double-booked this room for the same weekend. It ended up with six people being stabbed to death and nobody even got down there. And after all that they averted the crisis. But this time, I don't know. I've got a bad feeling about this time. How you doing?" he asked the Door.

"Three more," the Door said, wiping a hand against its cardboard.

"Well hurry it up. George is probably looking for us now."

Ten minutes later only one door remained. Sansano started to sweat. It had to be this one, and it had to work. As the Door cracked it open, another rush of freezing air came into the room. Only this time there were no pipes or towels. Instead there were steps.

Sansano rose to his feet. "Thank Christ for that. Right, let's go."

Before any of them had a chance to move, the stairs appeared to waver, obscured by bulks of greying darkness which began to bundle into the room like clouds of cotton. As the clouds started to form into shapes the room turned to ice. In the ice, limbs and faces began to appear. Angry faces.

Had the room on the tenth floor been occupied, it would have sounded like three heavy statues had toppled in the room above. But even had someone been in that room they'd never have heard the faint scratching at the door as rapidly stiffening fingers struggled to prise it open.

* * *

It was a while before Leo had another customer. And he wasn't a customer at all.

"So you haven't seen him?" the magician asked. "Dressed the same as me. He did say he felt a bit sick and was going out for a breath of fresh air, but that was ages ago."

Leo shook his head, smiling sadly.

Suddenly the man shivered. "Maybe it's the air conditioning in here or something. You know, I haven't felt right myself for a while." Leaning over the counter, the magician lowered his voice. "It's a strange place this, isn't it?" he said conspiratorially.

"I suppose so," Leo answered in his normal voice, the trace of a smile still on his lips, "but I suppose all hotels are strange to some degree."

The magician gave Leo a funny look. Thanking him, he went back towards the elevator. But Leo didn't notice.

He was too busy thinking.

3.: Smoke and Mirrors, Piss and Wind

"Nobody's seen him," Nick said above the furious splashing of water coming from the bathroom. "I've looked everywhere." Thirty seconds later the steady rush of water showed no sign of stopping. "What are you doing in there, taking a leak or drawing a bath?"

"I expect he's... hang on, here comes another one" — the sound of Jerry's urine was momentarily cancelled out as his sphincter got in on the act, emitting a long, loud rasp — '...got the same thing I have. My guts haven't been right since we arrived. I wonder if I'm going down with something. Is it me or has it turned cold in here? Hang on, here's the sequel..." a quieter but no less noxious emission began to drift through the open door as the tinkling water stopped. "Whew! Not bad as sequels go," Jerry said cheerfully, moving the smell around artfully with his hands, "a *Jaws 2*, I reckon."

"Maybe it's as well I couldn't find him," Nick said, turning his face away. "That doesn't even smell like a fart. What have you been eating? Sewage?"

"I agree with you on that," Jerry said as he closed the bathroom door, "about Ray not coming back. We both know he lets the act down. It'd be no great loss if he didn't show. Which reminds me — there's something wrong with the cabinet. When he went in before he left, he was still there when I opened the door. The catch must be jammed or something. So," Jerry said, making elaborate gestures towards the cabinet, 'if you'd be so kind..."

Nick folded his arms and stared at Jerry. "You know I don't go in the cabinet."

Jerry sneered. "Listen, Nicky boy — whoever heard of a claustrophobic magician? Did Houdini try and worm his way out of stepping into the sack and chains? No, he didn't. If Ray was here he could do it but he isn't. So, if you want to go down there with any kind of act, get in."

"A minute," Nick said, walking towards the black box, "a minute and no longer."

"Perhaps Ray has vanished after all," Jerry said, closing the door behind Nick. Tapping various panels of the box, he spoke again. "He wouldn't be the first in this place — it's supposed to be honeycombed with secret rooms and shit. Maybe he's wandered off into one. That's what happened to that girl. Did you hear about that?" Inside the cabinet a small muffled voice spoke. "No? Well, some girl found out how to get into the passageways and got lost in there for a while. She made the mistake of opening a secret door which led into the room of some very heavy gentleman who weren't too pleased to see her. I don't know the exact details, but she ended up getting stabbed and they shoved her back in." *Tap Tap Tap.* "Anyway, she was crawling about in those passageways for ages — they found blood all over the place. When she eventually did find a way out it was up through somebody's closet or something, just as they were reaching in for a suit. And the crooks got off scot free because of their expensive lawyer. Typical, huh? I'm done," he called to Nick, "coming ready or not." With a hearty tug Jerry opened the door. "Ta-DA!"

As it should be, the black interior of the box was empty.

"Nicky boy, we have lift-off. I'll have you out in a second." Closing the door again, he quickly reopened it.

"Oh."

Nicky boy wasn't there.

"Er, having a few problems out here my friend," Jerry called out. "Nicky? Nick?"

No answer.

"Listen," Jerry said, his voice higher than usual. "Third time lucky, okay? There's no need to panic." Once again he closed the door. Then opened it again.

Something came out of the cabinet this time, but it wasn't Nick. The something walked past him, a translucent body beneath a shock of pink hair. As it approached the wall the outline of the body vanished completely; only the hair stood out temporarily against the burgundy wallpaper like a stain. Then it too disappeared. Jerry gulped noisily.

In a kind of frenzied calm Jerry went back to the cabinet and closed the door. Then he opened it again. Closed it. Opened it again, closed it again.

He was still doing this an hour later when he heard the sirens outside.

In that time nothing else came out of the cabinet.

* * *

Hotels were strange places all right. Like well-upholstered dumping grounds. This was because people didn't respect them. The idea that people just "pass through" a hotel was nonsense — they always left something behind, no matter whether they stayed a month or a night. There was the baggage people brought with them, both physical and mental — their quirks, their suppressed energies and extremes of behaviour; away from home people became more playful, outlandish, took more risks, became increasingly desperate because the chances were they weren't coming back.

People die in hotels. All the time.

Sometimes naturally, other times not. Sometimes they died for the silliest of reasons. And that creates ghosts, whether you can see them or not. And this was an old hotel, with a lot of ghosts. And unlike the paying customer the ghost remains. But they needed to move on like the rest of us. Ghosts were like small children that don't know how to behave properly. Sometimes they're shy and keep out of the grown-ups' way; but sometimes they demand attention and explode into violent rages. And ghosts don't always discriminate.

Usually, when a ghost got the chance to move on, it had to take it.

Leo hoped that was about to happen. Because it was getting pretty crowded down there.

4.: The Magic in Old Hotels / Loose Ends

"I don't like it down here, Boss," Artie said, un-crumpling himself from the car once more, "it gives me the creeps."

George shielded his eyes from the sun's reflection off the sea, the white glare of the arcing gulls. "Don't you ever give it a rest? She's dead, she can't hurt us. Now get that idiot out of the trunk."

Artie hadn't just meant the girl and he suspected George knew that. He'd seen things down here, unfriendly things. Opening the trunk, he pulled the semiconscious man from within, standing him up as George came forward.

"Hey!" George prodded him in the ribs. A pair of woozy eyes snapped fully open. "Now. It's nice and quiet down here, we won't be disturbed. So you can either tell me where my goddamned powder is, or you can tell me where Sansano is. I don't mind which. But whichever you choose you do it quickly, because –" he curled his hand into a fist.

"Boss, wait." Artie's voice sounded puzzled, frightened.

"What now?" George snapped. He was still looking up into the man's eyes.

Artie's voice dropped, mingled with the cawing of the gulls. "That — that isn't him, George."

"What?"

"That's a different man to the one I shoved in the trunk. I mean, the clothes are the same, but –"

Instead of just the eyes, George looked at the whole face. Slowly, a look of utter disbelief spread across his face. Artie was right: it wasn't the same man.

"What the hell is going on today?" George shouted up at the gulls.

* * *

There were three main ways to get into The Sprawl.

There was the smugglers route (the one which Leo knew George sometimes used), which was little more than a narrow crack in the Cliffside down on the beach.

The second was through one of the doors in room 1127.

The third way was to walk through the walls and keep heading downwards.

All that energy. All those ghosts.

The Sprawl wasn't just the ultimate dumping ground for secret things; it was also the ultimate hiding place. All that energy... but ultimately all that energy had to be released. It needed a catalyst.

Unwittingly, Leo provided it.

* * *

"I should tell you," George said, chewing on his cigar as he followed Artie and the quivering figure through the gap in the cave wall, "I don't really care about what happened earlier — with the birds, I mean. Or the fact you seem to have grown a new face. I just want what's mine. Then we can all leave."

Nick began fidgeting with his collar. "I — I don't know how this happened. I — I was in this cabinet in our room, and the door closed, and it went cold, and — I've — I've got to get out of here," sweat was running from Nick's brow into his eyes, "I don't like closed in spaces."

"Oh, that's okay," George told him, his voice equal parts reassurance and sarcasm. "This place isn't closed in at all. See?"

Following George's hand Nick looked up into the clammy darkness. Wherever he was it had the damp atmosphere of a cave; only he couldn't see its roof. It was even colder than in the cabinet; his freezing breath jumped out of him in nervous puffs of smoke. Somewhere in the murk, small drops of moisture fell into invisible pools. It was like the atmosphere in the hotel. Only much, much worse.

"Look," Nick told them, "I really have to get out this place –"

"JUST-TELL-ME-WHERE-THE-POWDER-IS!" George screamed, slapping his hands against his legs after each word like a petulant child. "JUST TELL ME!"

It took almost a minute for his voice to stop rebounding off the cave walls, by which time Artie knew that George was at least as scared as he was. The three men looked at each other, unsure of what was supposed to happen next. Finally, George spoke.

"Okay," he said, barely above a whisper. "Okay. Then where is Sansano? I'll speak to him."

"Sansano?" Nick whispered back. "I don't know any Sansano."

"Boss," Artie whispered.

George looked round and saw Sansano and two other men standing a matter of feet away.

"Talk of the devil." George said, eyeing one of the costumes. But his usual cockiness had gone: something was very wrong here. Then he saw the pink haired girl next to them. Behind her there were others — dozens of them coming forward, circling him. Stepping backwards, Nick managed to move away without being noticed.

He was only a few feet from them when the whole cave became a huge screaming echo chamber, each scream louder than the one before.

Disoriented by panic, Nick stumbled through the cave looking for the exit, his hands clamped over his ears. When he eventually found the way out he was too frightened to notice that the cave wasn't freezing any more, or that the screams at his back were fading out.

As his eyes readjusted to the sunlight he staggered along the beach, his brain trying to comprehend what had happened. Above him to his left he saw the hotel.

At least he thought that's what it was — only its shape kept altering somehow; it was as if another building was vying for position with it. Later he'd say it was like making yourself cross-eyed as a child, so that one landscape imposed itself over another; only Nick knew that there wasn't another building up there, just the hotel.

Despite the heat from the sun, Nick was shivering again. Walking along the beach, he prayed a road would appear out of nowhere, away from the cliffs and the hotel.

* * *

Miki, she'd been called. She'd shown up at the hotel one day, looking for work, pink hair all over the place like a badly made nest. She was funny, bright, lively. And unfortunately adventurous. Leo thought she could start a conversation in an empty room. And she probably had. Many times.

He'd managed to get her a job in the kitchens- said she was so grateful that she'd do him a favour in return someday, even if it took her the rest of her life to do it. He didn't see a lot of her after that but she seemed happy enough. One day in a lull she'd asked him about The Sprawl. Where was it, How do you get in? I don't know how you get in, he lied. Besides, he told her, it was supposed to be dangerous down there.

Then one day she didn't show up for her shift.

How she found her way in, he never knew. He only knew one thing for certain — the day she'd turned up at his kiosk, he should have sent her packing.

* * *

Later, when Pestilence came out of his room on the eleventh floor, he didn't feel particularly refreshed by the short nap he'd had. Perhaps it was all this talk of the end of the world, or even the lurid costume he was wearing (his *papier-mâché* sores looked especially revolting under the hotel's sharp lights). There was an eerie atmosphere about the place, as if it was waiting for something to happen. This thought didn't make a lot of sense to him. Going back to his room after the buffet, the first thing he'd done was throw the whole lot back up into the bathroom sink; but the sudden purge had made him feel even worse. Laying on the bed, he closed his stinging eyes. For a second he thought he heard frantic cries close by, but he was suddenly too tired to care.

Pestilence dreamed. He was in the belly of a vast and diseased animal, and the stink of it was slowly killing him. He had to escape. But each turn he took, every new cavern he entered only led him further into the animal's stomach. The dream ended just as a gigantic rushing whoosh came down one of the animals' glistening tubes towards him.

Waking up, Pestilence decided he was going to leave the hotel before the weekend was over: he'd face the end of the world at home. But first he'd have a drink downstairs and let everyone know he was going.

He was passing the room next to his, room 1127, when he saw the door was slightly ajar. It was propped open by a hand, its stiff, unreal fingers beckoning him. Recalling the cries he'd heard before he fell asleep, he moved closer.

The hand belonged to what appeared to be a man in a devil's costume sleeping on the floor. But then he spotted the knife stuck in the man's chest, and the blood. And then there was the smell. And through the crack in the door he saw another two men who weren't sleeping either.

The end of the world was making everybody crazy, Pestilence decided.

He went back to his room to pack.

* * *

Normally, the sight of someone leaving the hotel without paying would have roused him into some kind of action, but Leo knew this time was different. Perhaps it was the costume the man was wearing. He knew something was about to happen. Folding his arms, he waited.

It didn't take long. The other people in the lobby had barely had time to notice the strange whooshing sound building around them when the glass doors leading to the ground floor rooms shattered under the force of countless frantic, flapping wings; and by the time everyone had dropped to the floor to avoid being beaten by the wings the lobby was empty again. There were still people on the ground when someone came running through what remained of the lobby doors and started shouting about dead bodies on the eleventh floor.

In his mind's eye Leo was sure that the first bird to break through those doors had a shock of pink feathers.

She never did do him that favour, he thought sadly.

Picking up the phone on the kiosk counter, he called the police.

* * *

Hearing the sirens, Jerry had the terrifying idea that they must be for him. First Ray had gone missing, then Nick. This hotel had a terrible history. Strange things happened here, people died horribly.

Men went into magic cabinets and never came out again.

He opened, closed and opened the black lacquered door again but nothing happened. He had to get Nick back before the police came up. He grasped the cabinet door again.

For a brief moment, sanity returned. He was being stupid. Whatever it was that was going on here, it had nothing to do with him. Ray and Nick were probably just playing a trick on him, that was all. They'd be hiding in some hidden part of the room right now, laughing at him. But he realised that couldn't be true either: he'd known Nick all his life and he was definitely claustrophobic. He really hadn't wanted to get into the cabinet. And as for Ray, he was the most humourless man that ever walked the earth; he wouldn't know a joke if it came up and introduced itself. So, closing the door once more, Jerry tried the cabinet again.

Open, close. Open, close. Open. Still nobody appeared. He slammed the door shut.

He couldn't carry on like this. There were police downstairs. He'd get them to come up and have a go. If he looked foolish, he looked foolish. So be it. But before he went he'd try it again, one last time.

Open. Close. Open –

Standing inside the box, a look of pure astonishment on his face, Ray looked like he'd been dragged through a hedge backwards. He stared at Jerry with large, haunted eyes.

Jerry did two things.

One: he turned as white as a sheet.

Two: he produced a sequel to *Jaws 2* even better than *Jaws 1*.

* * *

Later, after things had calmed down and the police had taken statements from bewildered customers, he closed up the kiosk and went to the manager's office.

"Quite a day, all in all," he said to the secretary.

She looked at him strangely, although not unkindly.

"I don't know how you can be so calm about it," she told him. "The whole thing's been horrible."

"Well," he told her, sitting down at his desk, putting his feet on the edge, "the end of the world. It's bound to make people do silly things."

"It won't be *the end of the world," she said scornfully. "It never is. They get people all worked up for nothing, is all."*

"Maybe," Leo replied. "But maybe the hotel needed it to happen."

She looked over the top of her glasses at him. "Not for the first time, Leo, you've lost me. Doesn't it bother you, all that damage, the cost to the hotel's reputation? Your father must be spinning in his grave! I don't know why you keep that kiosk going anyway — being out there didn't stop what happened today, did it? There's more important things –"

"I know, I know," he interrupted. "But I've told you before, I promised him. He said there was more to running a hotel than hiding away at the back — you needed to be out there, at the front, keeping a real eye on things. I happen to think he was right." His expression changed. "There's more to running a hotel than the people, you know."

He sat in silence for a few moments, tapping a cigar on his desk. After a while his secretary spoke. "Cheer up, Leo," she said, half laughing, "it's not the end of –"

Looking up at her he smiled. "No," he conceded. "No, I don't suppose it is."

A minute later, there was a knock at the door.

* * *

Leaving the hotel, Pestilence had wondered if the funny little guy at the kiosk would report him for not paying his bill. But how could he know? For all he knew he was going out for a breath of fresh air — heaven knows he needed it — his senses had been that badly shaken that he couldn't even remember where he'd parked his car.

It was as he was walking around the parking lot looking that he saw his reflection in a car window and saw that in his hurry to leave he'd forgotten to take his costume off, it was so comfy. No wonder the guy was giving him funny looks — Pestilence didn't pay his bill!

As he continued to look for his car he wondered if perhaps he *should* go back and pay, but then remembered that wasn't the only thing he hadn't done — he hadn't reported the bodies he'd seen in 1127 either; if he went back now it'd look bad. No, screw it — why should he pay his bill after witnessing something like that? The whole place was a madhouse-

Hearing what sounded like a hundred windows breaking, he turned back towards the hotel. At least he thought he had — when he looked up at it it seemed to resemble some kind of ugly gothic prison rather than the place he'd just marched out of. Still, it wasn't his problem anymore. Turning away, he focused his attention once more on the parking lot, and the certainty that wherever his car was now, it wasn't there. Because now, none of the cars were in the parking lot — it was just a wide open concrete expanse of nothingness.

Before he got the chance to swear and wonder what was happening, he heard a huge whooshing noise in the sky, like the one he'd heard in his dream, coming towards him. Blocking out the sky, a great squadron of birds descended on him, flapping around him, pecking at his clothes. He managed to bat most of them away but a pink one refused to move, no matter how many times he managed to hit it, its beak jabbing at first his chest then his legs. Then, after what seemed an age, it too finally flapped away.

Letting out a great breath he looked down at himself. No real damage had been done — his clothes were badly torn and his turned-out pockets were full of holes, but other than that-

That didn't make sense. But looking down at the concrete he saw nothing but tar, feathers and bird droppings; no coins, no notes.

"Hey! Bring back my money!" Pestilence shouted after the bird as it flew over towards the beach.

* * *

Hearing the shout in the distance, Nick looked up from the sand but there was nobody there.

This wasn't right, he thought again. This wasn't right at all. How long had he been walking along this beach? It'd got so he daren't even look at his watch to find out. It felt like he was going to be stuck here forever.

Then, with the echo of the voice he'd heard still hanging in the air, Nick saw a bird with pink feathers floating down towards him, lower and lower. *It's going to crap on me, I know it,* he thought, a split second before it all came hurtling down at him. Hunching himself against the impact he waited for the rain to stop.

When several drops of it hurt him he realised it couldn't be what he thought it was. Looking down at the sand, he picked up the several coins and notes he found there, along with a huge pink feather. Running it between his fingers, it suddenly occurred to him that he should go back to the hotel. Jerry and Ray would be wondering where he was.

To his surprise, he found his way back there quickly, and found himself standing outside the manager's office. Knocking on the door, a part of him rebelled against what he was about to do; he wasn't usually so public spirited.

"Yes?" the man now standing in the doorway said.

"Er, I found this outside," Nick said. "Thought it must belong to someone at the hotel."

But the manager wasn't looking at the money; he seemed more interested in the feather.

"Ah," he said smiling, "she managed it after all then."

"Pardon?" Nick said, handing everything over.

"Oh, nothing," Leo beamed. "Just someone doing me a favour."

Shaking his head, Nick walked away.

ABOUT THE AUTHOR

JOHN TRAVIS HAS had nearly forty stories published in various books, magazines and journals in the UK and abroad, in places such as *Nemonymous*, *The Urbanite*, *The First Humdrumming Book of Horror Stories*, *All Hallows*, *Supernatural Tales*, *Fusing Horizons* and online as a guest writer for Simon Clark's *Nailed by the Heart* website. His most recent appearances to be found in *Triquorum 2*, *E'CH PI EL #3* and the hardback anthology *At Ease With the Dead*. Plus, just released, *The British Invasion*.

Currently he is working on a new novel, *The Designated Coconut*, the second in a series featuring a feline Private Eye, set in a world which is now run by mutated animals. The first novel, *The Terror and the Tortoiseshell*, is being looked at by a publisher, while another publisher looks at a collection of his idiosyncratic short stories. And you'll never guess who's publishing his first collection next year. Novellas, apparently. *It Came Through the Leslie Speaker*, if you can believe such a thing.

www.humdrumming.co.uk

HUMDRUMMING TITLES BY JOHN TRAVIS:

The First Humdrumming Book of Horror Stories [CONTRIBUTION]
It Came Through the Leslie Speaker [FORTHCOMING]

OUR MAN IN THE SUDAN

SARAH PINBOROUGH

"I WANT TO see the body," Fanshawe said.

His eyes burned and his sockets were gritty as he blinked, as if the infernal dust that covered everything in this back end of beyond hell hole had somehow coated the inside of his eyelids too. Sitting in the leather-backed chair in Clift's office, sweat itched under his collar and he fought his fingers' urge to creep up and at least loosen his tie and undo a button or two. Instead, he just lifted his chin slightly and made a valiant effort to ignore it.

His shirt clung soaking to his back. It wasn't helping his rising irritation. He was tired, not so much from the flight that had landed at two o'clock that morning, but from the constant heat. It had been a baking black furnace when he'd walked across the runway to fight for his suitcase in the tatty terminal building, and there'd been no respite since. It seemed the air-conditioning on some floors of the Nile Hilton was refusing to work and, unfortunately, he'd been placed on one of those floors. He suspected from the weary expressions of all those who made it to the buffet breakfast, that it was all rooms which were affected, but the management refused to confirm or deny.

Blasted heat. He hated it. Crisp, elegant European winters were his choice; civilised and organised. This African climate left him cold, and even his own poor joke couldn't raise his mood.

On the other side of the desk, Clift smiled. But then it was probably easier for him to do so, dressed casually as he was in shorts and a T-shirt and making no apology for it. The First Secretary poured thick, sweet, black tea from a tall, metal pot.

"We'll have to have it local style today, I'm afraid. Had a blasted power cut and the night watchman didn't start the genny." He slid a cup and saucer across the desk. "He was probably asleep. Wouldn't be the first time. Anyway, all the long life's gone off."

Fanshawe stared at the cup but didn't touch it. How anyone could drink anything hot in these temperatures was beyond him.

"The body?" he repeated.

"Ah yes. The body. Well, that is a touch embarrassing as it happens." Clift took a sip of his own tea and sat back in his chair. With his tan and easy grin he didn't look at all perplexed by the heat. It didn't endear him to Fanshawe. Neither did his next sentence.

"I'm afraid we don't have the body. Not anymore."

Fanshawe stared. Outside, in the white brightness below, car horns blared loudly and two torrents of guttural Arabic raged over each other.

"What do you mean, 'you don't have it'?" His own Queen's English was as dry as the occasional patches of Khartoum grass and scrub that he'd passed on his way to the Embassy.

Spreading his fingers, Clift shrugged. "It was the coffin, you see. God only knows where our standard issue has got to. We haven't needed one since that poor sod flipped his Land Rover and broke his neck on the way back from Port Sudan, and that was a couple of years ago now." He shook his head slightly and frowned. "I'm not even sure it was replaced. I'd only been in post a couple of months then, and you know how these things are."

Fanshawe wasn't entirely sure that he did. In the cool sophistication of Europe's Embassies, those on Her Majesty's diplomatic service wore suits and ties, and typed everything in triplicate. He swatted a fly away and raised an eyebrow. "Go on."

Clift took another sip of his tea and leaned forward, his arms resting on the desk. "We tried to borrow one from the Germans but then one of their buggers bloody went and died too and so they needed it back. Didn't want to ask the Yanks or the Russians. They'd have had a bloody field day with that." He peered at Fanshawe. "We telexed the FCO. They said he had no next of kin so, to be honest, we didn't think anyone would be that concerned. In the end we just buried him."

Fanshawe sighed and looked over to the window. Even through the thick mosquito gauze stretched across it, he thought he'd have to flinch in the white of that sun. Maybe it reflected back up from the dusty, dirty cream of the ground. Maybe that's why it seemed so endlessly bright under the empty blue skies of North Africa. He chewed the inside of his mouth slightly. He'd wanted to see the body. There were things he needed to verify.

Clift rummaged in the desk drawer and pulled out a folder. "The doctor examined him and was pretty sure he'd had a heart attack." He slid the death certificate over so that it sat next to Fanshawe's untouched tea.

"Local doctor?" Happy to bring his eyes back to the more comfortable view of the seventies furniture which had seen better days, Fanshawe picked up the paper.

"Yes; we're a minimum staff in a post like this. He's a good chap, though. Did his training in London." Clift lit a cigarette, the match barely touching the side of the box before bursting into flames. "I have to say, I don't really understand this interest in Cartwright's death. He seemed like an ordinary Second Secretary. So, what's the story?"

Fanshawe refused the offered cigarette, even though he was a smoker himself. The smoke and the dust combined would probably make him choke. Watching Clift, he wondered how long one had to spend in a place like this before one acclimatised. 'Too long,' was the only conclusion he could reach.

"He was MI6," he said, eventually. "He'd had some trouble behind the Iron Curtain so he was laying low here. Having some R-AND-R while things quietened down."

Clift laughed. "Well, a year out here is certainly long enough to be forgotten. Are you worried the Russians tracked him down? If so, I wouldn't be overly concerned. It's too hot for spying games out here. I doubt they'd have the energy for it." He laughed again.

Fanshawe smiled tightly. "Probably not."

"It seems like you may have had a wasted journey. Sorry about that."

Shrugging, his shirt still stuck to his skin, Fanshawe stood up. "It's a week until the next BA flight back to London, which gives me time to take a look around. Perhaps check his files. Just to be sure."

Clift nodded. "Of course. Anything I can do to help just let me know."

"I'm going to want a full report on his death and this… irregular burial procedure." He paused. "Where did you bury him? The cemetery?"

Under Fanshawe's superior tone, Clift had lost a little of his laid-back manner. "Um, no. It takes forever to get the paperwork for a foreign national to get a plot there, and in this heat and with the power cuts we've been having..." he paused. "Well, you just can't keep a body around for long.'

'So, where did you bury him?'

Feeding a fresh sheet of paper in the typewriter before answering, Fanshawe noted that at least Clift had the decency not to look up as he spoke.

"Out on the edge of the desert near where he lived. Like the locals do. There are bodies in unmarked graves all along the border of Omdurman and the Sahara."

Unmarked. Fanshawe reconsidered the cigarette.

* * *

The first time Cartwright had telexed back to London, they'd had the whole team working for ten hours trying to unscramble the message. He wasn't supposed to be in any kind of contact while lying low in Khartoum, let alone sending encrypted sentences at two o'clock in the morning local time. Fanshawe had smoked a lot that night. Cartwright was one of the best. It wasn't unfeasible, if a little against the unwritten rules of play, for one of his opposite number to have tracked him down.

Eventually, a very tired young woman knocked on his office door, shaking her head. 'We've been through all the codes, sir. It doesn't make sense in any of them.' She shrugged and Fanshawe waved her away. He looked down at the original sheet of telex paper with the single sentence printed out on it.

It's all in the sand.

What the hell could Cartwright mean?

As it was, Cartwright was silent for just over a month before the next telex landed on Fanshawe's desk. It had been a long five weeks at the London end, during which Fanshawe maintained the protocol of radio silence to protect his hidden man. If Cartwright had something to tell them, he was going to have to get in touch again. In the meantime, all the encryptions were frantically being re-written. Perhaps they were compromised. Perhaps that's why Cartwright had chosen an ambiguous statement instead of using his allocated code. When the next message came it was as indecipherable as the first.

I can hear the thunder of hooves; the screaming of the dying beasts.

After staring at both messages side-by-side for far too long for sanity to be maintained, Fanshawe was ready to scream himself. He felt as if he were stuck on the last clue of the *Times* crossword with no hope of getting the answer. The sentences were imprinted on the back of his eyes. He carried them everywhere with him.

He waited for Cartwright to get in contact again. But there was nothing. Instead, two months later, came the telex that said he'd been found dead in his house in Khartoum. And so here Fanshawe was: hot, bothered and no closer to being able to solve the puzzle.

"I think I might go back to the hotel for a while. Catch up on some sleep."

Clift nodded, and Fanshawe was sure there was just a touch of relief in the way the younger man's shoulders dropped slightly.

"The driver downstairs will take you, sir. Call me if you need anything. Otherwise I'll pick you up tomorrow morning on my way into the office."

* * *

By the third day Clift picked him up from the Hilton, Fanshawe had given up on the shirt and tie completely, settling in favour of an Aertex collared T-shirt over cream slacks. His eyes burned from lack of sleep. It seemed that no one in the building had been capable of fixing the air-conditioning beyond the ground floor level. Fanshawe had stopped asking when that might be rectified. This was primarily because he was mildly concerned that he might commit an act of murder if anyone else was foolish enough to give him the answer "*Bukrah, in sh'Allah.*" *Tomorrow, if Allah wills it.* So far Allah was very much against the idea.

As the Land Rover bounced across the uneven, rocky and pot-holed dusty tracks that served as roads, Fanshawe squinted out through the open window. Beyond the shallow ditches that ran along each side of the street, old women sat on low stools hawking their piles of paper bread and watermelons to any passers by. Their skin was as cracked as the ground they came from, eyes black suspicious raisins in a desert of wrinkles as they watched the two white men drive by.

Clift paused at a cross-roads, waiting for the *mêlée* of trucks and buses so over-loaded with people hanging from the sides that they might tip over at any moment. Watching the insanity, Fanshawe was so busy trying to decide which potential accident was going to happen first that he didn't see the man approaching and jumped when he appeared at the window, waving the necklace at him.

"Jesus Christ." He pulled in a little, away from the leathery hand intruding his space trying to force him to touch the jewellery as if perhaps this would oblige Fanshawe to buy it. The metal and ivory pendant dangling from the shoelace strap looked tarnished and battered.

"*Y'ella,*" he muttered in disgust at the skinny man on the other side of the car door, whose free arm below the hem of the well-worn Adidas T-shirt, was loaded with necklaces and bracelets all with the same charm attached. The man's response was to lean in closer, words rushing in thick guttural Arabic, too fast for Fanshawe to follow.

Clift revved the engine and pulled the Land Rover forward, leaving the man standing in the street behind them, still waving and shouting at the dust trails of their tyres.

"Sorry about that," Clift said. "Seems they've been selling those bloody things everywhere. Must be the latest local fashion."

Winding the window up a little to prevent further intrusion, but still allowing in whatever hot breeze the car's motion could create, Fanshawe shook off the unsettled feeling and stared at the strange dips at the side of the road.

"What are the ditches for?" he asked Clift. Around them the huts and corrugated iron shacks slowly turned into rows of low, one-story buildings that made up the houses and shops as they came nearer into the centre of the capital city. They looked like they'd been forged from the sand around them. Maybe there was brick and plaster somewhere under their creamy surfaces, but it was well-hidden. The dust had claimed them, as it seemed the dust claimed and coated everything.

"There's your answer." Clift nodded over to the right. A thin man who could have been anywhere between twenty-five and forty lifted the folds of his white *jelabiah* and squatted at the edge. Fanshawe frowned.

"Is he...?"

"Yes, 'fraid so." The car bounced past the man. "The ditches are the closest you'll come to public lavatories in Khartoum. Damned health hazard, but there's no telling the locals." Clift continued, swerving to get past a battered truck that pulled out without even pausing. "The German that died? That was because of those ditches. We had the first of the big rains. Came out of nowhere and flooded the roads. The German's jeep got stuck in a pothole and he got out to try and clear the wheel. Found himself knee deep in sewerage. He must have had a cut that got infected because it was dysentery, and then blood poisoning, and then all over. Poor chap."

Fanshawe said nothing for a while. He couldn't imagine water in these streets. The ground must devour it within a day; no amount of rain could be enough to quench the thirst of this parched land. The car made its way through the increasingly busier streets. Wild brown dogs panted under parked cars, ready to dart out to claim dropped food or to snarl at anyone that got too close. Men and women talked and laughed and sat outside shops or on the wrecked pavements in dusty mixes of tatty western clothes, Arab *jelabiahs* and bright tribal dresses; a *mélange* of fabric and dark skin. Flies settled unnoticed on dark flesh.

Somewhere in the distance a Muezzin began a call to prayer. Slowly all activity ceased and prayer mats unfurled, for a few moments the majority of the city on their knees, facing Mecca. Fanshawe wondered if the man crouching by the ditch had finished in time. Turning into the Embassy car park, they passed three exceptionally tall and ebony-black men who stood frozen on the corner, staring impassively into the compound at Clift and

Fanshawe. They carried long sticks, which for a moment Fanshawe thought might be spears. Tribal men, not Arab men.

He sighed as the Land Rover came to a halt. 'It's not quite Bonne, is it?' He said, eventually.

'No, sir.' Clift stepped out into the heat. 'It's not quite Bonne.'

* * *

By midday, Fanshawe had finished his second sweep of Cartwright's office. He'd taken the phone apart, checked the light sockets and even the air-conditioning vent, yet there was no sign of bugs. Sweating and fed-up, he sat back in the desk chair. Maybe Clift was right. Maybe it was too damned hot out here for spying games. Maybe Cartwright had just got a touch of sunstroke and then died of a heart attack. These things did happen.

He pulled at the top drawer of the desk, tugging it open even though it was stiff. He wasn't convinced by his own argument though. Cartwright had undergone a full medical after the fiasco in Moscow and passed it with flying colours. His heart had been in perfect working order.

Yanking the drawer free, he checked its contents. Pens, paper, a stapler. All basic and ordinary and as expected. He pushed the drawer and it caught again. Something was stopping it running smoothly. Frowning, he slid a hand over the rough surface of the drawer's base. An envelope was cello-taped there. Fanshawe ripped it free and emptied the contents onto the desk.

Photographs. At least twenty. Spreading them carefully out so he could study each one, Fanshawe clenched his teeth slightly. They were pictures of the desert. There wasn't a single soul in any of them, just the endless sand and occasional black rocky outcrop under a bright cloudless sky. Leaning forward he searched their edges to see if maybe they lined up, like some kind of jigsaw puzzle, but it was a fruitless task. To all intents and purposes, they were just random holiday snaps. So why had Cartwright hid them? Were the Russians or East Germans planning to use part of the desert in some way? It didn't seem likely. So what the hell had the man been playing at?

The office door opened and a trolley appeared, carrying white mugs and a large urn, pushed by a grinning Sudanese man, the darkness of whose skin was emphasised by the crisp cleanliness of his white *jelabiah*.

"Tea, sir?" There was surprisingly only a hint of the thick Arab accent in his intonation; a far cry from the dusty Sudanese who had thrust his arm so rudely into the Land Rover that morning. The second surprise Fanshawe felt was that he did indeed feel like a cup of tea, despite the acrid heat.

"Yes please. With milk if there is any."

"Certainly, sir." With one hand he poured a splash of milk into a cup and then placed it under the urn. The tea poured, hot steam rising up from it, and then with the same hand the man carefully placed it on the desk. Looking at the pictures, he smiled.

"Interesting photographs. Deceptive, aren't they?"

Fanshawe had been about to sip his tea but paused. "How do you mean?"

"When you see the desert like this it looks flat. But of course, it is not."

Fanshawe stared at the images spread out in front of him. The ground looked level to him.

"Look there," the tea *wallah* pointed to a slight undulation in the sand. "It looks just like a ripple on the surface, yes?"

Fanshawe nodded in agreement.

"But," the local continued, "it is not. Just beyond that is the drop of a dune, maybe six feet or more. The desert is full of them." He shook his head slightly. "But to those who do not know the Sahara, it appears flat."

Fanshawe stared at the picture more closely and thought he could just see, in the hint of the shadows on the golden ground, what the man meant. "Are there such drops in all of these photos?"

The man's eyes scanned the display and nodded. "Yes, I think so.

"When the Mahdi fought the British at Omdurman, they used the land's deception as part of a battle strategy. While some stood and lured the British forward on the flat sand, others would wait in the drops between the dunes with their swords ready. As the cavalry charged at the enemy, they didn't see the drop until it was too late. The Mahdi's men would hack at the surprised horses' feet with their swords as they galloped and both beast and man would fall screaming into the pit." He smiled at Fanshawe. "Not bad for native thinking, eh Sir?"

Fanshawe nodded. "Not bad at all."

Looking at the clean cups, the perfect whiteness of the man's outfit and the way he stood tall and with dignity, Fanshawe's curiosity got the better of him. "You seem over-educated for your position. And your English is perfect. Surely you could be better employed elsewhere."

The man shook his head sadly and then revealed the stump of his right wrist. "Like many others, I've moved up from the South. I was a teacher of Politics at the university in Juba." He shrugged. "But then, apparently I stole a small item from the market and despite my protests of innocence..." His words drifted off as Fanshawe stared again at the man's missing right hand.

"A man with a criminal record finds it hard to get good employment, even here in the north. But I can't complain. I have good pay and conditions." The tea man smiled. "God save the Queen."

'Yes, quite.' Fanshawe muttered, but any slight empathy he'd felt for the man disappeared as something else he'd said gripped his thoughts. He sipped his tea as Cartwright's second telex typed itself out in his head.

I can hear the thunder of hooves; the screaming of the dying beasts.

"Did you know the man in this office? The man that died?"

The tea *wallah*'s eyes slipped away and he shrugged. "A little." He paused. "Did he take these pictures?"

"Yes."

"I thought so."

Fanshawe frowned. "How did you know?"

The man sighed. "They say we all walked out of Africa in those first days of mankind and then spread to the four corners of the globe. Perhaps the desert calls some of us back. I think maybe your friend was one of those people." He started to wheel his trolley out. "I think he became fascinated with the desert. The sand was in his eyes from his first *haboob*. He became different."

* * *

The Sudan Club was a small oasis of green in the middle of the dry city. Sprinklers turned on the vast lawns and from where he sat in the bar, Fanshawe could see the swimming pool glinting blue under floodlights keeping the dark away. Perhaps somewhere else people would notice the tattiness of the paintwork and chips in the floor tiles, but after four days of African dust and heat, even to Fanshawe, the private club whose membership was only open to those with British passports seemed like an idyll; a visit back to the glory days of the British Empire. And at least the air was cool, fuelled by a generator which ran somewhere out at the back of the building, its throb like gentle background music. It seemed the city danced to the beat of the generator drum, always one or two roaring somewhere, so that in the end you barely heard them. Maybe the silence of bare feet on sand would be more disturbing.

Leaning on the marble bar, he sipped his drink. It was the perfect mix of gin and tonic, just a large enough splash of the first, poured over huge rocks of ice, before being topped up with mixer. Enough of these and he wouldn't need his anti-malaria pills. Still, it felt like it had been a long day.

He'd spent the afternoon at Cartwright's house across on the western side of the wide muddy Nile, out past the edge of the town of Omdurman. He'd hoped to find an answer there for why the agent had moved from the centre of Khartoum, to the dustier, disappeared streets that bordered the desert, where only scrubby dry grasses and bare-footed goat herders lined what should be pavement. In the capital Cartwright could have gone to the hubbub of street 15 and bartered for eggs, sure that at least two or three of them wouldn't have been broken on the uneven journey by the time he got home. Instead, nonsensically, he'd moved to the back-end of the back-end of beyond.

Impressive as the house appeared — rising up on two levels, with a three gates to get in, and a balcony which ran all round the top floor — there was a sense that it was unfinished. Where there should have been gardens surrounding the building, there was only dirt, the lawns never laid. At the front of the property there was a high, metal gate and impressive walk to the double-fronted, heavy wooden door, it seemed that Cartwright favoured the low gate at the back that squealed open onto a short path leading to the servant's quarters on the right, and the door into the kitchen, straight ahead. It was by that gate his car was parked.

The servant's quarters were empty, although there was evidence that Mahmood, the boy, was still living there even though Clift claimed not to have seen him since Cartwright's death. A small jar of coffee and a pot of rice sat on a low chipped Formica table by the narrow camping bed, above which, on the uneven walls that looked made of mud, hung an amulet of ivory and tarnished metal. Its diamond shape was less regular than the one that had been thrust so rudely through the Land Rover window that morning. This one looked older. The symbols or letters that were battered into its surface made no sense to Fanshawe and he left it where it was and headed to the main house.

In the spotless kitchen, the fridge was empty apart from a bottle of Gordon's gin. A case of Schweppes tonic sat on the tiles alongside it and for a moment Fanshawe stared at them. The city of Omdurman seemed to be fine for electricity. The gin was cold and smooth blocks of ice filled the trays in the small freezer section. Tempted as he was to pour himself a drink, as much to fight his frustration as cool himself down, he resisted, and instead methodically did as he was trained to do, working his way through the various electrical appliances, sweeping each room for cameras and bugs. It was painstakingly slow work, but as with Cartwright's office at the Embassy there was nothing. All he found was precise neatness, a well-made bed, and ironed shirts in the closet. Not even any photographs, although there were slight tacky marks on the walls of the second bedroom as if perhaps pictures of some kind had been stuck up until recently. He'd stared at those marks for a long time but they refused to speak to him.

Eventually he went out on the balcony. The sun-baked tiles burned his feet through his shoes and, shading his eyes with his hand, he looked out over the ocean of desert that filled his view. Was this why Cartwright had moved? Simply to be closer to the desert? Staring at the dunes, which looked flat even though he knew better, he bit the inside of his cheek. What was so special about the desert? It glared back at him.

Clift picked him up at five, just as the heat of the day was turning its rage inwards, and they'd driven in almost silence to the club. Fanshawe was sure there had been a slight edge of smugness in Clift's expression as he'd, asked "Everything in order?" Fanshawe could hear the unspoken words echoing underneath the louder ones. *Sometimes heart attacks just happen.* Maybe it was just the heat addling his tired brain, but experience told him that smugness like that came from someone who thought they'd got away with something.

He wiggled his glass at the barman who nodded and waited for Clift to finish the last mouthful of his food before he spoke.

"So why did he move from the first house? Omdurman's a good forty-five minutes drive from here. It doesn't seem practical."

"He got an infestation of ants. Red ones. Those bastards really sting when they bite." Clift pushed away the remains of his chicken and chips in a basket so that it sat next to Fanshawe's, ready to be silently cleared away.

Fanshawe stared at it, mulling over Clift's words. Meat still hung uneaten from the tiny half-skeleton; just more greasy Western waste in a starving country. No one would boil those bones for chicken stock. Fanshawe idly wondered how the local men that worked at the club continued with their benign smiles and nods of subservience. Perhaps one day someone would drive by The Sudan Club to find confused white heads stuck on poles at its gates, mimicking Gordon, brows still furrowed. *What did we do?*

"He moved out while it was being exterminated. And just never moved back."

Fanshawe looked up from the basket, firmly back on his business. "There was no mention of ants in his file. That just shows that he requested a move. To that particular house, in fact."

As if appearing to support Clift's argument, a small black ant industriously carried an impossibly unwieldy crumb over to the far edge of the bar. It seemed to Fanshawe that ants and flies were a way of life in this part of the world. Ants wouldn't bother Cartwright, however painful their bite was. And he would know better that to draw attention to himself, even in a minor way.

"Paperwork isn't one of our strong points." Clift shrugged. "Not on things like housing. The Embassy's too small for a dedicated Housing Officer."

The barman replaced Fanshawe's empty glass with a fresh one. The room was relatively quiet apart from a fat man sitting further down from them who was laughing loudly, either with or at a much thinner middle-aged man and his rather bored looking pale wife. Fanshawe thought perhaps Khartoum was not the best place for the pale-skinned to find themselves. He had a feeling you could burn in the shade here if your skin was so inclined.

"What's a *haboob*?" he asked suddenly, and was sure that Clift twitched.

"*Haboob*?" The twitch again; a small tic in the man's cheek. "Where did you hear that word?"

"It was something the tea boy said." *Cartwright changed after the first* haboob. That's what the *chai wallah* had implied.

Clift lit a cigarette. "It's the local name for a desert sandstorm. We've had a few over the past couple of months. The season for them really starts now. You can feel the potential for one in the air most days." He drained his glass; almost half his drink gone in one go. "They're quite a sight."

Fanshawe thought he could make out the first beginnings of a bead of sweat on the younger man's hairline, even within the cool embrace of the chugging air-conditioning. He lit a cigarette of his own.

"The tea boy said Cartwright was quite fascinated with them."

Clift's eyes slid away. "Yes, I suppose... Although he only saw his first one a couple of months ago. By the end of the season I'm sure he would have got used to them." He sucked almost a centimetre of the Marlboro into blazing red and orange.

Fanshawe watched him. How old was the first secretary? Thirty maybe? He suddenly looked younger. Clift may well go far within the ranks of Her Majesty's Diplomatic service, but he would never make MI6. Not with that tic in his cheek. He sipped his drink. It really was very good.

"Perhaps," Fanshawe said softly, "Cartwright moved to be nearer to the desert."

Clift stared at the bar. "Maybe."

Behind them, the thin man and his pale-skinned wife said their goodbyes and headed out into the night. The fat man stayed where he was, a fresh drink placed in front of him. He smiled at the barman.

"*Shookran.*"

"*Afwan.*"

"*Afwan* yourself."

Over Clift's shoulder, Fanshawe could see the barman laughing along with the man's English / Arabic joke, but there was a sense that he'd heard it far too many times before. He took the tip though, before returning to cleaning and polishing glasses.

The bar paused in silence for a moment and then Clift pushed his stool away and stood up. "I think I'll head home." He busily picked up his wallet and car keys, avoiding eye contact. "Do you want a lift to the Hilton?"

Fanshawe shook his head. "I'll get a taxi later. Think I'll enjoy the air-conditioning for a little while longer."

Clift nodded. "I'll pick you up in the morning then." As Clift moved, Fanshawe caught a glimpse of shoelace around his neck; thin, black and local.

"I'll be there."

Sliding his glass round in his fingers, enjoying the cool condensation, Fanshawe watched him go. *Heart attack. Haboob. Omdurman. Sahara.* All of those words were wrapped up in the tic in his young colleague's face. But what was he hiding? Cartwright going mad? Maybe he was poisoned with a slow-acting agent. Maybe that's why he changed. *After his first haboob.* And why was Clift wearing a pendant like the one they'd seen this morning?

Turning back to the bar, he found that the fat man was watching, sharp eyes peering out from sockets dragged downwards with the weight of his cheeks. Despite the jowls, he managed a grin.

"Jasper Vincent. Freelance journalist." He raised his glass as a welcome. "How are you finding Khartoum?"

"Is my newness that obvious?"

Vincent laughed and, although it was loud and brash, there was an earthy warmth in it. "Your skin doesn't look like leather yet."

"Fair enough. Alan Fanshawe. It's a flying visit for me. Just got a bit of work on at the Embassy. Freelance, you say?"

Vincent nodded. "Even the BBC doesn't keep a man out here full time anymore. Not now things have calmed down. I started with them, but then went native and couldn't face heading back to London or anywhere else for that matter." He paused. "I presume you're here about that British dip that died."

Fanshawe carefully sipped his drink. "You heard about that?"

"It's a small town. Where ex-pats are concerned, word travels." Ice that clung to the last hope of solidity clinked within his glass. "And I was here when that chap who just left and the doctor came in right afterwards. They seemed pretty shaken up. They drank a lot at any rate, and neither of them was laughing."

Signalling the barman to replenish their glasses, Fanshawe was far too well trained to push for more information. It would come soon enough from a man like Vincent. And asking was often the very best way of not finding out.

Vincent stood up, sweat holding the creases and crumples in his linen trousers from where he'd been sitting. "Let's take these out on the terrace. It should be pleasant out there now."

Leaving the cool brightness of the bar, Fanshawe followed the fat man out to a metal table and chairs on the red dusty tiles. Yellow bulbs gave out a warm glow above them and, although the air was hot, there was just the lightest touch of a breeze. Taking his seat, Fanshawe listened for a moment to the loud calling of the crickets and other insects who, in the gloom of the lawns and cacti and bushes, seemed determined to drown out the generator's soft thrum.

Under the glow of one of the lamps, a small sea of black lay in the pool of light. He tossed an abandoned bottle top into it, and the mass rose as one for a moment before fragmenting, the huge flying ants clattering their wings into each other as they hovered before settling back down, drowning the discarded metal disc. Fanshawe shivered a little in disgust. The place was all wrong; dark, alien and wild.

"How on earth could you choose to stay here rather than go back to London?"

Vincent stared out into the darkness, his stomach and arms overflowing from the metal confines of the chair.

"Africa is a strange place," he said, eventually, "and maybe Sudan is one of the strangest within it. Some people view it as a kind of *terra media*, lying between and linking Africa and the Arab world. Others see it as lying on the fault line between two peoples, torn between them and unable to unite. Maybe it's both of those things. They certainly have their share of problems with the South. That's what brought me here: reporting on the civil war. But Sudan is more than that. In the face of the white man its peoples are all one. The Dinka, the Arabs and the Nuer and the other smaller tribes, they can do what we can't begin to; they all understand the land. They understand the power and truth of living on the edge of poverty and with the vast Sahara challenging them to survive it."

He paused, and Fanshawe smiled. The man had a way with words. He could have made a good career for himself away from this filthy hellhole. "And you fell in love with that challenge?" Fanshawe was cynical. With his wide girth and the ruddy face of someone destined for an early grave due to far too much enjoyment of the finer things in life, Vincent did not look like a man that wanted the challenges of poverty. In fact, he looked like a man a year away from a heart attack. Fanshawe would believe *that* death of this man with as much conviction as he couldn't believe it of Cartwright.

Vincent grinned. "No. I fell in love with a Dinka woman. A tall, ebony beauty full of the strength and quiet promise of the desert. You don't get women like that in England. Trust me."

His own smile falling a little, Fanshawe watched Vincent's chubby wrist as it reached for his glass. Around it hung ivory and battered metal.

"What *is* that? They seem to be everywhere. Some damned local tried to sell me one today and even Clift's wearing one."

Vincent's chubby fingers teased the bangle for a moment. "Ah, my magic charm. The wife gave it to me. She insists I wear it in *haboob* season, and I'm not going to argue with her."

That word again. *Haboob*. Fanshawe's jaw clenched. "I don't understand the fascination with the bloody desert and sandstorms," he muttered; the gin not strong enough to relax him.

Peering up at him, Vincent's convivial appearance had melted away. He looked thoughtful. Almost pensive. "Your man lived out in Omdurman, didn't he? I heard stories about him. Wandering out in the desert in the full heat of the day, taking photograph after photograph of the dunes."

Fanshawe sighed. In his years in the service he'd learned there was no point in being secretive with information that was already out there. "It would appear that he had become a little obsessive about the desert before his death, yes." *It's all in the sand.* He paused. "After his first *haboob*."

Vincent nodded as if all the things that were leaving Fanshawe so confused, were making perfect sense to him. "Yeah, the natives said the spirits in the *haboob* had got him." He sat back in his chair, comfortable in the heat.

"People think that Sudan is a Muslim and Christian country, most of its people one or the other. And in some ways that's true. To the Western world anyway, where we have a habit of only seeing the people we think matter. But the Dinka and the other tribes from the south, they have their own religions. Older ones. And maybe darker and more powerful ones too."

The crickets roared louder and Fanshawe couldn't help but wonder if they were trying to silence the journalist who considered himself native, but was so obviously not of this land.

"*Haboobs* are amazing to see." Vincent looked up into the night sky around them. "You might see one tonight if this wind holds to its promise." Fanshawe lifted his head. The other man was right: the breeze was getting stronger.

"And sandstorms are all *haboobs* had been for maybe centuries, until the Dinka started fleeing the south, crossing the desert and bringing their religions with them. It was as if they woke something with their steady march across the sand that had slept for too long." He smiled. "The true religion of the desert dwellers."

Fanshawe wondered for a long moment if the journalist was slightly mad or maybe had a touch of sunstroke or was just drunk. Perhaps there was no real information to be had here. The flying ants shifted a little in the pool of light and he fought a ripple of revulsion.

"What did the doctor say was the cause of death?" Vincent asked.

Fanshawe peered over at the fat man. "Heart attack. Why? What else could it have been?"

Vincent laughed a little. "Well, that would depend on whether you believe in the spirits in the desert."

"I don't understand." Fanshawe wondered if perhaps he was just being lured into a game; some old public school trick of getting one over on the new boy.

"The Dinka believe a great God lives in the hot earth beneath the endless layers of sand. Most of the time he sleeps in the coolness of the ground away from the sun. But for two or three months of the year, he's restless and sometimes wakes and reclaims the land, striding through the desert and leaving a huge rolling storm of dust in his wake."

Vincent looked over at Fanshawe. "The Dinka say that when he walks the desert, so do the spirits of those that died in it, all of those that fell or are buried there. They can revisit the living, carried within the cloud. That's why some of the locals bury their loved ones out on the edge of the city: they hope that they'll return."

Fanshawe sniffed. Bloody native hokum. "That's an appealing legend. But you don't expect me to believe it, do you?"

Vincent grinned, his cheeks squashing his glinting eyes. "No, I don't. But I'll tell you this, so you know." He leaned forward, resting his forearms on the table. "It wasn't Clift and the Doctor that buried him out in the desert. It was Mahmood, his servant." He paused, Fanshawe was sure for effect, before continuing.

"The story goes that your man wandered out in that last *haboob*, right into the middle of it, to see if the things he thought he'd glimpsed and heard were true. He came back hours later, a walking dead man; his eyes and ears full of sand and muttering incoherently."

Fanshawe stared. If Vincent hadn't used Cartwright's houseboy's name he'd have been laughing and on his way to find a taxi. As it was, his mind was racing. Could Vincent be in the pay of the Russians? And why would the Russians create such an elaborate story when he'd already been told by his own people that Cartwright had died of a common place heart attack? Around him it seemed that the hot night crept closer, threatening to smother him.

"How do you know this?"

"I told you, word travels. And I'm married to a Dinka. 'The white man who thought he saw the dead walking in the *haboob*' has been the talk of the Dinka for a few months. They take these things seriously."

Leaning back in his chair, Fanshawe appeared smooth and relaxed, despite the edge in his nerves. "Go on."

"Mahmood wanted to call the *Faquih* to purge the spirits, but the Englishman collapsed on the floor and gripped Mahmood's arm and wouldn't let him go. He held the houseboy like that for a full five minutes until the desert really claimed him and he died. They had a pact you see. Mahmood had promised that if anything happened to him, he'd bury him in the old traditional ways out by the desert. When he called the Embassy man out who saw the state of the body and went for the doctor in a panic about a bloody coffin, Mahmood took the body to the edge of the desert and buried it before disappearing with whatever money your man had given him."

"Isn't Mahmood an Arab name? Why would he believe any of this?"

"Arab father, native mother." Vincent shrugged. "Most Sudanese have a healthy respect for all the religions. When you live in poverty, with disease and death always ready to grab you, it's advisable to keep your options open."

They sat in silence. Behind them a light bulb flickered but kept its hold on the rare stream of electricity. The outside of Fanshawe's gin and tonic glass was damp under his fingers as he finished his drink.

"So, you think Cartwright believed that the dead walked in the *haboobs* and wanted to become like them? And you believe that?"

Vincent shook his head slightly. "I believe that *he* believed it." He held up his fat wrist with the charm attached. "The amulet is supposed to keep the desert spirits from touching your soul. It protects you from the *haboob*." He smiled. "Maybe I've been here long enough to start hedging my bets too."

* * *

It was at about five o'clock in the morning that Fanshawe felt the breeze carrying the tiniest particles of dust through the mesh of the mosquito gauze stretched across the open hotel room window. He sat up, his heart thumping in his chest for no good reason. Wind tickled his face. More breeze than he'd felt in nearly a full week in the Sudanese capital.

Pushing back the covers, he pulled on his trousers and without stopping for a shirt strode to the balcony doors and stepped outside. Despite the hours of darkness that had passed, the tiles were still pleasantly warm as was the metal rail that he gripped. He barely felt them though, as he stared out at the land on the other side of the river, the wind dancing around him, teasing him, laughing at him.

He'd never seen anything like it. In the distance, small, white one-level houses disappeared into the foaming sand surging across the land. A tidal wave of brown stretching across the width of his view thundered across the furthest parts of the city. Watching it rise up from the flat cream land, its facing edge billowing like clouds ballooning forward, Fanshawe could only guess at its height. Maybe fifty feet? Sixty? Or was it as much as a hundred feet in the air, endlessly rising towards the African sky.

Fanshawe's mouth dropped open in awe, as it claimed more of the city below, battered trucks and cars lost beneath its rolling movement, the desert like a murky cloud so huge and heavy that it had dropped from the sky, spreading out on the land and swallowing everything it touched in the whistle of its wind.

Against the silent backdrop of the pale pink horizon, the *haboob* raged. Fanshawe squinted. Despite the grit that pelted painfully into his bare skin he leaned forward. It couldn't be. It just couldn't be. For a moment out in the wild madness that had been the desert, he thought that the sandy shape of a huge horse's head, its mouth wide against the bit as it galloped, rose up through the cloudy edges of the sand storm before collapsing back below, as if something had… cut it down.

Gripping the edge of the balcony so tightly the bones of his knuckles threatened to tear through his skin, he blinked the screaming horse away. It was replaced by another. And another. As the sand charged forward, Fanshawe was almost sure he could hear the battle cries, both orderly and foreign, carried on the wind that brought the sand from Omdurman to the borders of Khartoum and was sure, just for a second, beneath the wailing and screeching of the wind, that the cry of "*Al nasr lana*!" *Victory is ours.*

He stared until his eyes were bleeding water from the onslaught of dust, and then just as the foamy surf of the desert tidal wave touched the far shore of the Nile, the wind dropped. Within moments the desert had fallen, becoming simply silent dust and sand covering everything it had touched.

* * *

He stood there for a long time, feeling the small particles of crushed ground fall slowly through the still air, pulled back by gravity, their tiny weight still too heavy to sustain their flight without the power of the wind. They tickled at Fanshawe's skin and scalp. It seemed to him that in that dawn moment of complete peace, the city sighed.

* * *

The day was quiet in the city. Fanshawe made some pretence of working in Cartwright's office, but in fact spent much of his time staring at the desert photographs, spread out in front of him, a code within a code. Clift seemed relieved that he had no more questions for him and kept himself hidden away, and when the *chai wallah* came round he merely watched Fanshawe cautiously for a moment or two before sinking into his subservient role and pouring out the tea and milk with his one good hand before wheeling his trolley away again. Fanshawe caught a glimpse of metal and ivory around the man's neck just before the door closed behind him.

The burning air was thick as honey and seemed so still Fanshawe thought that not the breath of any god could lift it, but at four in the afternoon the hint of a breeze teased its way into the hubbub of Khartoum. Away from the desk, looking out of the window, the glass panes blurred with dust in front of the mosquito screens, Fanshawe chewed his lip and was convinced that he felt the city and its various people tense up.

Without saying a word to Clift, he slipped out of the Embassy and told the reluctant driver to take him to Omdurman. Staring at the shapeless streets and hawkers that lined them, he watched the wind tug at the *jelabiahs* and yashmaks and Adidas T-shirts, making its presence increasing felt. Somewhere beyond the pretence of civilisation the desert was stirring. Breathing. Claiming its life.

At Cartwright's house, he let himself in. His heart thudded to a stop for the briefest moment before he slowly closed the door behind him and crouched to examine the floor more closely. His eyes narrowed.

Where the day before the marble floors had been spotlessly clean, sandy footprints now wandered aimless through the house, as if they'd come looking for their owner.

Fanshawe's cool MI6-trained eyes scanned the room, and he walked carefully to the sink, picking up the glass that sat on the draining board. Around its edge were crusty brown lip prints that glittered in the fading light.

Holding the glass in one hand, he stared at it and the footprints scattered on the ground and thought of the photographs still in his pocket, and the horses heads that had rose through the storm that morning, and that final cry of *Al Nasr Lana*, until eventually the wind outside howled as the sun set and his reverie was broken.

Without turning the lights on, he put the glass down, took a clean one from the cupboard and made himself a large gin and tonic. The ice cubes tinkled loudly as he padded into the gloom of the large lounge. Sitting in the cushioned high back chair, he casually crossed one leg over the other, sipping his drink before letting the glass rest on the scratched wooden arm of the regulation Embassy furniture. He'd mixed it perfectly and as the gin tingled to his head, the tonic buzzed sharply on his tongue.

After half an hour the first tendrils of sand began to whip at the sides of the house. Fanshawe, perfectly still in the chair, smiled. He'd come to Khartoum for answers. In the encroaching embrace of the *haboob*, he wondered if perhaps he'd get them from Cartwright himself.

ABOUT THE AUTHOR

SARAH PINBOROUGH WAS born in 1972 in Stony Stratford, Buckinghamshire, UK where her family have their home. She spent much of her childhood travelling all over the world — her father, now retired, was a diplomat and so her early years were spent trawling the Middle East — before at 8 years old she packed her trunk and headed off to boarding school for a ten year stretch, the memories of which she says still provide her with much of her material for horror writing.

She now lives about five miles from where she was born with her cats, Mr Fing and Peter. She is a member of the British Fantasy Society, The Horror Writers' Assocation and — along with fellow horror authors Sarah Langan, Alex Sokoloff and Deborah LeBlanc — the writing collective MUSE.

She really doesn't know what people that don't write do with their time. Housework, probably.

www.sarahpinborough.com

www.humdrumming.co.uk

THE HACK

JAMES COOPER & ANDREW JURY

I DIDN'T KNOW which was worse: the house, the room itself, or the landlord's pitiful attempts to acquit himself of all of the building's many shortcomings.

We were standing in the hall, discussing terms. I could smell dank laundry and TV meals that had passed through the digestive tracts of three generations of dole cheats. The landlord, whose name was possibly Ralph — I'm pretty sure that's how he introduced himself — seemed to be of a mind that the house was some wilful beast which existed solely to thwart his ambitions to tame it. He was small, sweaty, and grey, and had a mouthful of tiny yellow teeth, which he seemed to take a perverse delight in revealing to me at the most inopportune moments. I had taken an instant dislike to him from the moment his nervous, over-excited little voice had answered the phone the previous day. *Oh yes, yes,* he kept saying. *You can come over whenever you like. I'm here. I'm always here. No need to ring ahead... But the buzzer doesn't work. You'll have to knock. Just not too hard. Some of my tenants... well, you know...* His voice had exactly matched his physical presence; he was one of those men who always seem to be standing just an inch or two too close for comfort, and who take a mysterious pride in knowing it.

Ralph was currently talking about the water heater, which, like the electricity meter and the gas oven before it, was also showing signs of having 'a life of its own'. At this point, I had just about tuned him out like a Talk Radio station, and was instead trying to locate the source of another sound, one that at once was both familiar and anachronistic. From the moment I had set foot inside the house I had been aware of it, but it was only now, standing there in the hall, that I recognised it for what it was.

"Is that a typewriter I can hear?"

Ralph gave me one of his sly, wolfish grins and pointed to the room directly across from the one I had by now decided would be my own.

"That would be Mr. Calloway," he said without further elaboration.

I was aware that some kind of game was being played out here. Not wanting to indulge him — or at least, indulge him on his terms — I just stared, first at Ralph, then at Calloway's door, while feigning a kind of laconic interest in the whole affair.

After another moment had passed in silence (apart from the clattering of Calloway's typewriter), Ralph said, "Calloway's our very own writer in residence," in a peeved, almost childish tone, and when I turned back to face him, I noticed a minute curl of the man's lip. "Or C.J.P. to his friends."

"C.J.P.?"

"Your guess is as good as mine."

At this, Ralph laughed, though it didn't sound like a joke but rather the residue of some ancient dispute. I moved closer to the door and he immediately leaped forward and laid a hand on my arm.

"Careful! Mr. Calloway is not the kind of tenant who likes to be disturbed." He laughed nervously, as though embarrassed by his reaction. "At least, not when he's *in situ*."

"*In situ*?"

"His words, not mine. Our Mr. Calloway keeps himself to himself at the best of times, but when he's working, nothing must come between him and the written word."

Only now did Ralph realise that his hand was still on my arm. We both looked down at it at the same moment, at which point he embarked upon a slow release of his grip one bony finger at a time.

"You should know that Mr. Calloway often works late when he's in the groove. Sometimes right through the night. There have been some complaints, but our Mr. Calloway has what you might call a persuasive manner. If it's going to be a problem..."

"It won't be a problem."

"I'm just saying..." Ralph grinned again.

"I'm okay with it," I assured him. "I'm a nocturnal beast myself."

Ralph's grin faltered for a moment, as though he didn't quite know how he should interpret this, and I took the opportunity to ask him what kind of books Mr. Calloway wrote.

"Oh, the sort of thing that goes down well in airport lounges — or so I'm told," Ralph said in a nudging, confidential tone that suggested it was what I probably wanted to hear. When I didn't reply, I could tell that he was aware that his observation had actually revealed more about himself than the literary merits of Calloway's novels. I also realised that I had just forfeited my "right to a little latitude", as Ralph had called it, when it came to the deadline for my rent.

"You're saying he's a hack?"

"Not at all," said Ralph quickly.

"I haven't heard of him."

Ralph shrugged and looked across at the door.

"He makes a living," he said. "And his rent is always on time."

This was followed by a smaller, more ambiguous smile.

"Rent." I repeated the word, and when he nodded, I realised the conversation had turned full circle. My hand went to my back pocket, and with the ponderous dexterity of an amateur magician, Ralph produced a rent book from inside his jacket.

"One month's payment. In advance," he said.

He was standing so close that I could see the fine hairs of his top lip quivering, and it struck me that the whole time we'd been talking, there had been the steady, almost rhythmic *clack-clack* of those heavy, old-fashioned keys working overtime behind Calloway's door.

* * *

As grim as life in the apartment could be after a heavy day at work, it soon became apparent that the assurances I'd given the landlord in order to secure the room had been offered in haste. The boiler was a certified death trap, hissing in the sullen heat of the kitchen like a trapped animal, leaving me to sweat over an oven that should have been re-calibrated while it still had a chance. The room was sweltering, and whenever I tried to cook anything the meat was invariably seared. There was also a lingering smell of swamp gas after every meal as emissions from the oven and the boiler mysteriously coalesced. The overall effect was lethal, and after a cursory scrub of the pots I'd make myself scarce. I'd take what I needed for the night, usually a glass and a bottle of scotch, close the kitchen door, and wait to fall asleep on the couch. If I woke up with a hangover and nothing more, it was a bonus.

More irritating still was the constant *clacking* of Calloway's typewriter across the hall. While not as dangerous as the exhaust from the ageing appliances, it was unquestionably more frustrating. The guy seemed to type endlessly, irrespective of the time of day, and the discordant thud of the keys became a dogged accompaniment to my day. As if dissatisfied with his daily output, Calloway would also type through the night, and I often wondered if he'd simply destroyed his earlier work and was rewriting the same sequence over and over again, following a terrible pattern, tapping out the same dozen pages in dizzying twelve-hour blocks.

It also occurred to me that the man might be sitting in his room like an idiot, blindly striking the keys, determined to stumble upon some arbitrary masterpiece that had thus far defied the greatest literary minds. How else to account for the almost constant pounding of the keys? He seemed only to rest for about four hours out of every night, which meant that he was typing for the other twenty. How many writers had the discipline and energy to work like that? I was no artist, but I had a pretty good idea how difficult writing could be. I remembered with horror the numbing emptiness I felt when trying to write essays at school; how exhausting it was to spend even an hour in front of a flickering screen.

Some nights I preferred to leave the house and walk the streets rather than listen to the relentless beat for another second. Even then, imagining myself lost in the urban jungle, I could still hear the echo of Calloway's typewriter in my ears, like the distant thud of war drums. Its rhythm was almost metronomic: hour after hour at the same pace. But then there were those other times when all would go quiet behind the writer's door. The ensuing silence was often so shocking, so deep and empty, that I would be jolted out of the alcoholic stupor that now passed for my sleep. For a moment I would be paralysed, perhaps thinking this was some cruel joke, or else my mind playing tricks. And then after enough time had elapsed for me to be certain that I was not imagining the silence, I would pad across the room to press my ear to the door, thinking: *This is it! It's over.* Listening for those seven final beats: THE END.

Blessed silence.

And then, perhaps ten or fifteen minutes later, it would begin again: *clack-clack-clack*. The same tempo, a staccato beat, like Calloway was some infernal musician hell bent on mastering this single, implacable tune. I would return to my bed, until each depression of the keys was like a small incendiary exploding in the centre of my brain.

By the end of that first week, I was a mess, and there was still no sign of Calloway having completed his project.

When did he eat? How could he survive on such little sleep? How did he sustain his creative instincts? Did he have no other life at all?

Just what the hell was he doing in there?

Once or twice during those early days, I ran into Ralph on the stairs, and though he never mentioned it outright, I could tell by his sly little grin, and the way he observed the bags under my eyes and my grizzled appearance, what he was really thinking. I wanted to lodge a complaint with him, or at least canvass the opinion of the other tenants, some of whom must have been of a similar persuasion when it came to Calloway's night-time vigil, but each time I even considered such a course of action, I would remember that first conversation outside Calloway's door, and a kind of stupid, stubborn pride would prevent me from opening my mouth. No, I would deal with the situation myself: which, I knew, meant not dealing with it at all. And only then did it strike me that I had started to believe that Calloway's typing was something I had no control over; that I was reacting to it in the same way I would to a noisy radiator or the sound of æroplanes passing overhead.

I had developed Ralph's mindset: I'd started to believe that the sound of Calloway's typewriter was just part of the wider influence this house exerted over its tenants; that his being perpetually '*in situ*' was symptomatic of the building's own agenda, like the faulty boiler and the capricious oven.

That's when I came to a decision. I would give Calloway one more night's grace. If he hadn't finished his project by then, or else dropped dead at his keyboard, I would take matters into my own hands.

* * *

The next morning, on waking from another night of troubled sleep, I noticed that a brown envelope had been slid beneath the door of the apartment. Nothing fancy, just a standard A4 envelope with my name typed on the front.

My first instinct was that Ralph had decided to forego another face-to-face visit to collect the rent; but the fact that my name had been *typed* rather than handwritten triggered a different association, and the vague impression I'd started to form of the mysterious Mr. Calloway began to surface as though emerging from a mist.

With nothing to work from other than the incessant clacking of the man's typewriter I'd summoned a dozen archetypes to help define him: the smoking jacket drawn across a bulging gut, lush Minnetonka slippers, a Galalite cigarette holder protruding from thin, dissembler's lips. None of it accurate, I was sure, but the image had become so fixed in my head it was almost impossible to dislodge. Calloway might well be a hack (had to be if he was churning out material at such an improbable rate), but the idea of trying to visualise a *real* writer was so far removed from my own existence that I had no frame of reference to apply. I realised that my composite was absurd, of course I did, but the possibility that he might look exactly like the average man on the street just didn't register. Calloway's lifestyle was so different to my own — or so it seemed — that it was only natural that I create a thoroughly disparate idea of him in my head.

I tried to imagine him stooping to push the envelope beneath the door. A shock of white hair falling freely across his brow;

a soft, vulnerable chin; delicate eyes behind *pince-nez*, fluttering from side to side as though the constant shuffle of the typewriter carriage had conspired, over time, to knock them loose.

I smiled and bent down to retrieve the envelope, imagining Calloway doing the same thing in the blackest hours of the morning, his back aching, knees creaking, his eyes panning across the tiled floor.

I held the envelope in the palm of my hand and wondered at the contents. It was almost weightless and, when I tore it open, I came close to tearing the paper inside.

I hesitated, uncertain whether I wanted to initiate any kind of communication with the man who regularly kept me up at night, and then pulled out three sheets of premium bond A4. The top sheet contained a curt message that I barely had the wit to understand:

It'll stop soon. It's nearly done.
Read this and see what you think.

The message was signed ***C.J.P. Calloway*** in an elegant script that reminded me how childish my own signature was by comparison.

I looked at the message again and felt almost cheated. If it was intended as some form of apology, the note was a long way wide of its mark. The first sentence sounded desperate, as though Calloway was trying to convince himself that the burden of typing the damn book might eventually be brought to an end; how the rest of it might apply to me though, I had no idea. Why would I have any kind of vested interest in the work itself and its completion, other than to secure for myself the glorious prospect of a solid night's sleep?

I flicked to the page behind and realised that Calloway had indeed granted me access to his work-in-progress, the monster that had been terrorising my nights for the last three weeks. I read the title at the top of the page and failed to control a snigger. Calloway's *magnum opus*, the beast that, judging by the effort he was investing in it, had to be wrenching him apart, was called *The Face of Death*. I couldn't imagine a cheesier title and I was almost tempted to put the pages down there and then. But for some inexplicable reason, Calloway had seen fit to entrust the opening chapter of his work to me. I had no idea why, other than that he had to be aware of how intrusive his typing had become and had decided to offer something personal in return.

I glanced at the first paragraph of the manuscript and felt a smile steal over my face. This is what Calloway had typed:

> **Evan Daniels passed the car in the night and felt a rush of fear. His heart beat savagely in his chest, and the lights that came on behind him as the car pulled onto the road illuminated a grimace of terror on his face that made him look for all the world like a demon from hell. They were coming for him. Just as he knew they would. And this time they would not stop till he was dead.**

As I'd guessed, it was the highest form of hokum imaginable and I wondered how on earth a story such as this, which was really nothing more than beach fodder, could have demanded such a gruelling schedule of work. Surely Calloway wasn't devoting twenty hours out of every day to *this*? It was bog-standard fare of the lowest possible denominator. If the opening paragraph was anything to go by, the tale would surely write itself. It was riddled with clichés, and it occurred to me that if this represented Calloway's best work, what kind of drivel had he chosen to omit?

I read the paragraph again, puzzled as to why Calloway would feel the need to labour over a tale that was, even in the kindest of lights, nothing more than warmed-over tripe; prose that would have seemed more than a little threadbare even eighty years ago when the penny dreadfuls had given rise to the pulps.

I continued to read and found myself smiling at the lurid description of the car chase, the brash heroism of Evan Daniels, the sensational melodrama of the plot. I was by no means equipped to criticise the man's creative output, but Mr. Calloway's work-in-progress seemed, even to an untrained eye, something of a damp squib; a hoary old chestnut of a book that even I knew didn't really merit a second glance.

Was he working on something else in there, perhaps; a second, weightier tome that would one day confound the literary world? Given the pages he'd been willing to share with me, it seemed unlikely that *The Face of Death* was the *only* narrative in which he was immersed. Maybe the more profound work was still under wraps; the novel that Calloway sweated over into the early hours of each and every day.

In which case, why was he trying to throw me off the scent with *this* garbage? I glanced again at *The Face of Death* and felt a sudden urge to confront the man who I now realised had been playing me for a fool. I didn't want snippets from some shallow pot-boiler; I just wanted Calloway to have the decency to stop typing in the middle of the night. Was it too much to ask that the man show a little consideration to his fellow tenants?

I opened the door to my apartment and heard Calloway's fingers dancing across the keys of his typewriter. It was so commonplace now I had almost become inured to the dreadful thud of it, in the same way that people living next to runways gradually filter out the noise of approaching planes.

I marched over to Calloway's door, mindful of the fact that now was probably not the best time to challenge him, given that I was still in my underwear, and knocked firmly on his apartment door.

The *clack* of the typewriter stopped and I was thrown slightly by the sudden silence that descended on the hall.

"Mr. Calloway? Are you in there?"

There was no response. The echo of the last key he'd struck was still ringing in my head, but other than that there wasn't a noise to be heard.

I knocked again. "Mr. Calloway? I'd like to talk to you for a moment. I know you're in there. I just heard you typing."

Silence. Not even the remote shuffle of a man half-heartedly trying to hide. He'd just stopped typing; was probably sitting in his chair smoking a cigarette, waiting for the disturbance to recede.

I slammed my palm on the door and returned to my apartment, feeling sick.

Within five minutes the typing had resumed.

* * *

If Calloway had been writing this narrative, he might have described the following few nights as a '*living nightmare*' or a '*waking hell*'. I guess he wouldn't have been too far off the mark, either. By now, I felt like a lab rat in the final stages of a sleep deprivation experiment: I was irritable at work, incapable of concentrating on anything for more than a few seconds, always tired but unable to sleep. The sound of Calloway's typewriter was now a constant accompaniment to my every waking moment, like a bizarre case of tinnitus. I heard it at work, on the street, and in the supermarket. I even incorporated the sound into my dreams, on those rare occasions I managed to doze off. Over the next few nights, those thudding keys overlaid all of my thoughts, conscious and unconscious, and I developed something like an addiction to them, preferring to stay at home and endure the actual sound of Calloway's typing than be held hostage to its echo in my head.

The evening after Calloway had delivered that first chapter to me, I came home from work to find another identical envelope had been slipped under my door while I was away. There was no note attached to the manuscript this time, though by now it was easy to believe that a man who worked so late into the night that the sound of his typewriter eventually competed with the clink of milk bottles would quickly dispense with even the idea of social etiquette. Instead, the fat envelope was crammed with chapters two and three of *The Face of Death*: about sixty pages in all. I took out the first page and read the opening lines, and then tossed the envelope to one side. Later, I thought. *Much* later...

I started to prepare a meal that I didn't feel like eating, and once again my mind turned to why Calloway felt an obligation to share his work with a total stranger. Surely he had an editor or an agent. Or had he simply misinterpreted my knocking on his door the previous night as evidence of some kind of connection between us? Perhaps he thought I was coming back for more. Was he that insecure? Ralph had assured me that he was a professional writer, that he made at least enough to pay his rent on time. Reading those first few pages the previous night I had found that almost impossible to believe, but at work, on a whim, I had Googled Calloway's name and discovered a back catalogue incorporating thirty novels and three collections of short stories spanning a period of four decades. If he was not actually a name, at least in the household sense, then from what I could gather from the blogs and message boards, he had a small, loyal fan base, most of whom had grown up with his work and cherished him for his lumbering prose and corny plotlines — like an eccentric uncle who appeared once or twice a year, and was entertaining enough not to turn away from the house.

When I returned home from work, it had been silent behind Calloway's door. By the time I had finished my supper, however, it came as no surprise that he was up and running again and, perhaps goaded by the sound of his typewriter, I kicked off my shoes and began to read the second chapter of *The Face of Death*:

> **Evan Daniels stared at the dead woman sprawled across the motel bed. What the hell? He'd been faced with a choice - her or him - and in that split-second he'd made it. In the past, he might have agonised over her demise, but the time for regrets had passed. The woman was just another victim in a chain of events that were spiralling out of control. And all the time, while he sat here trying to make sense of it all, they were getting closer, until he could almost feel them...**

Jesus, I thought.

And read on.

* * *

The next night, chapters four, five and six were waiting for me when I returned home from work, the envelope almost bursting apart at the seams. Some of the pages were creased and torn at the corners, as if on a whim he'd crammed them in at the last minute. When I saw that he hadn't even taken the time to type my name, it occurred to me that C.J.P. Calloway might be a little insane.

I didn't really care. The story had its hooks in me by now, and no sooner had I opened the envelope than I was immersed in the continuing adventures of Evan Daniels.

The quality of the prose hadn't improved, and the story arc was following a trajectory that was as predictable as it was strangely seductive. Worse still, the death count was off the chart. Calloway must have been churning out this kind of tat year in, year out, but still I was drawn to it the way a tongue is drawn to a rotten tooth. I even read it during my lunch break at work, though I have no recollection of putting the manuscript in my briefcase. Perhaps it was the mere proximity of Calloway's physical presence that was pulling me into the story — the idea that he was writing the novel specifically for me rather than with some notional reader in mind. Or maybe the hypnotic *thud-thud-thud* of the typewriter keys was acting like a spell upon me, burrowing into my subconscious night after night. The truth was, I didn't care. I was just like any other addict — all I craved was my nightly fix, a fact that was brought home to me about a week later, when, after a two hour period during which I hadn't heard a single sound emanating from Calloway's room, I had to resist the urge to cross the hall and ask why in the hell he *wasn't* typing.

It wasn't until the next morning that I found out why.

C.J.P. Calloway, along with almost everything he owned, had departed during the night.

* * *

I stepped into the hall and had an unimpeded view directly into Calloway's apartment. The heavy door that usually faced me across the landing was wide open and for a moment I was shocked by the change in circumstance, disoriented by the sudden deviation in our routine. The unspoken arrangement that had developed between us had been simple: there was the enigmatic *clack* of the typewriter, the forced perspective of being miles apart, and *The Face of Death*, Calloway's homage to the trashy stories of a lost generation that would now remain forever untold. Even as I thought of the book and Calloway's unexpected presentation of it, a part of me felt oddly touched that he had chosen to include me in the story's birth. I was still uncertain as to why he might have selected me, but there was no denying that we had forged a rather peculiar dependency: Calloway in need of an audience for his work, me with a curious appetite to read it. The idea that the book might have come to an untimely end made me feel nauseous, as though an old friend had moved on to pastures new.

I stared into Calloway's apartment feeling numb. His room, what I could see of it, looked exactly like mine, and I wondered if my ambivalence to discover what had happened to him during the night stemmed from an unconscious desire to never actually find out. There was no denying, as I stared with glassy eyes into Calloway's apartment, that the greater disappointment for me lay not so much in the departure of the *man*, but in the interruption of his unfinished work.

The sudden appearance of an individual in overalls and dark boots broke my concentration, and I momentarily thought I was staring into the dull, uninspired eyes of Calloway himself. It was only when the man moved over to the bed and began stripping back the sheets that I realised I was staring at Ralph, the tedious landlord, to whom I suddenly remembered I owed rent.

I tried to retreat without drawing his attention, but my flickering shadow must have caught his eye and he was upon me before I could close the door.

"Your friend left you something," he said, crossing the hallway and, rather irreverently I thought, bundling Calloway's dirty sheets into a ball. He reached beneath the bedding and produced a familiar-looking envelope, considerably slimmer than any of the others that had preceded it. I took it from him wordlessly, glancing at my name on the front.

"You don't seem surprised," Ralph observed.

I felt something turn in my gut and pointed at the open door. "How long had he been here?"

"I'm not sure. About a year. Maybe longer. I'd have to check my records to be certain."

"Was he working the whole time?"

"Give or take a few weeks." He looked down at the sheets, as though the answer to the whole mystery of Calloway's disappearance might lie within the writer's soiled linen. "I was hoping you might have some answers," he said, nodding at the envelope in my hands, and I could see that he wanted me to open it right there and then. "You and him..."

"I never spoke to the man," I said.

"You didn't?"

I shook my head.

"Writers, eh", Ralph said, as if his daily rounds brought him into regular contact with them all the time. "What about the typewriter?"

I stared at the little man, not sure if it was a question or an accusation of some kind.

"All that time, all those sleepless nights, and he just leaves it behind," said Ralph, his fingers dancing over an invisible keyboard. "Can you believe it?"

I shook my head, for once agreeing with him.

"I'm not sure what to do with it," Ralph said now. "Seems a shame to just dump the damn thing. Do you want it? Might even be worth something..."

"Sure. I'll have it," I said quickly before he could fully develop the gleam that had appeared in his eye. "I mean, if that's okay with you..."

Ralph seemed to do a quick calculation in his head before dropping Calloway's sheets in a pile at my feet and returning to the writer's room.

A minute later, he stumbled out with the typewriter clutched to his pigeon chest.

"Christ. The fucker weighs a ton."

I relieved him of his burden, staggering slightly beneath the machine's deceptive bulk despite my best efforts to appear nonchalant.

"No wonder he left it behind," Ralph said, rubbing his arms and glaring at the typewriter. "He's probably decided to join the rest of us in the twenty-first century. You've got a computer, right?"

"Right," I said.

I retreated towards my flat and was in the process of closing the door with my foot when Ralph poked his head through the gap. The muscles in his neck were still knotted and a vein at his temple pulsed like a cursor.

"I meant to ask you," he said with a casual air that was totally at odds with his florid appearance. "Did you ever find out what C.J.P. was up to in there?"

I lowered the typewriter on to my desk and shrugged, not wanting to spend another minute in the man's company.

Ralph waited for a moment, and when he realised I didn't have any dirt on Calloway — or at least none I was willing to share with him — he said, "Writers, eh?" and closed the door.

* * *

Inside Calloway's final envelope to me was a single sheet of A4 stationary with these words typed in black ink on a fading ribbon:

EVERY ENDING HAS A NEW BEGINNING.
I LEAVE THE REST TO YOU.

I don't know how long I stared at those words. I hadn't for one moment considered the possibility that he might not know how to end the story; I found it even harder to countenance the idea that his unquenchable inspiration could end so abruptly, and with nary a backward glance save for this mysterious coda I now held in my hands. Where had Calloway gone? Why had he left me this note? And what did he mean by '**I LEAVE THE REST TO YOU**'? Was he talking figuratively, as in a reader putting a finished book back on the shelf and imagining the characters' subsequent lives — or was Calloway proposing that I actually finish the novel myself?

I put the sheet of paper to one side and paced the room for a while. I had placed Calloway's typewriter on the desk next to the window where it now seemed absurdly out of place, dominating the room like a prehistoric relic on loan to a village museum. It was almost twenty years since I'd used a typewriter. Like almost everyone else under thirty-five, I was a child of my time: I owned a wireless laptop, communicated constantly via e-mail and text, and disdained last year's model above all else. I had bought an iPod that I hardly ever used, and downloaded films instead of renting them. And yet here I was, a 21st Century Boy, completely overwhelmed by an urge to sit at my desk and pound away on Calloway's ancient typewriter; to hear once again the satisfying clatter of those heavy, cumbersome keys striking the page; to experience for myself that connection between a writer, his material and his machine.

I rolled a sheet of blank paper into the typewriter. That's right,

I *rolled* it in. And it felt good. It felt *hands-on.* And when I looked down at my own hands, I saw ink marks on the fingers. And that was good, too. The keys bore the nicks and marks of Calloway's late night exertions: most of the consonants were discoloured, the vowels were barely visible, and the space bar had been battered out of shape. As an experiment, I tapped out my name, depressing each key as though they might have been booby-trapped by Calloway himself, and the sound reverberated satisfyingly around the room. As I did so, I imagined my fellow tenants raising their heads from whatever diversions they were immersed in: *Oh, God. Didn't he leave? I thought we'd heard the last of all that...* and found that I didn't care a jot. At that moment, I comprehended what Calloway must have understood all along: that the creative process was a noisy, chaotic, and infinitely complex affair; that our generation, spoiled by forgiving cursors, predictive texts, and on-screen auto-corrections, had overlooked those facts in its headlong rush for speed and utility.

I experienced what Calloway must have felt during those long solitary nights in the room across the hall.

And almost without knowing it, I had inserted a fresh sheet of paper into the typewriter and started to write.

* * *

Six days later I had written ten new chapters of *The Face of Death.*

At first, I would return from work and write for three or four hours before going to bed, but by the end of the week my sessions at Calloway's typewriter — as I still thought of it then — were taking me through to the early hours of the morning. On Friday, with nothing to get up for the following morning, I worked through the entire night for the first time — and most of Saturday and Sunday, too — dressed only in a pair of shorts and my bathrobe. Immersed in the story, I called my office the following Monday and took the next week off, before setting about writing what I believed would be the last few chapters of the novel. By this time, I had quit shaving and stopped combing my hair. I bathed only when it seemed absolutely essential, which was hardly ever, and subsisted on a diet of vitamin pills and baked beans eaten straight out of the can.

By the end of the second week, as my trousers began to sag around my waist, I had added another two hundred pages to Calloway's manuscript, and yet I was still no closer to an ending. It wasn't so much that the story was out of control, but rather that it seemed to have created a life of its own. Puzzled by this, I put aside a few hours to read the manuscript in its entirety, and realised that the first couple of chapters were little more than a pastiche of Calloway's hard-boiled style. But as the story moved forward, I developed my own style — or, perhaps more fittingly, another style had emerged from the narrative; one that was every bit as pulpy as his, and perhaps only indistinguishable to another reader by its occasional idiosyncrasies. And yet the novel *had* come to feel as though it belonged more to me than it did to him, as if first by imitating his style, and then replicating his actual routine, I had somehow *overthrown* Calloway. Perhaps by the simple acknowledgement of this fact — that the novel was mine now — I might speed it towards its conclusion.

Throughout the next week, my neighbours both awoke and fell asleep to the sound of my typewriter clacking away: twenty hours a day, seven days a week, the way Calloway had worked in those last few days.

I stopped eating altogether, and when my boss called to ask why I hadn't returned from my holiday, I resigned over the phone and broke the connection before he could ask me for an explanation.

A couple of times during this period, somebody, probably Ralph, knocked on the door. Not sure if I was up to date on my rent or not, I wrote him a cheque and slipped it underneath my door. The amount was enough to cover the next few months, though I was confident I wouldn't need more than two weeks at the rate at which I was working.

But despite my best efforts to finish it, the story continued to claw its way back from any possible resolution. By the end of the month, with more than six hundred pages added to the original manuscript and still no end in sight, I was starting to panic. I had not eaten for days and the flat was beginning to smell. Desperate for inspiration, and needing some fresh air, I left the house for the first time in weeks. The sun hurt my eyes, and it was all I could manage to put one foot in front of the other. For a while I thought

I was being followed by an odd character with loose trousers held together by a length of cord double-knotted at the waist, until I realised it was my own reflection in the shop windows as I strolled by. I no longer recognised myself, and by the time I found myself in a park, slumped down on one of the benches, it occurred to me for the first time that I had murdered Evan Daniels more than a hundred pages ago and replaced him with his brother — a *twin brother*, no less.

I scuttled back to the house and scanned the manuscript again, not quite trusting my memory. There it was in black and white: Evan Daniels had been executed in the dead of night by a black-eyed assassin in an Armani suit, his body dumped in the desert. Two pages later, Brett Daniels, Evan's twin, arrived in town, determined to avenge his brother's death.

After that, there followed another three chapters which I had no recollection of writing.

I rubbed my eyes, tossed the manuscript to one side and stumbled out into the hall. I stared across at Calloway's apartment door and tried to remember when my mind had become so groggy, the exact point at which Calloway's book — now *my* book — had started to consume my life.

The door was closed, just as I remembered it. I stared hard at the gnarled wood and thought I detected a trace memory of Calloway's clacking keys somewhere on the other side. I strained my ears and stood perfectly still. Calloway's obsession had permeated the apartment to such a degree that its echo now seemed to inhabit the room. The subdued clacking I could hear — or *thought* I could hear — sounded like the pattern of derisive laughter the black-eyed assassin had produced upon drawing a blade across Evan Daniels' throat.

I stepped over to the door and placed my ear against the wood, wondering if Calloway had returned. The sound of the pounding typewriter seemed to be amplified in my head, but I couldn't determine whether the noise was originating in me or the empty room. It was like the weird acoustics that distort your perception when you place a conch shell against your ear and fool yourself into believing you're only a whisper away from the sea.

I placed a hand on the doorknob, expecting to meet resistance when it was turned, and found myself staring into Calloway's old room, the door having opened with a squeal of protest and nothing more. I vaguely wondered why Ralph might have left it unlocked, before taking a tentative step into the apartment.

It was exactly as I remembered: damp, dingy and thoroughly unappealing. The only difference now was that Ralph had at some point replaced Calloway's bed linen with a blanket and a discoloured sheet. The pillow that rested atop the mattress bore the impressions of countless heavy heads, weary with disappointment, and I wondered how much sweat had been dreamt into its foam.

The dimensions of the room mirrored my own right down to the last cornice. The furnishings too were essentially the same: bed and sagging mattress, chest of drawers, wardrobe, desk. They all looked as though they had congregated here together, aware that this place would be the death of them, unless they were saved from the furnace by some poor schmuck even more desperate than Ralph.

I stood in the centre of the room on the worn carpet, trying to figure out why on earth I had made this bizarre pilgrimage. Was it a case of returning to the source in the vain hope that inspiration might strike? That revelation, in whatever complicated form, might manifest itself here in Calloway's old room, declaring a path through the story he and I had unwittingly collaborated upon? Even as I thought it, I became acutely aware of how I'd been seduced first by Calloway and then by his spiralling narrative. If there was an ending to be found anywhere, why not here, where the story had first taken wing? Calloway had spent so much time in this room it seemed reasonable to assume that a part of him might remain here, his fingers ghosting over my own, instilling in me a desire to type.

I shook my head, feeling groggy with one senseless speculation after another. What the hell had I been thinking? A quick glance around the apartment confirmed what I already knew: there was nothing here. No ghost; no inspiration; no end.

And yet, a part of me knew this wasn't true. No room, no matter how dull, ever fully voided itself of the people it had housed. There was always *something* left behind, no matter how negligible. And although I'd never met Calloway, I knew from his work that he would have found some way of making his mark on his apartment; his personality seemed too *chaotic* for him not to.

With this in mind, I moved over to the chest of drawers and pulled open each one, unsurprised to discover nothing more than the acrid stench of mildewed clothes, the items themselves, much like the man, long gone. It was a similar story at the desk and the wardrobe, though what I was actually looking for I could barely even begin to define.

I walked back to the apartment door and took one last look around the room. In the far corner, where a flaking radiator pipe disappeared into the floorboards, a flap of carpet had been pulled up and imperfectly replaced, revealing a dark matrix of wood.

I scurried over and bent down to inspect it. The carpet here was even more worn than elsewhere in the room, and I pulled the flap away from the floorboards with a mounting sense of discovery. What I expected to find there I had no idea, but it suddenly dawned on me that Calloway had disappeared a little too abruptly. What if someone had slit the man's throat and buried the body in the very room where he had hidden himself away — Ralph, perhaps, in a pique over unpaid rent; or an irate neighbour, finally driven to extremes as a result of Calloway's incessant typing. It wasn't beyond the realms of possibility. More bizarre crimes than that had been committed in places such as this; Calloway had written about most of them as Evan Daniels had meandered through the pages of *The Face of Death.* Perhaps it was someone's idea of poetic justice, a way of seeking retribution for Calloway's uncompromising last few months...

I shook my head and took a deep breath. I was getting more than a little carried away; the story of Evan and his twin brother was beginning to influence my thinking. If there was melodrama to be had here, it almost certainly wouldn't be in the form of Calloway's body buried beneath the floor.

I lifted the carpet and stared at a loose floorboard, suddenly wondering what the hell was waiting to be discovered underneath. I placed a hand against the ridge of the wood and prised my fingers between the floorboard and the circling current of air. I braced myself and pulled, expecting nothing more than a ripped nail for my trouble, but the board came up cleanly in my hand.

For a moment I was unable to process the sight that lay before me. I gasped and took an involuntary step back, ludicrously thinking that Calloway's body might have been less of a shock.

Underneath the floorboard, packed between the wiring and the pipes like insulation, were hundreds of sheets of white A4 paper. They had all been typed on — at least, all those that I could see — though I suspected there were dozens, *hundreds*, of pages that the poor light and the wooden boards conspired to hide. They had been stuffed into the floor space with such demented purpose it was impossible to gauge exactly what kind of imprint each sheet contained.

I pulled a handful of creased pages into the light and quickly ran my eyes over the content. Evan Daniels featured strongly, as I'd expected, and I recognised Calloway's exaggerated flourishes and the uneven signature of his battered typewriter immediately. I read a couple of set-pieces and marvelled at how shamelessly he manipulated the reader. The man had the flamboyance of the pot-boiler down to a fine art.

I reached under the adjacent floorboard and discovered that the sea of paper had encroached beyond its allotted space and swept into every nook and cranny it could find. I retrieved another handful, coughing at the amount of dust and filth I disturbed, and began to wonder just how far the tide had spread.

The latest batch of papers I'd rescued were almost yellow and the print had faded considerably, but the essence of the story was the same: more bravura performances from Evan Daniels as he eluded the black-eyed assassin in the rain.

I felt a sudden chill. The black-eyed assassin? Hadn't that been my idea? I tried to remember when the character had first been introduced, but my memory of the narrative itself had become increasingly hazy, let alone the intricacies of who wrote what. I thought I heard a bark of laughter out in the hallway, but realised it was just the floorboards creaking beneath my weight.

I scanned another sheet, trying to smile at Calloway's trademark elaborations, until my eyes fell upon something that jarred me from the page:

> **There had been a time in Bret Daniels' life when the death of his brother would have gone un-mourned. But now, with the blood of his brother still warm on the black-eyed assassin's blade, he vowed to take his revenge.**

I dropped the page onto the floorboard and held my breath. I could see dust motes spiralling in the afternoon sun, and tried to imagine the story working itself loose in my head, turning in slow motion like the dust and languidly falling apart.

I read the page again and tried to remember exactly when Brett Daniels had been written into *The Face of Death*. Hadn't it been after Calloway's tenure of the story had elapsed? A *long* time after...? My spinning brain offered nothing conclusive, just a jumble of disorganised pages and typewritten words.

I stood up and ran across the hall. I didn't need to rely on my own complicated memory of events; I had the exact same elements of the story already written down. I was sure of it. Proof positive that I was not delivering myself into some violent insanity.

I hurried into my apartment and began scratching around on my desk, poring through the most recent pages of the manuscript. Within minutes I had it; a virtual copy of Calloway's buried text, typed on the same machine:

> **In a past life, the death of Brett Daniel's brother would have been unlamented. But now, with Evan's blood still heating the black-eyed assassin's blade, he knew he wouldn't rest until his brother's death had been brutally avenged.**

I felt the first stirring of panic as I tried to determine what the hell I'd stumbled into. Was it possible that both Calloway and I had driven the narrative down exactly the same path? A kind of collaboration gone mad? I tried to smile at the whimsy of it, recognising how easily such an idea might feature in *The Face of Death*, the irony of it almost too much to bear. How long Calloway's pages had been stuffed away under the floorboards I had no idea, but they were certainly not pages I had been privy to during the course of my initial foray into the book. The first volume of *The Face of Death* — Calloway's volume — had not even *hinted* at Evan Daniels' death. That had been all me. And yet now, with Calloway gone, one of his earlier drafts, long since buried and forgot, had seemingly served as an unwitting blueprint as I attempted to bring the story to a close.

I thought back to all the pages under Calloway's floorboards, possibly *thousands* of them, wedged into the entire cavity, as though he were somehow nesting in the very heart of the failed story he was trying to conclude. I thought too of my own attempt to draw the tale to a close, the meandering product of which was staring at me from the desk, and wondered whether we'd both merely explored, in the thousands of pages that had been written, every single plot twist it was possible to conceive. Was that why we'd both ended up writing more or less the same sequence? Because there'd been nowhere else for the story to go? Could it be that straightforward? The thought made me feel giddy and I dropped into the swivel chair beside the desk. Maybe that was it, I thought. The story had been guiding us the whole time, moving us back and forth between what had already been written and the resolution we had yet to write. With this in mind, wasn't it inevitable that eventually we'd both arrive at exactly the same point?

I smiled. Hugely improbable, no matter how much I wanted it to be true.

A thought suddenly occurred to me and I turned in the swivel chair and began rooting through the papers on the desk. At the bottom of the pile I found the envelope in which the initial chapters of *The Face of Death* had been slid beneath the apartment door. I stared at the black characters typed across the front and felt sick.

My own name stared back at me, my new name: **CALLOWAY**.

I closed my eyes and thought I heard the black-eyed assassin drawing his blade at my back.

* * *

I knew I had to possess every single page of Calloway's hidden manuscript and, having managed to persuade Ralph to help me rip up the floor in the name of Health & Safety, I began stripping Calloway's room of its buried text.

As we worked, Ralph kept up a constant rant of bile and disgust, wearing me down with his profanity.

"How the hell a man can do something like this is beyond me?" he said, pulling up another floorboard. "It's not natural." He cast an accusatory glance in my direction. "Did you know he was doing this shit?" he asked.

I shook my head and tried to ignore him, but he seemed to think that I knew more about Calloway than I was letting on.

"What are you going to do with it all?" he asked.

I glanced up, wielding another ream of creased pages in my sweaty palm, tired of fielding his inane questions.

"Read it," I said. "Every last page."

By the time we'd finished excavating Calloway's apartment and transferring the manuscript into my own room, I was feeling exhausted. Ralph was still busy nailing the floorboards back down, muttering under his breath about Calloway's craziness, which, apparently, he'd been conscious of all along.

I closed the door on his nonsense and turned to look at the apartment. Every single item of furniture, as well as every available square inch of floor, was covered in Calloway's meandering prose.

I sat down and started to read.

* * *

Over the next few weeks I devoted all of my time to reading the various adjuncts of *The Face of Death*. The first thing I did was build the manuscript into more manageable piles and place each one into an empty box I'd reclaimed from the supermarket. The apartment now housed over *sixty* boxes of differing sizes, and by my calculations Calloway's undisclosed manuscript currently stood at a staggering *ten thousand* sheets of A4, all of which had been secreted beneath the floorboards.

There were, however, one or two anomalies. I'd retrieved the pages almost as randomly as they'd been stashed away, and the narrative had lost all meaning as a result of the disorderly arrangement of the sheets. It was rare, then, for one page to lead smoothly on to the next.

As disconcerting as this was, it also became quickly apparent that the pages I was attempting to read had been printed on more than one typewriter. The robust, almost blurred characters of Calloway's typewriter was occasionally replaced by the nuanced print of completely different machines. Did this mean that Calloway had simply changed typewriters? Or did it suggest that *The Face of Death* was a collaboration that ranged much further than Calloway and myself?

I collected three of the sheets that had been clearly typed on unrelated machines and placed them against the last page I myself had written using Calloway's salvaged typewriter. There was no question about it. They were utterly dissimilar in every regard. I looked at Evan Daniels' name on each page just to be sure.

Evan Daniels **Evan Daniels**
EVAN DANIELS EVANDANIELS

If nothing else it was conclusive proof that I wasn't losing my mind, and I clung to it with the relief of a drowning man being thrown an inflated ring.

As the days turned into weary weeks, I became immersed in the fragmented story of *The Face of Death*, realising that the lack of structure in the disorganised pages added a whole new dimension to the tale. I had to work harder as a reader to help *define* the narrative, and I began to store sections of the story away in my mind, compartmentalising like an academic in order to piece them together at a later date when additional features were disclosed.

At some point I was aware of Ralph leasing out Calloway's apartment to a new tenant, a girl, I think, and I could hear him reciting the same glib inaccuracies in order to impress her that he had done when I'd first arrived, only this time the '*writer in residence*' was me.

I blocked Ralph and his endless dissembling from my mind and focused instead on the manuscript. It was a story without end, despite the fact that I stumbled across several attempted finalés during the course of my reading and even discovered THE END typed impetuously on more than one occasion. It never was; the story, and its potential, was limitless. One poor soul had simply stopped in the middle of a sentence and typed **THEENDTHEEND THEENDTHEENDTHEENDTHEENDTHEENDTHEENDTHEENDTHEEND** for a dozen pages or more, without recognising the irony. This was what the writing of the story could reduce you to, and I noticed as I glanced at that repeated declaration that there were several dark spots staining the paper that I didn't care to consider for too long.

There was a newly-discovered joy though that I welcomed. My old world had become a faded memory of someone else's spoiled narrative, something I worked hard to forget, but *The Face of Death*, the exploits of Evan Daniels and the black-eyed assassin, these were the structureless dimensions that had come to govern my life.

The pitifully configured narrative that I pored through each night was so compelling in its complexity that I had taken to imitating its style when I typed. I no longer wrote in traditional linear prose, but instead co-opted Calloway's arbitrary framework to produce a story that meandered beyond anything either one of us could have dreamt up alone. When I wasn't reading, I was typing, and vice-versa, until my days became a blur of uncoordinated composition, spent piecing together fragments of a drama whose protagonists were ever-changing and whose set-pieces never failed to surprise.

I was vaguely conscious of the other tenants whining and banging on the door from time to time, but my mind was usually elsewhere, delving into the new fiction Calloway and I had unwittingly produced. There were even times when I looked back over work I'd just finished where I was absolutely certain that I was reading Calloway's prose and not my own. Similarly, when I read some of his private manuscript, the thousands of pages that hadn't seen the light of day in God knows how long, I could unequivocally remember conceiving some of the ideas, arranging them in my head, and pounding the typewritten words onto the page. *The Face of Death* had become *our* story; not just a collaboration, but a *merging* of minds, to the point where I could no longer say with any degree of certainty which part of the story was Calloway's and which my own.

It was about this time that I began to recognise just how grungy I'd become. My beard was like knotted tumbleweed clinging to my chin and my body odour had become so rank even I had trouble enduring it. When I looked in the mirror my eyes were all but lost in a sallow, pale face, much thinner than I remembered, and surrounded by a bird's nest of wild, unmanageable hair. I looked like something that had been dragged backwards through time.

I took a pair of scissors to my hair and beard and hacked away at the coarsest clumps. I then shaved, cutting myself repeatedly in the process, and took a long, lingering shower, scrubbing at my body and hair until my fingers hurt. When I'd finished towelling and talcing myself down, my hair looked a little uneven, but the overall effect was substantially better than when I'd begun.

I stared at myself in the mirror and saw a new man staring out at me through the glass. The look pleased me and reminded me of my imagined impression of Calloway, all flowing hair and carpet slippers, a man ideally suited to the pursuit of literary distinction.

With this image in mind, it occurred to me that Calloway deserved better than to be hobbling around the room in his underwear and bare feet. I slipped on some relatively fresh clothes and snuck out of the apartment, feeling a sudden urge to recreate my own vision. I needed to stock up on paper anyway, and while I was out I treated myself to a few luxuries that I knew Calloway, in his prime, would have appreciated.

When I returned to the apartment, I slipped on the new robe and slippers and placed a cigarette in the cheap holder I'd managed to purchase from a tobacconists on the High Street. The *pince-nez* I'd stumbled across in a charity shop for next to nothing and they balanced on the bridge of my nose as though they'd rested there for the best part of my adult life. Furthermore, the old lenses seemed to have corrected my mild astigmatism, and my vision seemed substantially sharper for having the spectacles perched on the end of my nose.

It was far from perfect, but the effect was startling and when I looked at my new self in the mirror I even *felt* different, as though I'd begun to channel a more direct purpose, a greater sense of who I was and what I was about to achieve.

I moved over to the swivel chair and sat down, chewing on the cigarette holder. I suddenly felt full of ideas.

I rolled a sheet of paper into Calloway's typewriter and felt a surge of adrenaline. I stared for a moment at the blank sheet, collecting my thoughts, and received a fleeting chill that made me pause to consider what I'd become. I looked deeper into the grain of the page. The black-eyed assassin stared back.

* * *

There was no denying that over the next few weeks my output significantly increased. The last time I checked I'd added over two thousand pages to *The Face of Death* and the manuscript was growing fatter by the day. My writing was more intense than ever, and the story was being propelled at breakneck speed towards what appeared on the surface to be a definitive end.

And yet, I never felt truly satisfied with it. The ending I had in mind hovered on the horizon, but it always remained tantalisingly out of reach. Until it suddenly dawned on me: the reason I was dissatisfied was staring me in the face, and had been all along. The story would never be brought to a satisfactory conclusion, because it literally had no end. You could plan for one, even write one, perhaps, but that would never finish the story off because it would always be *passed on* to someone else.

The thought struck me like a physical blow and I had to stop writing until the nausea began to recede. I stared around the apartment at the countless boxes, feeling a mild sense of dislocation. That was it, I thought. It was that simple. The book had no end because it was unending.

I looked back through the manuscript and tried to calculate the number of different typewriters that had been employed down the years to add their cacophony to *The Face of Death*. It took me the best part of a morning to differentiate the pages, but by the time I'd finished I'd managed to isolate at least a dozen different machines. *The Face of Death* was a collaboration all right; a collaboration that incorporated at least a dozen different contributors.

I looked at Calloway's typewriter and froze. I felt something in my bowels give way. If everything I'd just considered was true, wasn't it logical to assume that Calloway himself might be without end? I glanced down at the robe and the slippers and the *pince-nez*. If this was *my* idea of the man, how might he have appeared to others? It seemed only natural to assume that the *real* C.J.P. Calloway could quite easily be five, ten, even twenty years deceased. Perhaps it wasn't just the story that was passed on; perhaps the very idea of Calloway himself was bequeathed too.

I tried to smile, but the notion terrified me, though I couldn't quite articulate why. I followed the trail of my hypothesis deeper into the darkness and began to realise how blind I'd become. It wasn't just *The Face of Death* we'd collaborated upon, those faceless hacks and I; we'd been involved in a far more intimate collusion, each of us reimagining Calloway in our own image, each generation redefining him as we saw fit, collaborating in order to recreate a man who had been revealed to us only in the concentrated violence of his work.

The man who had spent his days and nights typing in the apartment across the hall had no more been C.J.P. Calloway than any of the rest of us. Doubtless such a man had once existed, but the original Calloway was so far removed from what *The Face of Death* had become that I suspect he'd no longer be able to recognise his own creation. For all I knew, the original tale might have been a legitimate thriller, critically well-received and stylishly penned, rather than the rambling trash it had been reduced to.

I looked at myself and felt extremely old and tired. I was dressed like an old fop and I flung the robe and slippers and other paraphernalia onto the floor, disgusted with myself.

I went to bed and dreamt of a dozen different Calloways pursuing me down a darkened hall.

* * *

When I awoke I knew exactly what to do. *The Face of Death* was a collaboration; it always had been. And would be again, I was sure. To that end, Calloway, and his unending novel, needed to be passed on.

I seated myself at the old typewriter and rolled in a final sheet of A4. I considered how best to frame my tribute to Calloway and his work and typed:

**There's something missing, but I'm not sure what.
Any ideas?**

I signed the bottom of the sheet: *C.J.P. Calloway*.

I pulled a large envelope from the desk drawer and placed the note inside, along with the last fifty pages I'd contributed to *The Face of Death*. I sealed the envelope and wrote APARTMENT 4 on the reverse.

Before I had time to change my mind, I went out into the hall and stood facing my collaborator's old apartment, my hands shaking, the looping strands of our unfinished narrative playing themselves out in my head. I tried not to think of the young woman behind the door as I took a nervous step forward and reached out.

The wood was cold to the touch and, though I sensed closure, I knew too that something more meaningful was about to begin.

The Face of Death hung over everything, like a recurring dream, and as I slid the envelope under Calloway's door, I remembered the black-eyed assassin. Wondered if he had memorised my name.

ABOUT THE AUTHORS

JAMES COOPER LIVES in Nottinghamshire, England, with his wife and son. He is the author of the novel *The Midway* (Crowswing Books, April 2007), and is the editor of the anthology *Dark Doorways* (The Prufrock Press, 2006). His début collection of short stories, *You Are The Fly (Tales of Redemption & Distress)*, was published in September 2007, by Humdrumming.

He has also sold over thirty short stories to small-press magazines and anthologies in the last three years, including *Cemetery Dance*; *Black Static*; *Postscripts*; *Hub*; *All Hallows*; *Midnight Street*; *Not One of Us*; *Cold Flesh*; *Daikaiju 2*; *The Harrow*; *Black Petals*; *When Graveyards Yawn*; and *Red Scream*.

He is currently heading-up a project for Humdrumming entitled *In Conversation: A Writer's Perspective*, interviewing some of today's leading practitioners of dark fiction, including Ramsey Campbell, Joe R. Lansdale, Tim Lebbon, Greg F. Gifune and Graham Joyce.

He is also at work on his second novel, *Gothic Revival*; and a new collection of short fiction.

ANDREW JURY LIVES in Leicester. His story "Mary's Room" was nominated for a BFS award in 2007 and his work has appeared in *Cemetery Dance*, *Nocturne*, *Lighthouse V*, *Dark Doorways* and many others. He is currently working on his first novel.

www.jamescooper.org.uk
www.humdrumming.co.uk

HUMDRUMMING TITLES BY JAMES COOPER:

You Are The Fly (Tales of Redemption & Distress) [COLLECTION]
The First Humdrumming Book of Horror Stories [CONTRIBUTIONS]

Are you having trouble being as excited as you used to...?

Then try books!

BENEATH THE SURFACE

— A COLLECTION —

BY SIMON STRANTZAS

WITH A FOREWORD BY MARK SAMUELS

ISBN: 978-1-905532-50-6

Below this world lies another — a world from which all nightmares are born, and to which all our dreams are sacrificed for our very survival.

Collected here for the first time are a dozen tales culled from the surreal genius of Simon Strantzas. Tales of grief, of loneliness, of guilt. Tales of things that live beyond our understanding, that watch us with a malignant indifference. Tales of the liminal places that separate our world from *that* other world, and where all barriers between the two have begun to fail...

There, can you feel it? That shiver down your back? Something horrible has begun to rise from beneath the surface.

...he explores, through surrealistic metaphor, the kind of existential angst so skilfully portrayed by Aickman... very moving, very disturbing and elegantly written.

— **Peter Bell**, author

Scared the hell out of me... his deeply paranoid and slightly hallucinogenic prose provides a striking personal metaphor for loneliness and exclusion.

— **Gary McMahon**, author of the *Year's Best Horror* included story "Hum Drum"

Weirdly metaphorical, and genuinely strange...

— **Gary Fry**, author of *Sanity & Other Delusions*

OF SHREW-MICE AND TATTOO'D MEN
— A COLLECTION —
BY GARRY KILWORTH

WITH AN INTRODUCTION BY BRIAN ALDISS

ISBN: 978-1-905532-64-3

An entertaining and beautifully crafted collection of fantasy, science-fiction and horror stories from a master of the genre.

In the Country of Tattooed Men, the nights feel hollow and are full of the sounds of the jungle: danger is everywhere, Tattoos hide all from the prying eyes of the world. On Murderer's Walk, the cards are dealt for the ultimate game. There can only be one loser: pray you do not hold the ace of spades. And from York to London, Northampton to Southend, the boys are surfing Spanish style. It's exciting and exhilarating and potentially fatal...

Garry Kilworth's powerful and striking anthology from the past, present and future is now presented in this expanded collection, featuring fourteen additional stories. Winner of the British Science Fiction Award and the World Fantasy Award, many of his books have seen publication across the globe and in over seventeen different languages.

His characters are strong and the sense of place he creates is immediate and strong

– ***Sunday Times***

A British writer who shows great versatility and invention... Kilworth has a fertile, wide-ranging imagination.

– ***Library Journal***

A masterpiece of balanced and enigmatic storytelling... Kilworth has mastered the form.

– ***Times Literary Supplement***

THE FIRST HUMDRUMMING BOOK OF HORROR STORIES
— AN ANTHOLOGY —
SELECTED BY IAN ALEXANDER MARTIN

ISBN 978-1-905532-01-8

Spawned from Horror and Fear come the familiars of Terror — 12 awesome tales to haunt your days and chill your dreams — every single one now published for the first time.

All these never-before-seen stories:

- "The Door", by GUY ADAMS
- "And Then There Was Blood" as well as "In Each Dark Body There Lies", by JAMES COOPER
- "In the Absence of...", by GARY FRY
- "One's a Crowd", by RHYS HUGHES
- "Thumbwood", by DAVIN IRELAND
- "The Kraken", by MICHAEL KELLY
- "Sacrificial Anode", by GARRY KILWORTH
- "Hum Drum", by GARY McMAHON
- "Pale Light in the Jungle", by SIMON STRANTZAS
- "Dissertation on a Mouthful of Seaweed", by JOHN TRAVIS
- "Bathtub Fiction", by CAROL WEEKES
- PLUS! an INTRODUCTION by: MARK MORRIS!!

All that — PLUS! a packet! of CRISPS! — for a bit more than A FIVER!

(reader must supply own crisps)

The First Humdrumming Book of Horror Stories *is, I hope, the forerunner of many subsequent volumes.*
— John Berlyne; *SFRevue*

A nice collection of stories in the tradition of the classic anthologies from yesteryear. Very recommended.
— Cesar Puch; *HorrorWorld*

Short-listed for the **British Fantasy Society's** 2007 Best Anthology Award

YOU ARE THE FLY
(TALES OF REDEMPTION & DISTRESS)
— A COLLECTION —
BY JAMES COOPER

ISBN 978-1-905532-34-6

You live in a world darkened by the threat of global terrorism, where the very worst of human nature can be seen in the faces of young and old alike.

You walk the streets and sense their fear. They are not just afraid of you; they are afraid of everything. The married couple whose relationship is falling apart. The next-door neighbour who furtively stares across the fence. The street children you used to know.

This is the dawning of a new dark age. An apocalyptic vision of life in the 21st Century, when only the horror of what you've become remains.

Your journey has already begun.

You Are the Fly (Tales of Redemption & Distress): 16 subversive stories that illuminate the human condition and escort you to the very brink of the unknown.

Only those of you who endure shall be redeemed.

The first collection from the prodigious talent of James Cooper, whose stories have already garnered some phenomenal devotion:

Though James Cooper's love of the traditional horror tale is evident in his writing, his fiction is anything but formulaic. His work is thought-provoking, passionate, slightly offbeat, and delves as deeply into the often very real horror of the human condition as it does elements of the fantastic. A fresh new voice in dark fiction, James Cooper is a writer on the rise, and deservedly so.

– Greg F. Gifune, author of *Dominion & Deep Night*

"The Other Son" is excellent… in a different league…

– Graham Joyce

DEADBEAT: MAKES YOU STRONGER
BY GUY ADAMS

ISBN 978-1-905532-37-7

"I think you're missing something, what did you notice about the woman in the coffin? ...She was breathing. Not a common habit amongst the dead."

It's the middle of the night and, in a dark suburban churchyard, a group of men are loading a coffin into the back of a transit van.

But why would you be taking a full coffin away from a graveyard and, more importantly, why is the occupant still breathing?

The matter obviously needs thorough investigation by the best, most capable authorities.

Which is a pity as the only two witnesses are a pair of drunken ex-theatricals with reasons of their own to avoid the police.

Tom Harris (nightclub owner)
and Max Jackson (habitual barfly)
are on the case.

God help us...

...a world away from the bloated procedurals that have come to dominate the crime field, harking back to a time when fiction could be quirkier and less boundary-conscious. Tell a good tale, be scary, be funny... easy to say it, much harder to pull off. Deadbeat manages all three.

- Stephen Gallagher; author of *Oktober*,
The Spirit Box and *Valley of Lights*

Short-listed for the **British Fantasy Society's** 2005 Best Novella Award

Frankly, it's just like every other
Pulp Crime/Horror/Zombie/Comedy/Thriller
you've ever read.

DEADBEAT: DOGS OF WAUGH
BY GUY ADAMS

ISBN 978-1-905532-14-8

"High on life..."

There's a new drug running rife amongst the Undead community. Once ingested it simulates all of the symptoms of the living, faster pulse, perspiration, the intoxicating rush of blood through your veins...

Not that Max or Tom would be stupid enough to try it of course, they're far to busy smashing their senses to a pulp working their way though Deadbeat's new cocktail menu.

But people start vanishing from the Soho streets and some of their customers disrupt big band nights by keeling over dead.

For the second time.

Which is when Max & Tom decide it might be worth looking into, if only to stop profits dropping too far.

In a lifetime of bad decisions, this may rank as their worst yet.

Deadbeat: Dogs of Waugh *is the second in a series of adventures set in the secret underbelly of contemporary London, a place where the dead walk, magic can be bought on street corners and anything is possible.*

Long-listed for the **British Fantasy Society's** 2007 Best Novella Award

Frankly, it's just like every other
Pulp Crime/Horror/Zombie/Comedy/Thriller
you've ever read.

STITCH
BY MARK MORRIS

ISBN: 978-1-905532-42-1

Welcome to The Crack

Autumn term at Maybury University and, as the nights draw in, so does an atmosphere of menace. Dan Latcher — a previously quiet and withdrawn student — blossoms overnight into the forceful illusion-working leader of a charismatic student movement, 'The Crack'; an organisation with the power to shape and alter its followers' personalities, pushing them on to mindless heights of pleasure and pain.

When hitherto bright, vivacious fresher Stephanie Peele becomes one of his converts, her worried room-mate Annie enlists the support of fellow student Ian.

While the campus is further beset by an unknown knife-wielding psychopath, Annie and Ian pit their strength against the forces of evil as personified by Latcher and his infinitely more potent puppet master, Peregrine Stitch, voraciously sucking-in new converts body and soul…

This special edition also includes the following bonus material:
- *a brand new introduction by the author*
- *an interview conducted at the time of the book's original release*
- *a bonus short story "Warts and All" written the same year*

making this the definitive edition of Mark's second novel

A big, blusteringly red-faced, glowering novel of neo-religious cults, bizarre sex and rarely plumbed levels of almost impenetrable blackness… the essence of true horror.

— Peter Crowther, *Fear Magazine.*

A sizzling banquet of the bizarre that simply demands to be read.

— Julian Lloyd Webber, *Sunday Express*

THE REACH OF CHILDREN

— A NOVELLA—

BY TIM LEBBON

FOREWORD BY MICHAEL MARSHALL SMITH

ISBN: 978-1-905532-58-2 [VERY SPECIAL EDITION]
ISBN: 978-1-905532-59-9 [SPECIAL EDITION]

The Reach of Children, the latest novella by Tim Lebbon, is a story of childhood, bereavement and hope, and explores just how far some people — living, or dead — will go to protect the ones they love.

Daniel is ten years old when his mother dies.
She dies young, and with so much left to give.
He does not understand.
He cannot let her go.

After the funeral, his father begins talking to a large wooden box that suddenly appears beneath his bed. And when Daniel whispers to the box one day when his father goes out… it answers back.

It's a voice he does not know.
But this voice knows so much.

The novella comes complete with a Foreword written by Michael Marshall Smith, as well as an Afterword by Mr. Lebbon, making this so much more than a simple novella: this is a towering monolith of a must have book for both the 'Lebbon Acolyte' and general horror reader alike.

…Lebbon's writing … is profoundly moral, which is the hallmark of a serious writer, not merely a writer who takes his writing seriously.

— *All Hallows*

WORLD WIDE WEB

— & OTHER LOVECRAFTIAN UPGRADES —

BY GARY FRY

ISBN: 978-1-905532-40-7

H.P. Lovecraft isn't dead. He survives. From parody to pastiche, from *homage* to quite deliberate attempts to deny his influence, modern horror writers have wrestled unspeakably with the master for years. In this collection of Lovecraftian tales, Gary Fry takes the un-dead writer to task in a sequence of pieces which explores everything that can be done with his fiction.

Here you'll see how the Mythos can be used to inform contemporary concerns, to provoke laughter, to make you think, to employ alternative narrative devices, to be experimental, and more.

One novella and six short stories, including an introduction by Mark Morris and an afterword from the author.

Cosmic terror awaits you; indifference is not a choice you can make. Read this book and shudder as the dreadful entities gather and the world grows dim and dangerous…

Gary Fry has been behind some of the most sophisticated — and scary — work of recent years, and this superlative collection is no exception.

This is a writer with important things to say and the talent to make them compelling.
— Melanie Tem

…powerful ideas that resonate with me.
— Adam L.G. Nevill

The prose is so polished and vivid, and the suspense maintained so powerfully and adroitly…
— Russell Blackwood

Fry's writing is assured… effortlessly drawing the reader in to the story and making him care about the characters.
— Peter Tennant; *The Third Alternative*

…powerful …with many effective and imaginative touches.
— Ramsey Campbell

LESS LONELY PLANET

BY RHYS HUGHES

— A COLLECTION —

ISBN: 978-1-905532-52-0

A collection of inexplicably joined short stories and tales from Rhys Hughes, the author who is to convention what apricots are to armadillos.

32 tales about life, non-melodic sounds, cats, adventures, love, bread, circuses, pyramids, ducks, and more!

Since time immemorial, the planet Earth has revolved around the sun on its own, carrying one species of technically advanced hominids, a handful of basic urges, a dozen or so original plots. But a very slow collision with the rogue world Happenstance is about to change all that.

The two celestial bodies will fuse together into a single object, doubling the surface area, trebling the population, quadrupling the number of resonant archetypes, multiplying by a millionfold the virtues of hyperbole!

A less lonely Earth means more high adventure, more low morals, more medium rares. Oh yes!

Rhys's previous appearance under the Humdrumming banner was the story of military overthrow "One's a Crowd", which appeared in *The First Humdrumming Book of Horror Stories.*

ALL YOUR GODS ARE DEAD

BY GARY M^C^MAHON

WITH AN INTRODUCTION BY MARK SAMUELS.

ISBN: 978-1-905532-40-7

Can you see all *the colours of pain?*

Who is sending Doug Hunter mysterious e-mails that seem to be from his murdered brother, Andy?

Why are severed human body parts being discovered in drains and rivers across the country?

What is the real meaning behind the graffiti that ominously states "All your gods are dead"?

When Doug travels to Leeds, where six months ago his brother's defiled and mutilated corpse was found on an abandoned industrial estate, he is drawn into a web of religious mania, orchestrated torture, and deceit.

There he encounters the Church of All Sufferance, a strange sect comprising of bald, androgynous men and women who claim that they are able to see "all the colours of pain".

Then, when he meets and reluctantly starts a relationship with Andy's ex-girlfriend, all the pieces of a bizarre cosmic puzzle begin to slot into place, and Doug realises that the bloodied acolytes who call themselves the Sufferers have dark and monstrous plans for the entire world...

All Your Gods Are Dead *comes with my highest recommendation for anyone who wants to read the best new fiction the horror genre has to offer.*

— Joe Kroeger; *Horror World*

Short-listed for the **British Fantasy Society**'s 2007 Best Novella Award

RAIN DOGS

BY GARY M^C^MAHON

WITH A FOREWORD BY CONRAD WILLIAMS

ISBN: 978-1-905532-47-6

It is raining...

Guy Renford is fresh out of prison. His life is in ruins; his wife and daughter are estranged. So he returns to the Yorkshire town of Stonegrave to try and recover what he once held dear. But a presence is watching from behind the endless rainstorm, something that wants revenge and has not come alone.

...and still it rains...

Rosie sees ghosts, and has done since childhood These sorrowful visions of drowned schoolgirls are linked to a past she fled to America to escape. But you can never run from your destiny, and something is calling Rosie back to rainy Stonegrave, the home of her worst nightmares.

...and rains...

Slowly the lives of these two people are drawn together in a town cut off by floods, and at the height of the storm they will be forced to battle a relentless foe that uses the deluge as cover, stalking them from within a merciless onslaught of rain.

Rain Dogs *is a rabbit punch to the back of the head... a cracking début... Gary M^c^Mahon is a skilful writer and an able cartographer of these badlands.*

— Conrad Williams;
from his introduction

Gary McMahon is a very bloody good writer indeed. His writing is heartfelt, accomplished and soulful, and his stories are both serious and mature. Gary has a bright future ahead of him.

— Tim Lebbon; award-winning
author of the "Noreela" novels

If you are interested in purchasing any of our titles for yourself or others (and thereby demonstrating your superior intellect and discernment), please direct the attention of your web-browser to the address below.

We thank you kindly in advance for supporting these fine writers and their works.

www.humdumming.co.uk